Sweet Deals

SWEET
DEALS

Brian Lysaght

ST. MARTIN'S PRESS, *New York*

Design by Laura Hough

Library of Congress Cataloging in Publication Data

Lysaght, Brian.
    Sweet deals.

    I. Title.
PS3562.Y4498S9   1984   813'.54   84-22885
ISBN 0-312-78081-8

First Edition

10 9 8 7 6 5 4 3 2 1

To Stephanie, then and now.

Sweet Deals

1

Up above San Francisco, once the people get left behind, once the air gets cold and the trees replace the buildings, the world gets better in a thousand different ways. The highways are a metaphor of the change. Route 101 in L.A. is the Hollywood Freeway, a painted lady if there ever was one, an exhaust-blackened, concrete hell that carries more pimps and murderers on its back in a day than any roadway in America. Up north the road has the same federal number yet is now the floor of the Golden Gate Bridge, a change the significance of which is lost on no one in Northern California. About a hundred miles south of Eureka the old whore truly gets religion, slimming down to an undivided two lanes, slicing the Russian River gurgling happy and wide alongside, carrying trucks to and fro through the Sonoma and Mendocino vineyards, lush green vineyards dotting golden hills. The towns have names like Clear Lake. Sometimes the road is dark from the pall cast by the giant redwoods and pines growing alongside.

On the windward side of the Coast Range lies the glistening Pacific and the most enticingly suicidal road in the state. Route 1 was a Depression-era project that only exists because there was more cheap labor than sense in those days. It is an undivided two-laner hanging high above the ocean,

I

flipping and turning as the hills follow the painfully gorgeous sea. Its only function is to present a visual siren ever trying to yank a driver's eyes and car down into spectacular oblivion.

The towns along Route 1 are every bit as incongruous as the road. Bodega Bay, Fort Ross, Salt Point, Gualala, Anchor Bay, Point Arena, Albion. The biggest of them has maybe five hundred people. Lumber country. Wine country. Wind-chafed fishermen. Strange naval installations with whirling beacons. Otters and sea lions and migrating gray whales. Crashing rocky coasts. Cold mist and fog. Not a sunbather or surfer for a thousand miles.

In the summer of 1980 a young peregrine falcon was feasting along a riverbed around Philo. Sated, he took to the skies and began following the Navarro River to Salmon Point. At the Pacific he turned south, sweeping along the coast ridge, scouting possible future homes in the crags, keeping his eyes open for a bit of dessert should it happen along. For twenty miles he saw nothing, got bored, and settled in on the edge of a bluff to primp. He was rubbing his notched beak against a rock when he spotted some movement a thousand feet below. Curious, he folded his wings back like a swing-wing fighter and plummeted down with the precision of a lance at 175 miles per hour. A hundred feet from the ground he opened his wings, caught a bit of wind, and flattened the flight, now skimming horizontally over the long beach. A restaurant clung to the coast road, its open deck balanced over the rock beach on twenty-foot pilings. The falcon buzzed the deck once, causing a large man sitting in a deck chair to forget his sunset and follow the flight of the bird. The falcon banked left, skimmed the waves for a hundred yards, and returned, flapping twice before coming to rest on a piling supporting the restaurant's deck.

Benjamin Aaron O'Malley applauded lustily, then lifted his Anchor Steam Porter in salute. The proud young bird gave a tip of his crown in acknowledgment and was gone.

2

O'Malley followed him with his eyes until the brown shape disappeared around the curve of the beach. Then he went back to his beer and his sunset.

O'Malley had been living effortlessly in the land of that falcon for a full three years now. For most of that time, until recently, he had asked little or nothing of this strange coast town and received tranquility and warmth in return. There had been a period of getting used to it, of course, of retuning an engine set to run at urban speeds, but in six months he had adjusted, aided by a discipline that had him on this porch every evening to watch the sun slide down the horizon toward its nightly Pacific disappearance. That was the pace of the town, with time measured in events rather than days: babies, funerals, great fishing, new lovers. And of course the angle of the sun, whether north or south, as it made its western splash.

At first the locals didn't know what to make of him: an Irish-Jewish escapee from L.A.; hell, there wasn't a church in town he could go to even if he was of a mind to, which he didn't seem to be. Later on they told him that as a city boy he'd never last; that he'd grow tired of the pace, bored with the lack of action. The prediction was once he had exorcised his ghosts, he'd need to go back to the places where people lived, even if only places like Eureka or Mendocino, huge towns with huddled masses of five or six thousand. At the beginning, O'Malley, with loud boasts, denied he would leave them. But they knew the truth far better than he did.

The night the peregrine falcon buzzed his perch, O'Malley had just such thoughts on his mind. What was once a fortune of a stake had been all but obliterated by three years of blissful unemployment. By stretching things out he could fashion another indolent year of Gualala sunsets; after that poverty was as inevitable as the daily drop of the sun. To stay would then mean long, hard hours of work for a sustaining wage. O'Malley loved the boats and often went out to taste at first hand the cold salt spraying off the green waves.

3

Those jaunts bore no resemblance to what he'd have to do to make a living at it.

A wiry, gaunt man came out and interrupted his reverie, sitting with a worker's sigh and wrapping a grimy hand around a cold beer. He slid a full one across to O'Malley. "That's 'cause I know you're going broke. My mother always told me to be kind to the poor."

O'Malley grinned. "Your mother's a saint. And you're a mind reader, Michael. I was just sitting here figuring out what boat I'll sign on with."

The fisherman's head flew back and he laughed loudly. "You'd last about a month. Then you'd get throwed in with the squirmy things."

"You may be right, Mike. You may be right."

"I got some good news for you, though."

"Oh yeah, what?"

Michael waved his beer toward the houses on the ridge. "Mary says bring you back tonight. Says she could never forgive herself if you starved in front of her eyes."

Christ, the whole town knew he was going broke. "It's not quite that bad yet, Michael."

"I know. But come on up anyway. We'll drink some beer."

"O.K.," he said.

Six days before and seven hundred miles south a haughty blond woman pushed resolutely through a set of double doors, ignoring the startled gazes of the men at the desks. She kept her eyes fixed on the high, brown desk in front of her. The man sitting behind it peered down at her with a look that was not unkind and only vaguely lustful. She swept wetness from her cheek in irritation.

"May I help you," he said.

"Yes. . . " she said, ". . . yes. It's hard to explain."

"What's hard to explain?"

"It's my husband. He's not there anymore."

4

She looked up resolutely, determined not to let the wetness reappear. He rubbed his nose to hide the smile.

"I see," he said. "You know we get a lot of that here. Sometimes it's best just to relax, have a sip of water"—he gestured to a cooler—"and sit down in one of those nice chairs. Maybe in a half hour or so you can call home. He probably snuck out to play some golf." He smiled at her again, this time the lust less vague.

Anna Bradley dropped her eyes and spoke directly into the floor. "Look, officer, I don't need you to patronize me. I am not a crazy lady. I'm here to tell you that my husband, John, is gone. He did not come home last night. Nor is he at work, because I tried there too. As for golf, while I'm sure he's heard of the game, I'm not sure he could tell you the size of the ball. In fact, I'm quite sure he hasn't played that or any other game in the thirty-odd years he's walked this earth." Her voice was hard as she looked into the desk sergeant's lined face. "Now, are you going to treat this seriously or do I go storming into that office over there?" She pointed to the right.

Involuntarily the sergeant's eyes swung in that direction. The door was unmarked but Anna had made a very good guess. The smile faded from his lips. "No, ma'am, you came to just the right spot." He bellowed out a name and a cop watching from the other side of the room stubbed out a cigarette and strolled over with practiced insouciance. He was young enough and insolent enough to let his eyes trace up and down Anna's body. "Get her story, Gibson," the sergeant barked.

"Name?"
"Anna Bradley—two n's."
"Address?"
"3720 Drury Lane, Bel Air, California."
"Phone?"
She hesitated. "Yes."

5

"I mean what's the number," he said. "I got to put it down." He grinned and shrugged.

"Well, there's the house number and my private line."

"Got to have both."

She looked quickly around the room. The novelty of her presence had worn off and the other cops had gone back to their business. She looked back to him. He had a young, simple face without guile, intelligence, or complication. His needs were spread across his face like a classified ad.

"Will you be working on this case?" she asked.

"Yes, ma'am."

"Tell you what," she said. "I'll give you the house number now for your records. If you find my husband, I'll . . . I'll give the private one just to you." She dropped her eyes and held her breath for a moment to bring pink to her cheeks.

"Yes, ma'am." He didn't grin, believing this the moment to appear professional. "Well, let's get on with this." He hunched over his pad. "Age?"

"Mine or my husband's?"

"His."

"Thirty-six."

"Yours."

"Twenty-eight."

"What did he do?" He caught himself. "What does he do?"

"He's an accountant, a CPA. Chief auditor of the international division." She named a motion picture studio.

"How about you?"

"I'm self-employed. Or to be accurate I suppose I should say unemployed." She let a moment go by without speaking. "I was left some money when my father died."

"How much?" The kid was nosy.

"Enough to remain unemployed for the foreseeable future."

"Fair enough. Let's go back to your husband. You say he's the head of it all?"

6

"Head auditor of the international division, yes."

"So he gets to touch a lot of dollar bills, right?"

"What does that mean?"

The cop shrugged. "I mean he's the accountant. He touches a lot of dollar bills. He's gone. One, two, three, right?"

Anna Bradley tried to breathe slowly. Her voice lost a touch of its patience. "Officer," she began, "accountants are not bank tellers. They review the books and records of the corporation, conduct audits, and provide financial services to management." She thought for a second about a way to simplify it for him. "They talk and write about dollars," she said. "They don't touch dollars."

"Okay. So how long you been married?"

"Three years."

"Kids?"

"No."

"Any running around?"

"Pardon?"

It was the cop's turn to be patronizing. "Mrs. Bradley, that's a simple question. You say your husband has left home. Was he running around with anyone?"

She shook her head vigorously. "No, John isn't the type. He is very proper and always has been. He graduated from college and went straight into the military. Four years as an Air Force officer. Financial officer, that is, not flying planes, of course. Then he came out, did postgraduate work, and began his career with the studio. His life has been a straight line. He is certainly not a sexual profligate." She looked into his blank stare. "That means I don't think he's running around."

"All right, forget it. Why do you think he's gone?"

She stood and spoke quietly, almost to herself. The cop had to strain to hear. "John is a creature of habit," she began, "the most dependable man I know." She smiled weakly. "For better or worse, that's why we got married. Anyway, Friday nights have always been special for us. John leaves work one-

7

half hour early and we meet at the house about five-thirty. I have a drink waiting for him, usually a small Scotch. John doesn't usually drink, of course, but Friday nights are an exception, sort of his reward for a difficult week. He has his Scotch between five-thirty and six, then we dress for dinner."

She composed herself for the hard part. "Last night it didn't happen. It's the first time it didn't happen in the three years we've been married. Five-thirty came and no John. I kept staring at that little Scotch on the table watching the ice melt. I called the studio to try to get his secretary, who frequently works late with him, but no luck. His assistant was gone too. So I went back, sat by the phone, drank John's Scotch, and started to worry.

"As the night wore on, I became frantic. I drank more Scotch to calm down and ultimately took two Valiums, which I know is a mistake. By eleven I felt terribly drowsy. I went into the bedroom and the room started spinning. I lay down for a moment to clear my head, with the thought of calling the police if John didn't show up by midnight. The next thing I remember it was ten in the morning. I dressed and came here immediately." She stared at him, her lip resolute, but the lip quickly turned to jelly, and in a moment her body was wracked with sobs. He tried to pat her, but she just kept crying. "I know he's dead, I know he's dead, I know he's dead," she said between sobs.

When her crying slowed, he tried to comfort her. "Look, I know it's tough. I'll do what I can. We get these things through here every day and nine times out of ten it's nothing. We check 'em out and it turns out the guy got a snootful and wound up in county for the night." He hesitated. "It doesn't sound like that happened to your husband, but you never know." He cleared his throat and picked up the pencil. "Why don't you give me some names and we'll follow up."

She nodded. "Allen Witkin, W-I-T-K-I-N, is the assistant. He lives in Santa Monica." She gave him the number.

"What about his boss?"

"John doesn't really have a boss. He reports directly to the board of management. But the person he's had the most contact with recently is David Perino, P-E-R-I-N-O, who lives in Beverly Hills."

The cop raised his head. "*The* David Perino?"

"I suppose so. Why? Is he famous?"

"Yes, ma'am. But not for making movies."

"I know. He's a . . . well, a consultant, I believe."

The cop smirked. "He may be. But he's usually doing his consulting with guys from Detroit and Chicago, if you know what I mean."

"I'm sure I don't. John told me Mr. Perino was a respected local businessman whom the studio hires on special projects from time to time. I'm afraid your imagination is getting the better of you."

The cop shrugged. "So forget it. Who's his secretary?"

"Monica Davis, she's in West Hollywood." Anna thought for a second. "She just changed it to Davis because she hated her real name. It was an unusual name, I could understand why she wanted to change it."

"That's okay, we'll just . . ."

"Glitzman! That's it, Monica Glitzman, G-L-I-T-Z-M-A-N. She's living over on . . ."

"Give me that name again."

"Glitzman, Monica Glitzman. Like I say, she lives in . . ."

The cop bellowed. "Hey, Harry." Across the room a bald head looked up from a desk. "Bring me that sheet." The bald head got up, walked across the room, dropped a single sheet of paper, and left with a brief sweep of the eyes over Anna.

"What's the matter?"

The cop was chuckling, looking at the paper. He flipped

9

it to Anna. "Monica Glitzman. Came in this morning." He watched her eyes grow wider. "She's gone too," he said unnecessarily.

O'Malley and Michael left their perch when the sun evaporated and walked back through the gathering cold. It was a hard climb up rapidly rising hills to the small ridge holding up the few dozen houses in the community. Michael didn't talk much until they reached the top; then he was puffing. O'Malley was barely breathing. Michael was impressed. "You're staying in shape, I'll give you that."

It was true. Stripped of the need to earn a living, life could be devoted to more pleasant pursuits, like long dreamlike runs along empty coast roads. O'Malley did it habitually, religiously, waiting with anticipation each day for the trance caused by the cold wind in his ears and the monotonous pounding of rubber on concrete. He did it as therapy, in the hope that for an hour a day the demons would leave him. Sometimes it even worked.

"Not much running on the boats, huh?"

Michael laughed. "Oh, you'll get your share, O'Malley," he told him.

Mary, the fisherman's wife, had treated O'Malley like her firstborn from the first day. She was a kindly, garrulous woman with a face lined deep with fifty-odd years of battering by ocean winds. When he first arrived she felt sorry for him, as many did, not because of what had happened in his past, but simply because they thought he was insane. Here he was, a lawyer, a man who could presumably make money anywhere, and by the standards of Gualala, a ton of money. Yet all he did for those first few months was stare at the ocean from the gummy window of a rented room at the Gualala Hotel. Later, when she learned his reasons, every maternal instinct in her formidable inventory responded.

She wrapped him in the bear hug she always gave him. He laughed and gave her one back. When she broke it she said, "It's pot roast tonight. Nothing fancy. We ain't L.A.

lawyers, you know." It was the same joke every time.

"In that case, I'm gone."

Mary went back to her kitchen. O'Malley wandered over to the window and looked down at the sea below. It was well past twilight and the boats were in, the men done pulling the fish from the holds and now in the last stages of wrapping the gear. He could see hoses being dragged from the pier to wash down the offal. The older men, the ones exempt from dreary cleanup tasks, were pulling off thigh-high rubber boots and casting hungry glances at the bar. It was Friday night and the checks were in the bank.

Michael came over and asked, "Goin' over tonight?"

"Sure." Friday night was party night, the night the whole town gathered for an evening of real fish stories. No wife, no matter how tight her rein, objected to Friday night.

Nevertheless Mike sensed something. He said, "You don't sound that interested."

O'Malley said, "It's not that. I'm doing too much thinking."

Mary came in and heard the remark. "And I know what you're thinkin'. You're thinkin' you can't sit on the porch the rest of your life."

O'Malley laughed. "That's what I'm doing?"

Mary said: "You bet it is. I know you went through a lot down there in L.A., and God knows that's a hellish place." Mary and the Ayatollah held one opinion in common, their view of L.A. She didn't quite call it "The Great Satan," but that was the general idea. Mary went on. "I know there's people got killed down there and all the rest, but you just can't sit on the porch and think about it forever."

"It's going away, Mary," he said quietly. "Day by day."

She shook her head vigorously. "It ain't gonna go away long's you sit and do nothing. You worked like to hell to get out of . . . where the hell was it?"

"Jersey. Bayonne. Great state, Mary. You know, Lou Costello. Bruce Springsteen."

"Never heard of it. Anyway, you scraped your way out.

Then you tried to love somebody and it didn't work. Hell, I know what that's like. Christ, you should see the ones I had before him." She jerked a finger at Michael.

"Hey, I never heard of . . ."

"Never mind," Mary said. "Anyway, you hear what I'm saying. What's done's done. You're a city boy, O'Malley, as city as a streetlight. Go on back." Then she punched him in the upper arm.

"Christ, Mary." He rubbed his arm and grinned at her. "We'll see."

After dinner Mike and O'Malley walked back down the hill. Mary said she'd come later. They didn't talk on the way down and O'Malley didn't even notice. When they got inside, Lainey behind the bar grinned at him and O'Malley grinned back at her, but his heart wasn't in it. Later on they would tickle and laugh in Lainey's big cedar bed in a room in the back, but right now even that thought didn't cheer him. He felt strangely alone and disoriented and for a moment thought of simply leaving, maybe wandering around in the dark of the beach for awhile to search for answers in the salt-scrubbed pebbles. Then Henry walked from the office in the back and yelled, "Hey, O'Malley, I got something for you."

He had to shout twice before O'Malley looked up. It wasn't unusual for Henry to have messages for him; the restaurant was like the town switchboard. He held up two fingers for Lainey and pointed one toward Michael, then walked over to Henry. He took the slip from the man's hands, squinting lightly as he tried to read the scrawl. "It's the number of some guy named Baird down in L.A.," Henry said. "Says he's got a big job for you."

O'Malley looked at it awhile before speaking. Then he said softly, "Mama, pack the bags."

2

It had been over three years since O'Malley had last seen L.A. and he wasn't really ready for it. The shock of recognition came when the stretch-727 swept east over the San Gabriel Mountains and began a landing rectangle that took it seventy-five miles inland. The plane then banked south, then west, finally taking its place in a queue behind eleven jumbo jets arriving from all parts of the world. Then it was seventy-five miles in to touchdown, a slow, casual descent over the whole of metropolitan Los Angeles, a postmodern megacity stretched flat to each horizon. At night ten million lights would blink harshly into the black.

Three years in the bushes will put the hayseed in anyone, even a jaded former habitué of North Jersey streets. O'Malley found himself staring open-mouthed at it all.

As he cleaned up in the airport bathroom he decided he at least *looked* a lot better than when last he faced an L. A. mirror. Then a dreaded office disease had ravaged him, leaving unhealthy eyes, pale cheeks, and more than a bit of softness in the middle. Three years on the Mendocino coast had made him no wiser, and certainly no richer, yet had considerably improved his mien. The farm-fresh food, sea air, and delicious Mendocino wines had taken away every last line around his eyes. They stared clear and bright from a lean face made ruddy by the good life. The face still sat upon a large frame just over two hundred pounds. Except now those pounds were tight.

*   *   *

He climbed into a rented Ford and headed in search of his friend Jerome Baird. He hadn't seen Baird at all in the three years prior to Baird's call, hadn't even spoken to him in fact. He decided if he had to do it all over again, that would be one thing he'd change. They had stood together, he and Baird, against all of them, the kid from North Jersey and the polished—if eccentric and lamentably ungainly—wizard from the top of the pile of bodies at Harvard Law School. They had nothing in common except a world view, that and a complete lack of understanding at what each was doing as part of the legal infantry of the great law firm of Jenkins and Dorman. They had left together, fought together, won together. And then had gone off to separate caves to lick the blood away.

Jerome Baird. A throwback in many ways. A man with the visage, manners, and breadth of knowledge of an Oxford don. From the eighteenth century, back when it was fashionable to have a comprehensive understanding of every possible academic discipline. Stress the academic, there, because Baird was equally bent on having a complete *lack* of information about anything that might be classed fashionable or trendy. That was one reason he looked the way he did, like a six-foot-six stick-man clothed by Goodwill. O'Malley thought there was a better than even chance his skinny frame would still be draped with the same suit.

The only thing O'Malley knew about Baird's whereabouts was an address on Sunset. He headed toward the west side, the fashionable side, figuring in three years Baird would have cashed in that incomparable mind for a very fancy price. It was the wrong side. When he ran out of land at the ocean he turned around and headed east, unnecessarily squinting at the descending numbers through twenty tedious miles of stop-and-go traffic. When he got to Hollywood he realized Baird was definitely not in the high-rent district.

The building itself was clean and ordinary: three stories, white, with a florist's shop on the bottom. A Mexican restaurant sat on the south side and something called a Scientology Testing Center on the north. Across the street, two nice-looking ladies in shorts smiled at him.

O'Malley ran up a set of more or less decrepit steps and into an empty reception area. The door to Baird's office was open. He walked in to find his friend staring thoughtfully at the street.

"A familiar pose," O'Malley said.

Baird turned and smiled broadly. "If it isn't the venerable Benjamin Aaron O'Malley, erstwhile felon, now Mendocino lotus eater. Welcome again to L.A."

"Accused felon, but thanks," O'Malley said. He looked around the room. "It was worth the trip just to see how successful you've become." The room was furnished with a wood-grained formica desk and metal chair, an aged and defeated walnut table, and a few tons of loose paper.

Baird looked around the room with him, then shrugged. "I started to spruce it up in your honor. Then . . ." He shrugged again, leaving whatever intervened unexplained.

O'Malley wandered over to the one window to look out on Sunset. Across the street two attractive young blonds in tight jeans were chatting amiably with an equally attractive young black girl. Occasionally, one would smile at a passing car. As O'Malley watched, a dark car pulled up, the driver had a brief conversation with the black girl, and then drove away with her. "The locals seem extraordinarily friendly," O'Malley observed.

Baird leaned forward to look. "Bread and butter, my friend, bread and butter." One of the two blonds left on the corner waved happily at Baird's face in the window. Baird waved back.

"Baird, I'm shocked."

"Don't be. These ladies are my clients, O'Malley, the same as the oil companies and banks used to be. And the business they're able to generate is really surprisingly large. Aside from the obvious, I also do their taxes, fight their domestic battles, manage their money. You'll be surprised to know my clients are the only ladies on Sunset Boulevard with trust funds for their children."

O'Malley was laughing. "You're kidding?"

"No, indeed." Baird played with his pencil, then said: "We each have to chase the ghosts in our own way, right?"

O'Malley nodded. They looked at each other for a moment. "But this case is different," O'Malley observed.

"This case is different," Baird said.

When Anna Bradley walked into Baird's office at 10:00 P.M. that night, O'Malley and Baird had already discussed the case for three hours. O'Malley thought he knew exactly what to expect.

He was wrong. The woman sitting across from Baird's desk was neither dressed in black nor heavy-eyed from weeping. Her pale green eyes were steady and sure. The hair was bright yellow, falling loosely over her shoulders. She was dressed in a crisp, tan suit. It was neither severe nor mournful.

Baird had told O'Malley that Anna was attractive. He didn't disagree, yet would not have called the woman stirring. Anna had taken the components of beauty and packaged them in a formal, learned way. Her mouth was full and fashionably rouged, the teeth even and white, the cheekbones high. The neck was long and slim, hidden for the most part in a high-buttoned white blouse. The blouse fell over full breasts to tuck around a slim waist. The skirt was conservative, the crossed legs slim. The jewelry was tasteful.

Every inch of Anna said she could imagine no life in which she did not have a great deal of money.

Baird introduced O'Malley. "Anna, this is the lawyer I told you about. We were together at Jenkins and Dorman." Anna nodded and held out a cool hand. "I've asked him to come down and help us," Baird continued. "As I said, it's not going to be inexpensive."

"Yes, you did," she said. To O'Malley's ear, the voice

16

had a tinge of British in it. Yet from what Baird had told him, the woman was as American as a freeway. She turned to Baird. "I must tell you I'm extremely anxious to begin this investigation. The suspense of not knowing where John is, or . . . whether . . ." She fumbled with the word, then left the obvious unsaid.

Baird nodded sympathetically. "I understand. Let me tell you first of all the two main things I believe we can do to help you. One is to put pressure on the authorities in Los Angeles to begin taking the case seriously. That will be my responsibility. If we're successful, a detective will be assigned full-time within two weeks. Then things should move much quicker." She nodded.

Baird gestured toward O'Malley. "But we have to assume the police may remain uninvolved. That's where O'Malley comes in. He'll do the leg work the police can't or won't, talking to people, knocking on doors, trying to understand the situation. The more he can find out, the easier it will be for us to convince the police to take this seriously."

She nodded again. "What do they think now?"

Baird spread his hands. "They believe what you would expect them to believe, Mrs. Bradley. They believe your husband ran away with his secretary."

"Of course." She turned to O'Malley. "You've never been a detective, I trust."

"No. Would you prefer a detective?"

"No, of course not." She turned back to Baird. "You understand this is very embarrassing for me. Nevertheless, I want my husband found, regardless of what questions must be asked or what publicity results. Do you understand?"

"I understand."

There wasn't a shake or a tremor in her voice. "And I hope you understand that too, Mr. O'Malley. I don't care who you have to talk to or how loudly they protest. Oh, by the way—money is absolutely no object. Do I make myself clear?"

"I understand." He didn't really, but he assumed Baird

would tell him what the woman was talking about. What was anybody going to protest about? The lady's husband had disappeared and she was trying to get him back. No one could fault her for that. He only half heard the discussion going on between Anna and Baird, thinking instead about the sort of man who would marry this woman—and then leave her. Her money would be a powerful inducement to remain. Would her full mouth and slim legs? Was Anna the sort of woman who used those charms to thrill her husband? Or were they ornamental, like the small jewels on her gold cigarette case. Anna opened the case and put a white cigarette between her lips, waiting patiently, and O'Malley decided the jury was still out on that one.

3

O'Malley drove his shiny Fairmont past the disingenuous sign welcoming him to Beverly Hills. The car stopped bouncing over the Sunset Strip potholes and began cruising like a jetliner. He felt a sense of peace brought on by sudden proximity to unthinkable amounts of money. On his right, an enormous mansion decorated before oil glut days by a crazed and now bankrupt Arab sat boarded and charred. It still sported dozens of statues with painted genitalia roguishly facing Sunset. At the sight of it he remembered again that money does not always buy peace, or even taste.

The Bank of America needs several branches in the Beverly Hills enclave to handle the flow. O'Malley walked into the air-conditioned foyer of one of them and knew immediately this was not a place that took itself lightly.

"May I help you?" a receptionist asked swiftly.

"Yes. My name is Benjamin O'Malley. I've got an appointment with a Mr. Whitworth Franklin."

"Of course, sir. Please have a seat."

He walked over and sat among some folks in tennis clothes. They weren't smiling either. Across the wide floor on the other side of the bank, hordes formed a hundred-foot queue for the privilege of offering another fifty bucks each to the bank with more assets than any in the world.

O'Malley didn't have to wait in any queues. Five minutes after his arrival a smartly dressed young woman with crisp manners, a gorgeous smile, and a tag on her breast that said "Carol Fields" asked him to follow her. They rode up eighteen stories without speaking and she led him to a plump armchair facing a staggering view of green hills. She poured coffee from a sterling set.

"This is terrific service," O'Malley told her. "I've got fifteen hundred in a passbook at Security Pacific. I'll be over tomorrow to transfer it."

The woman smiled indulgently. "Thank you, Mr. O'Malley," she said. "The people downstairs will be more than happy to help you."

He nodded with understanding. "I take it Mrs. Bradley has more than fifteen hundred?"

The woman didn't banter. "Mrs. Bradley is a valued customer, Mr. O'Malley," she said seriously. "As Director of Client Relations, I have the task of ensuring that the wishes of clients such as Mrs. Bradley are carried out expeditiously." She said it easily, without pretense or affectation. She was undoubtedly very good at her job.

"How much does it take to get that sort of treatment?" She didn't answer. "Okay, let me guess. Six figures."

Carol Fields smiled in a perfectly charming way. "Mr. O'Malley, this is the Bank of America. Clients with six figures are handled quite efficiently on our first floor."

O'Malley was whistling softly to himself at that one

when their chat was interrupted by the entrance of Mr. Whitworth Franklin. Franklin was slim and correct, dark-suited, with an affable manner. He was also obviously good at what he did. They shook hands and Franklin sat down. Carol Fields poured her boss some tea.

"I must confess, Mr. O'Malley, I'm somewhat in the dark as to the precise purpose of your visit," Franklin began. "I received a note from your Mr. Baird, who told me to expect you. The note had appended to it a note from Mrs. Bradley granting you full access." The correctness only partially hid his curiosity. "How may we be of help?"

"We've been asked by Mrs. Bradley to do a . . . a sort of investigation . . . into various of her accounts," O'Malley told him. "The purpose need not concern you."

"Of course," the man said. His disappointment did not show.

"So I'd like to ask a couple of questions first and then spend the rest of the morning going over the accounts, if I may."

"Of course," Franklin agreed. "What do you need to know?"

"First of all, what accounts do the Bradleys maintain?"

Franklin held out his hand and Carol Fields placed a tan folder in it. His eyes ran down a list. "A great variety, actually. Mrs. Bradley has a number of checking accounts—three in her own name and one joint account with her husband. Then there are the trust accounts; the CD's"—his finger was running down the page—"quite a few of those actually, with differing maturity dates. Then the bonds, the deposit boxes, more trust accounts, the stock portfolios, and finally the accounts we maintain for the executor of her father's estate." He chuckled. "There's even an old passbook account in here with ten thousand dollars she must have completely forgotten about."

"How long has she been a customer?"

"Mrs. Bradley has been a customer in her own name since 1954, when her father opened a Christmas Club for her. Her father was our customer for thirty years before that. Her grandfather"—his tone approached awe—"was a very, very good customer for a number of years before that."

"So she inherited her money."

Franklin nodded. "That's right. The trust accounts and accounts we maintain for the executor of the estate are by far the bulk of her holdings."

"Can she get at those?"

"Certainly. If approved by the executor. And the executor is quite generous."

"I hope so. It's her money." Old bank, old money, and apparently plenty of it for Anna.

"Where exactly did the money come from?" O'Malley asked.

"Anna Bradley's maiden name was Anna Kendall," Franklin said. "Her father was Edward Kendall, Jr. Her grandfather was the founder of Kendall Industries." O'Malley nodded, impressed. He had known Anna had inherited money, but this was big time. Kendall Industries was a massive California conglomerate into everything from chemicals to moon landings.

"That's amazing. How much of the Kendall stock did she inherit?"

"Why, all of it," Whitworth Franklin said simply.

O'Malley paused while the information sliced through the fog. He now understood all the attention he was getting. "O.K., let's return to earth," O'Malley said. "You said Anna and John had a joint checking account?"

"That's right."

"What was the average monthly balance on the joint account?"

Franklin shuffled through some figures. "Ten thousand five hundred dollars."

"And how much of that was deposited by him?"

More rustling. "Mr. Bradley contributed a monthly average of eight hundred dollars to that account."

"But I'll bet he writes more checks on it than that."

Franklin smiled. "Yes, he writes all the checks on the joint account," he said. "Mrs. Bradley uses her own account."

A kept man. So why would a kept man walk away from the feedbox? "What was the average monthly on her personal account, the one she used most?"

For the first time the banker betrayed a hint of nervousness. He licked his lips slightly. "That depends what year you're speaking of."

"What does that mean?"

"From 1975 through 1977, the average monthly was fifteen thousand dollars. Beginning in late 1977 and early 1978, it jumped to eighteen thousand five. Lately it's been running between twenty-two and twenty-five thousand."

"And what's the reason for that?"

"I'm afraid that is something you'll have to ask Mrs. Bradley," he said abruptly. He turned to his assistant. "Ms. Fields, please bring Mr. O'Malley the canceled checks from the 8456 account. January 1977 to date. And he'll also be needing another cup of coffee."

The lovely Ms. Fields sauntered away, returning with some young men with boxes of documents. She then gracefully poured him another cup.

Franklin left and took Fields with him, a disappointment but at least the end of a distraction. O'Malley began leafing through the canceled checks. Each year he found the normal crazy expenditures to the Beverly Hills shops, thousands upon thousands of dollars spent on shoes and jewels and clothes in stores he had never heard of. In late 1977, he began to detect the cause of Franklin's concern. The banker returned an hour later just as O'Malley found the last one. He sat down quietly next to O'Malley. The two men stared at each other for a moment and then O'Malley looked again at the separate stack he had erected of checks made out to "Cash." He had them in chronological order, the oldest ones on the top. The numbers got bigger the further down in the pile he went.

"They're all endorsed by the secretary," O'Malley observed. "Monica, the one he ran away with. And they're all signed by Anna." O'Malley looked up at Whitworth Franklin, hoping for a rational explanation.

Franklin rose. "I've been hoping for a long time someone would look into this situation," the banker said.

4

O'Malley bounded up the wide, granite steps of the fake library building and confronted the third guard of his visit. He handed that guard the green slips given him by the two others and was led down a skinny hallway. On the walls were framed black and whites of dead stars. At the end of the hall a fancy set of double walnut doors with a gold inscription heralded the quarters of Brenton Roberts, Vice-President and General Counsel. West Coast.

Roberts's desk virtually squeaked with cleanliness. It was glass-topped and offered a beautiful reflection of the forest of plants in his office. A single sheet of paper with an envelope attached lay neatly in his "in" box. As O'Malley walked in, a secretary lifted it with two hands and placed it in front of Roberts. Roberts signed with a flourish. The secretary picked it up with two hands and carried it carefully away.

Roberts turned to O'Malley. "Just no way to get out from under, I guess." He flicked away a speck of dust that had apparently been left by the letter. He wore the most beautiful tie O'Malley had ever seen.

O'Malley sat down. "I can see you're a busy man, so I'll try to be brief," he said. "As I told you on the phone, I'm a lawyer working for Anna Bradley. I'm trying to find out everything I can about her husband. I don't know if you can help or not, but this seemed as good a place as any to start."

Roberts's small eyes darted back and forth as O'Malley spoke, as though he wanted to always be sure the exits were clear. O'Malley thought the man's reports must read the same. "I really had very little contact with Mr. Bradley," Roberts began predictably. "He was our controller, of course. And I suppose we'd meet from time to time when it was necessary to give board reports. But we were not in the same chain of command."

"What exactly did he do?"

"What you'd expect him to do," Roberts said. "His job was to ensure the integrity of the financial records of the company. He was also responsible for all internal audits, required to verify the documentation supporting the figures."

"What does that mean?"

"It means it was his job to make sure no one inside the company was cheating the company."

O'Malley nodded. "Was he honest?"

Roberts squirmed. "I've not yet seen any evidence that would conclusively demonstrate Bradley did not act in the best interests of the company."

O'Malley laughed a little. "Do they have classes where they teach you to talk like that?"

"No," Roberts told him curtly. "I learned to be precise on my own."

"Well, are you willing to tell me what you suspect?"

Roberts hesitated. "No, but I'm willing to tell you that the company is presently conducting an investigation."

"Why?"

"Because the man occupied a responsible position and has disappeared under unusual circumstances."

"Who ordered the investigation?"

"I did."

"Who told you to do that?"

"No one. I decided to look into this on my own." He smiled as though he were very proud of himself.

"Who's doing the investigation?" O'Malley asked.

"I am."

"Is the investigation complete?"

Roberts hesitated again. "I'm really not authorized to tell you anything about our internal investigations," he said slowly. "Especially on a matter of this sensitivity." He studied his clean desk for a moment. "However, I wish to have one interview with you, not two. Therefore, let me say the investigation is completed but the results have not yet been made public."

"And you still haven't seen anything that shows the man's a crook?"

"I said 'conclusively.' Conclusively demonstrates he had acted in a manner adverse to the interests of the company. I remember exactly what I said."

"Do you think we can stop playing games, Roberts?" They stared at each other for a moment. "I'm a lawyer representing the man's wife and I'm entitled to some answers," O'Malley said evenly. "I certainly would prefer to get them informally, just between the two of us. But I'm not going to just walk away empty-handed, and this fencing just makes things take longer."

Roberts seemed to consider it, then nodded. "All right, I'll tell you our suspicions. The investigative report will reach the conclusion that there are no facts that conclusively demonstrate Bradley was corrupt. And that report is accurate as far as it goes. However, there is no question in my mind he was taking money."

"What do you mean taking money? Embezzling?"

"Not in the sense you mean it," Roberts said. "When I say 'taking money,' I mean taking money from persons outside the company in order to do favors for them."

"Bribes, then."

"If you wish."

O'Malley laughed again. "That makes absolutely no sense. Do you know how much money this man's wife has?"

"Of course. His wife is heir to the Kendall Industries fortune."

"So why would a man like that take bribes? And why on earth if he was taking bribes would he suddenly leave town? That just about guarantees an inquiry."

Roberts shrugged. "I'm afraid you'll have to ask John Bradley those questions, Mr. O'Malley."

"What do you base your suspicions on? Who was bribing him?" O'Malley asked.

Roberts rose and walked to the window. Then he turned to face O'Malley with his hands behind his back. "I don't mean to be coy with you, but this is where I must draw the line. These are my suspicions only, not the conclusion of the report. Besides, a detailed response to that question would require disclosure of confidential corporate matters. However, I can tell you this much. The foundations of my belief, among other things, are transactions that are explainable on no other basis."

"What sort of transactions?"

"Sales and purchases of product for the company."

"That just about covers the field, doesn't it?"

"In essence, yes."

"So what was wrong?"

"The prices."

"What about the prices?"

"They were high when they should have been low and low when they should have been high," Roberts said. His tone said O'Malley was not going to be asking questions forever.

"And you think he was on the take?" O'Malley asked quickly. "You think that explains it?"

Roberts shrugged and looked at his watch.

O'Malley spoke fast. "So why aren't you investigating further? Why not look into it?"

Roberts seemed vaguely uncomfortable at the question.

He looked toward the exits. "In my judgment further inquiry would not be in the best interests of the company," he said finally.

It would be rude to laugh, O'Malley decided. He had only known the man ten minutes yet knew Roberts didn't get to exercise his judgment on anything more weighty than when to take lunch. Except he had decided all by himself to look into this. He had not been the one who decided to end it.

"Let me ask you something else," O'Malley said. "What do you know about her?"

"Who?"

"The secretary. Monica."

Roberts's face wrinkled. "The woman is slime, Mr. O'Malley."

O'Malley did smile this time. "Excuse me, Reverend, but do you think you could climb down from the pulpit long enough to give me a sensible answer?"

"I have given you a sensible answer, sir," Roberts said stiffly. "The woman's morals are the morals of the gutter. She is a prostitute." Roberts sat very erect when he said the word.

"Roberts," O'Malley began pedantically, "the fact that a woman sleeps around doesn't make her a prostitute. It just makes her . . . well, friendly . . ."

Roberts leaned over the table and looked into O'Malley's face. He spoke slowly and with emphasis. "Mr. O'Malley, believe it or not, I know what friendly is. What I am telling you is that our investigators discovered that Ms. Monica Glitzman Davis or whatever other names she goes by was and presumably still is a certified, card-carrying, professional, and very high-class prostitute."

"Oh."

In return for getting out of his office, Roberts gave O'Malley permission to walk around and ask questions. For thirty minutes. O'Malley checked the directory and quickly went down the metal stairs and through a glass door marked "International Auditing." The secretarial area was in front of him and he thought he had died and gone to heaven. At each of fifteen desks sat an aspiring young actress, dancer, whatever, each lovelier than the last. Somewhere, somehow, back in time, someone must have made it big starting as a studio secretary. Ever since, the halls had been crammed with delicious young things looking for the same break.

O'Malley searched around for the oldest face he could find. That face was crowned by raven hair and looked out at the world through pale green eyes. A blue tag on her white silk blouse said her name was Brenda. She was probably twenty-three.

"Are you the boss around here?" he asked her.

Brenda looked up and gave him a grin that made his mouth go dry. "Right now, yeah. At least until Simmons gets back from lunch." She looked him up and down. "Where are you from?"

"Bayonne."

She nodded sagely. A girl on her way up couldn't afford to be uninformed. "I thought they usually sent black guys to do their buying." When O'Malley stared open-mouthed, she became flustered. "Wait, wait," she said. She went fumbling through a list, then snapped her fingers. "That's Gabon, not Bayonne." She went to another list, this one apparently alphabetical. "You're from France, right?"

"Right," O'Malley said. "Just across from New Amsterdam."

"So what can I do for you?" She smiled at him again.

O'Malley sat on the edge of her desk and looked down. Those green eyes would confuse any honest man, so he selected a point on the wall to look at while he talked. "I'm a sort of investigator," he said carefully. "I've been sent down to learn what I can about John Bradley and Monica."

"No kidding. They took the money and ran after all, huh?"

So much for Roberts's confidential investigation. "What makes you think that?"

Brenda shrugged and grinned but didn't say anything. She seemed to have a nose for knowing when she had something that someone else wanted. O'Malley realized the green eyes weren't nearly so soft as he'd supposed. Brenda might well be the kind of girl who didn't give up anything of value for love.

"Have you been interviewed by the investigators?" he asked her.

"Sure."

"And did you tell them what you know?"

She laughed at that. "You mean in gratitude for this great job filing Simmons's papers?"

O'Malley was beginning to understand. "What would it take to unlock those lovely lips?"

"More than a kiss, Mr. Frenchman."

"I'm prepared to give more than a kiss." Then O'Malley got it. "If I can get the kiss, that is," he said.

Brenda grinned as widely as O'Malley thought she would. "There's no one around here who can tell you more about her than I can," she said eagerly. She waved her arm around the room. "They're just kids. But she and I were tight. Like sisters, sort of. Monica and I roomed together."

Interesting. "Maybe you were even in the same business?"

Brenda's laugh was bright. "Yeah, we were both great typists." She grabbed some paper and wrote down an address and phone number. "I'm free from about eight on," she told him. "But I'd call a little earlier. Just in case I get a last-minute date, you know."

"I know."

Brenda studied him again. "And I know you're a real serious guy who's after real serious information. But maybe I can make it fun for you to get it."

O'Malley took the slip. "O.K."

29

*　　*　　*

O'Malley was walking briskly past Roberts's office on his way to the exit when he felt a harsh hand on his shoulder. The hand spun him around. O'Malley turned to see a crusty old man in a dark three-piece suit. The old man's face was flushed. He looked like a man who had always been angry.

"What the hell's going on here?" The words were shouted.

O'Malley looked at the man with faint contempt. "Who the hell are you?" he asked pleasantly.

"Never mind who I am," the man shouted. "I said what the hell's going on here. When I ask a question, I expect an answer." The veins in the man's neck were bulging.

"Fuck you," O'Malley said cheerfully. "How's that for an answer?"

The man turned purple and sucked in air as a prelude to more bellowing. Before he could get it out, Roberts came scurrying from behind the door.

"What's the problem here?"

"Is this the guy?" the old man demanded.

Roberts cleared his throat nervously. "Yes, David, this is Benjamin O'Malley. He represents John Bradley—or rather Mrs. Bradley—and he came in to . . ."

The old man cut him off. "To ask you questions. To pry around. To stick his nose where it doesn't belong. And you, being possessed of no more than half the wit you were born with, which wasn't that much, decided to let him do that. Do I have it right?"

"David, please," Roberts began.

"Get out of here," the old man ordered evenly. To O'Malley's absolute astonishment Roberts coughed once, spun on his heel, and walked meekly behind his large double doors.

O'Malley thought it was a great show. He clapped in appreciation.

The man named David turned to him, inspecting him

carefully. This time the gravelly voice was soft, well modulated, and very smooth. "O.K. Mr. Benjamin O'Malley, whatever the fuck that is, I'm going to make a little speech for you right here in the hall and I want you to listen very closely. Whatever that moron told you, you never heard, understand?"

"No. Who the hell are you? That was my first question."

The man considered it. "Perino," he said finally. "The name is David Perino."

O'Malley didn't say anything, just spent a moment studying the man. From everything he had read in the papers he expected Perino to be about seventy-five or eighty years old, yet up close the man looked fifteen years younger. Although the face was heavily lined, the man's arms and chest were strong and well-developed. The eyes were piercing, set deep within a perpetual scowl. Perino was a large man impeccably dressed in a very formal fashion. His near-bald head jutted forward in a combative pose. He looked as powerful and as dangerous as he was supposed to be.

"Pleased to meet you, Mr. Perino," O'Malley said finally. "I didn't know you were still, uh, active." Actually O'Malley had thought Perino was either dead or in jail. "What do you know about John Bradley? As a matter of fact, what are you doing out here at all?"

Perino's manner didn't change. He just moved closer and his voice became even softer. "You're not listening, friend," he said. "I didn't ask for conversation. I told you to forget whatever that moron told you. That's all I want. Understand?"

"Why?"

"Because it's my business. That means it's none of your business."

"Why is it your business?"

"I'm a friend of the boss. The top boss. Somebody you never heard of."

"I represent Bradley's wife."

"So I heard."

"Don't you think that gives me the right to ask questions here?"

"No," Perino told him, stepping still closer. "I think you should go away. That's what I think."

O'Malley cleared his throat and started to get a little nervous. Perino was not likely to enjoy playing games. "I heard there was an investigation. I think I'm entitled to know what it was about."

"I'll kill that little fuck." Perino said it softly and to himself. Then he spoke to O'Malley. "The investigation is all over. It concluded Bradley was a Boy Scout. Eagle Scout, I think."

"That's not what I heard. I heard the man's a crook."

"You heard wrong."

"You can't hide it," O'Malley told him. "There's an investigative report around someplace. That's going to set it out in black and white."

"It got lost. Now everybody's operating from memory. They remember him as a prince."

O'Malley smirked and felt more courageous. "What about the guy behind that door?" He pointed to Roberts's large gold-embossed doors.

"What about him?"

"He may be a moron but he remembers it different. What are you going to do about him?"

This time Perino laughed, a hearty laugh that had him throwing back his head. He went over to Roberts's door and pounded hard with a fist three times. Roberts came out looking as ashen as he had going in. Perino put an arm around him and led him over to O'Malley. He patted him gently.

"Roberts, our little friend here was telling me about some report on John Bradley. Know anything about that?"

Roberts's head was bouncing back and forth as if he were in the fancy seats at Forest Hills. He started coughing. Finally he spoke: "Not a thing, David," he said.

5

O'Malley called Baird from a phone booth on the studio lot cut in the shape of a cartoon animal. They agreed to meet right away for a drink.

Baird was sitting alone at the bar when he got there. Small scraps of paper were scattered over the full width of the dark wood. He was scribbling furiously, occasionally taking a sip and scribbling some more. When a scrap was filled with writing, he half crumpled it and jammed it in a pocket. His pockets were bulging.

O'Malley sat next to him. "Is this a refinement on the Dewey Decimal System?"

"Don't worry, O'Malley, I know exactly where every piece of information is," Baird said. He reached into his pocket and pulled out a pink slip, holding it aloft without looking at it. "My interview notes with Mrs. Bradley's accountant." He pulled out another crumpled slip. "My bill to Mrs. Bradley's accountant." He put them back. "This is a very sophisticated operation, O'Malley."

"I can see that. So what have you found out and written on your little slips of paper?"

"No, you first." Baird hollered, "Sam," and the bartender turned, shook his head, and came over with a bunch more of the bar tabs. Baird was using the blank part on the back. "One of my clients," Baird explained. "Go ahead."

"Well, I've been to the bank and the studio. Strange things at both places. So far it doesn't make a lot of sense."

"Start with the bank."

33

"First of all, you have no notion how much money this lady has. Total red carpet treatment for me. They had this wonderful head of client relations pour me coffee until the vice-president could come in himself. They're real interested in keeping Mrs. Bradley happy, and the same goes for anybody working for her. If the Bank of America has an account to offer, Anna has two or three of them."

"She's a rich heiress. We know that."

"Patience. I'm working up to the big stuff. Anna has two kinds of checking accounts, separate accounts for herself, and a joint account with John. The account he has access to averages about ten thousand a month, which is a fortune for you and me but is nothing in her world. Her accounts are different: big, fat, and sassy, with lots of checks going to lots of places on Rodeo Drive. Nevertheless, so far nothing strange. The strange part is the number of checks going to Monica from Anna's separate accounts."

When Baird heard shocking news his mouth had a funny way of forming a distorted "O," with lips pursed. His head usually remained fixed. He had that look now. "Would you run that by me again?" he asked.

"Sure. Our client was paying off the secretary, the one that her husband supposedly ran off with. And Mrs. Bradley wasn't the only one paying Monica off the studio books. It turns out Monica is in the same business as your clients on the Sunset street corners, although probably for a somewhat higher fee. I'll tell you about that later." Baird's lips made another little "O."

"The checks to Monica got bigger as time went on," O'Malley continued. "They started about 1977."

Baird was recovering slowly. "How much?"

"In the beginning, maybe five hundred a month. Later on, as much as two thousand a month."

"All signed by Anna?" Baird asked weakly.

O'Malley was disappointed. Baird shook his head to clear the fog. "That's right, you said they were from her

34

separate accounts. Just give me a moment." He grabbed his Jack Daniels and sloshed it back cleanly. He thought for a moment and then turned to O'Malley.

"She had to know you'd get to the bank accounts sooner or later."

"Maybe. So what?"

"What does that tell you?"

O'Malley shrugged. "O.K., maybe she wanted to find out. Maybe she was afraid to come right out and say so?"

"Why?"

"Gee, Baird, this is fun. A Socratic dialogue, just like law school." When Baird didn't respond, O'Malley sighed and spread his hands. "The easiest guess is she was being blackmailed."

"For what?"

O'Malley was getting exasperated. "How do I know? What do people get blackmailed for? Murder, rape, piracy, treason. The usual."

"Or an indiscretion?" Baird suggested.

"O.K.," O'Malley agreed. "That's typical."

"If an indiscretion, then John's disappearance with Monica is particularly ironic."

O'Malley nodded. "It also takes two people away from the feedbag, whatever the reason for the blackmail."

Baird grinned. "That's excellent." Whatever that meant. Then Baird abruptly changed the subject. "What happened at the studio?"

O'Malley thought for a moment. "I found out some interesting things and some more strange things. I still don't know what it all means."

"The suspense is killing me." Baird made a face to register impatience.

"Well, to start with, some functionary named Brenton Roberts tried to investigate John's conduct. To say he smelled a rat would be putting it mildly."

"Why John's conduct?"

"Because they think he's a crook."

"I repeat. Why?"

"I'm not sure," O'Malley said. "Roberts would only tell me his guesses. It had to do with selling or buying product quote unquote. Maybe he had an auditor go in and check the missing auditor. Anyway, Roberts thinks John Bradley was on the take from somebody or other."

"Who?"

"I don't know. Presumably people on the other side of the deal."

"One time or lots of times?"

"From what I could figure, lots of times. But Roberts wasn't talking."

"Lots of dollars, too?"

"I think so."

Baird thought for a moment, then said, "Where's the investigation going?"

"That's the best part. After I met Roberts I ran into a celebrity by the name of David Perino." Baird's head jerked up from his drink. "That's right, the one and only. Perino wants an investigation like Nixon did. Roberts is probably feeding his report to the shredder even as we speak."

"That's incredible," Baird said. "Anna mentioned John had dealings with Perino, but I had no idea we'd be running into him this soon." For the first time he seemed slightly unnerved.

"What do you know about him? Perino, I mean."

Baird leaned back, seeming to let his mind rifle through a mental card catalogue. "I looked into it a little," he began. "Wasn't hard because there's a lot written on him. Born Biagio Perrantonio 1905 or thereabouts in southern Italy. Not Sicilian, you understand, but close enough. Came to Ellis Island in the early twenties together with four generations of his family. The customs people gave them all a new name. Perino's father was one of the most famous of the early Mafiosi, operating out of New York as part of the Cap-

36

pici organization until his untimely demise in a barber's chair in 1939. By then young David was not only a full-fledged member of the New York bar but had graduated to become the Cappicis' principal tax advisor, a job that required more knowledge of the laws of Switzerland than the United States."

"How the hell you know all that?"

"I read, O'Malley. I do research. They're delightful exercises. Anyway, when the Cappici family decided to move into Las Vegas during the war, they sent Perino first to smooth the way. He was so successful, he was made counselor the next year. He stayed with the Cappicis until the early fifties, when he ostensibly left them to move to California and mingle with the movie crowd. He's been here ever since."

"You mean he practices law here?"

Baird shook his head. "According to the papers he's not even a member of the California bar. He just gives advice. And does favors for people. And gets things done. He's sort of a free-lance counselor, if you will, taking a piece of every deal he works on. He supposedly works by himself with some clerical help in an elaborate office in Century City."

"So how is he wrapped up with John Bradley?"

Baird waved the question away. "That we will have to find out. What else do you have?"

"Well, as I said, our girl Monica was a lady of uncertain reputation. The scandalous rumor is she does not give her love away for free. What I've also found out is Monica wasn't the only one with that sideline."

Baird shook his head. "Believe it or not, there was a time I didn't know anybody in that business. Go ahead."

"All that doesn't prove anything; as a matter of fact, it just confuses things. If Monica was a professional, it makes it kind of hard to buy the love angle."

Baird held up two fingers for his client, the bartender, and two more Jack Daniels appeared. "True," he said. "Let

37

me tell you what I learned downtown. There's a young cop dying to work on this case. I was excited until I talked to him. He sounds like he should still be down on the farm. Preferably pulling the plow."

"Even farm boys like long legs and green eyes," O'Malley suggested.

"That seems to be it," Baird agreed. "Anyway, the people who count have no intention of getting involved. So the way it is now, we're on our own. They're just sitting. They've got a missing persons out and John is now in a computer printout with tens of thousands of prepubescent Iowans."

"So what'll we do now?" O'Malley asked.

Baird finished his drink and rose. "More of the same for awhile," he said, a bit resigned. "I've got a meeting tomorrow with a captain and three lieutenants. Then I've got letters going out to every local official I can think of, and the press as well. Maybe they'll get sick of me and do something to shut me up. Like assigning someone decent to the case. Maybe not. What about you? Where are you off to tomorrow?"

O'Malley finished his too, and tipped the bartender. "Baird, you don't know what a hard worker you have," he told him with a grin. "I'm going back on the job tonight."

O'Malley drove back to the hotel for some room service dinner and a quick shower. Half an hour later, he was all but unconscious under the hot spray. It was a delicious feeling, soothing a long day of concentration. He heard nothing and felt nothing. All those lovely hot needles!

Then he got out of the shower, grabbed a towel, and strolled into the bedroom to find every worldly possession he owned lying ravaged in the middle of the floor.

He felt the hormones surge and raced through the still open door. The white towel flapped rakishly behind him. A man stood casually by the elevator. He wore a dark suit and his hands were in his coat pockets. The red arrow on the elevator was pressed down.

O'Malley was too angry to feel foolish or afraid. He walked up to the man. The man didn't take his hands out of his pockets. The fellow's face was pockmarked and his mouth cruel. He didn't look the least bit surprised to see O'Malley standing half-naked before him.

"Did you see anybody come out of that room?" O'Malley asked abruptly. He was standing no more than six inches from the man.

The man stared at him for a moment, then turned back to the elevator. He pressed the down button again.

"I asked you a question," O'Malley said slowly.

The man still said nothing.

"Let me ask it a different way. Were you just in my room?"

The man's hand started to come out of the coat pocket. O'Malley's right hand flashed down hard on the wrist. The man's wrist and forearm were wooden. Nevertheless, he couldn't pull the hand out of the pocket.

They stared at each other for a moment. The man smiled in a casual, knowing way and O'Malley felt bright beads of sweat erupt on his upper lip. Then, as comedic relief, the elevator suddenly opened. A woman gasped. The man pulled his arm free and stepped backward into the elevator. O'Malley let him go, watching the door close after him.

He went back to the room. His wallet lay defiled in the middle of the floor, its contents methodically strewn about. The cash sat untouched among the pieces of paper. All his clothes had been pulled from the drawers, separated, undoubtedly searched, and thrown as waste into the middle of the floor. Even the paperbacks from the airport had been ripped in half and tossed like dead things on top of the heap.

But O'Malley was nothing if not resilient. He looked it all over one more time, sighed, called the maid, and made a

drink. Then he lit a cigarette and blew smoke over the carnage, a primitive gesture to drive away the demons. It got rid
of about half the anger. The half that was left entertained
itself with the delicious thought of meeting the pockmarked
man again.

Brenda lived in one of a series of recently constructed
and what were supposed to have been enormously chic high
rises on the western part of Wilshire Boulevard. Set between
Beverly Hills and Westwood, the apartments and condominiums had arrived with fanfare and controversy, then
proceeded to slide down the toilet with the real estate bust,
bankrupting a host of Arab speculators in the process, to the
delight of the local media. Nevertheless, even half-empty the
units were prohibitively expensive. To live there required
much more wealth than any secretary could muster. Unless
she had a lucrative outside source of income, that is.

O'Malley drove past Brenda's high rise and continued
on into Westwood, then through the UCLA campus to Sunset. He passed through the august gates of Bel Air and on
down Stone Canyon Road. No secretary could afford to live
in this district either, no matter what her outside source of
funds. Nor could a head accountant at a movie studio. But
John Bradley had.

The Bradley house was nestled in a small cove of houses
just past the Bel Air Hotel. The sweep of the road gave the
house a large plot of territory in the rear. It was set well back
from the street, hidden by a row of erect Italian cypresses
standing at attention like Swiss guards. A narrow blacktop
driveway sliced through the trees toward the house.

O'Malley drove the Fairmont through the tiny gap in
the Swiss guards and parked. It was hard to tell if anyone
was home. The outside lights were already on, probably set
by a timer. Inside the house he saw a pale glow that could
have been anything. An incongruously nondescript American car sat alone in the driveway.

He went up to the large wooden door and rang the bell,

listening intently to the silence that followed. He tried again twice and was rewarded by more of the same. He reached for the knocker because it was there, without any real hope of success.

That done, he wandered over to the garage. It was a four-car affair, three-fourths full. A gorgeous black Bentley shimmered, even in the dark, flanked by a cream 450 SEL. At the far left sat something low, sleek, red, and Italian. Then O'Malley laughed with more genuine delight than he had felt in a long time. At the rear of the red car a familiar figure in a dark suit fumbled in the trunk.

The man had his back to O'Malley. He had a briefcase open and was examining some papers. To the man's left was a small door. O'Malley went over and opened it.

The man turned at the sound of the door. His eyes were wide, trying to focus in the dim light. The face was full of deep pits.

"Hi," said O'Malley good-naturedly. "You know it really is true what they say about a small world."

The man's face registered no emotion, not even surprise. He turned, shut the lid of the briefcase, and slammed the trunk of the Ferrari. The silver lock on the trunk was badly twisted. When he turned again, he held the briefcase in his left hand.

O'Malley felt strong, full of Gaelic spunk. He found himself giddy with anticipation. He clenched and un-clenched his large hands. "That briefcase yours?"

The man stepped forward. "I'm leaving now."

It was the first time O'Malley had heard him speak. The voice was dull; there wasn't a wisp of intelligence in it. The man sounded as thick as his arms had felt.

"To get out, you've got to talk to me."

"No," the man said simply.

"In that case, you know what you have to do."

The man waved his hand to the right and moved closer. "I want you to move out of the way."

O'Malley shrugged. "Sorry."

The man's right hand came up hard. O'Malley caught it on the shoulder, spun, and buried his head in the man's chest, coming up hard with the hands. He worked inside, looking for the soft spot in the belly, the solar plexus, around the back of the kidneys. In close quarters, he did well. The pockmarked man was hard, yet at each blow he let out an "Oof."

The man backed up against the Ferrari, felt it, and deftly moved to the side. O'Malley followed him, trying to get back into tight quarters. This time the man dropped the case, moved to get himself some room, and adopted a classic boxer's pose: left arm curled, right hand up high to protect the face. O'Malley laughed at the silly posturing. "O.K., John L.," he said cheerfully. "You do it your way." He charged forward like a ram. The man braced and snapped off three jabs that should have been on television.

O'Malley's head jerked back 180 degrees with each one, then flapped uselessly forward. Blood rushed from his nose as if from a faucet. His knees went weak and his head spun. A fucking boxer. A goddam, fucking boxer.

O'Malley had been in enough fights in his life to know the difference between a boxer and a street fighter. A boxer uses speed: quick, solid, jolting shots that snap the head so rapidly, unconsciousness results purely from the scrambling of the brain. A street fighter just hammers away like a black-smith at an anvil. Unconsciousness comes when the brain can't stand to watch anymore.

This guy was a boxer.

O'Malley cleared up a bit and decided to try again with a lot more caution. He inched forward, covering up the whole way. The man backed, planted the right foot, and fired three more shots, all deadly, all aimed right for the eyes. O'Malley caught them all on his forearms and felt the shock to his heels. He took another very reluctant step forward and the man hooked to the body, hitting flush, driving the breath out. O'Malley dropped to his knees in anguish. He heard the man laugh. Then he went all the way down, spun like a top on the ground, and took the man's legs out from under him like fat Jack hitting a wedge to the green. The man fell heavily, cursing, and tried to twist away, but O'Malley grabbed him and kept him down. The ground was O'Malley's territory: all wrestling, grunting, tearing and pounding; not a bit of finesse in it. O'Malley began to have a good old time, banging away with abandon and thinking about all those clothes strewn around the room. After a time he had the man around the throat, a thick red-haired arm under the man's chin pulling hard. He was braced and waiting for the man to go limp when the lights in the garage went on.

O'Malley was so surprised he released his hold. The man jumped up quickly, rubbed his throat, and moved away. In the doorway Anna Bradley stood open-mouthed.

O'Malley cursed under his breath. Anna's bare arms were filled with gaudily wrapped boxes. As the pockmarked man rose, she dropped the boxes and shrank against the soiled garage wall in fear. Dark stains spread across the pale print dress where it met the wall.

"Hold it," O'Malley began.

The man ignored him. He grabbed Anna roughly by the upper arm. He pulled her from the wall, then spun her to face O'Malley. The briefcase was still closer to O'Malley than it was to him.

"Tell him to move," the man ordered.

Anna was still too frightened to speak. Her eyes winced with the pain of the man's hands. Her mouth was open and silent.

"I said *tell him*," the man said louder. To emphasize the order he spun her quickly. His open hand flashed. The loud crack echoed through the garage. "*Now*," the man shouted. He turned her again toward O'Malley.

Anna's brown eyes filled with tears. She began speaking and choking simultaneously. "Pl . . . pl . . . please, Mr. . . . Mr. O'Malley . . ."

O'Malley stepped away quickly. The man walked to-

43

ward the case, always keeping Anna in front of him. O'Malley spoke to him as he walked. "There will come a day, my friend," he said. "A day we will work it all out, you and me." As he talked he tried to squelch the rising frustration, the sudden desire to act irrationally. He would not be the one to suffer for a foolish act.

The man reached the case and picked it up. He walked backward toward the small door, still keeping Anna in front of him.

"No," O'Malley said. "She stays."

The man again ignored him. O'Malley moved forward. "I said no. One more step and I'm coming."

The man slowed long enough to reach into his coat pocket. Even in the dimness O'Malley could sense the harsh metal. There was a loud click near Anna's right ear. "Sit down, shithead," the man ordered.

"You got it," O'Malley said quickly. He squatted like Yogi Berra on the filthy garage floor. The man motioned to the door with the gun, and Anna, after a brief look at O'Malley, walked through it. When they left O'Malley jumped up and ran to the small window. Anna and the man walked to the nondescript car that had been sitting in the driveway when O'Malley drove up. The man threw the case into the back seat and put the gun away, then turned to Anna. He looked at her tear-stained face as though considering something. Then he laughed and pushed her roughly away. She stumbled and fell in a lump into the soft grass abutting the driveway. A moment later an engine exploded and the man was gone.

When O'Malley reached her she was sitting stolidly, biting her lip. "Let me help you inside," he said.

6

Before they could get inside, an expensive German car pulled up. Anna groaned slightly, although she couldn't yet see the occupant. When the pale car stopped in the driveway, she tried to smile pleasantly.

"Harriet," she said brightly, "what a lovely surprise."

A small, nicely rounded woman got out of a white Mercedes. She was young and pretty, with a sassy, challenging look about her.

"Who was that guy driving out?" she asked. "He almost swiped me."

Anna spoke quickly. "A nobody," she said. "Selling something or other. I didn't buy it." She even managed a smile.

The woman named Harriet came over and the two women embraced, exchanging dainty kisses. "I'm here for the day and I had to stop over," Harriet said. "I wanted to surprise you." She looked at O'Malley and had a thought that seemed to delight her. "But if this is a bad time . . ." she began.

"Don't be silly," Anna said quickly. Whatever the problem, the decorous maintained decorum. "This is Mr. Benjamin O'Malley. He's my, uh . . ."

"Lawyer," O'Malley said, filling in the void.

"Great," the woman said. She walked over to O'Malley and held out her hand. "Harriet Resnick," she said. "I'm Anna's pal from the old days. We used to chase guys together, except Anna was usually hiding under the bed. Did anybody ever tell you you're cute?"

O'Malley tried to appear dignified but that didn't last too long. He found himself smiling, the woman's banter washing away the anxiety of the garage. Anna cut between them quickly.

"Some other time, my dear," she said. She grabbed Harriet and gave her a big hug. "I love you like a sister but you've sort of landed right in the middle of something. Mr. O'Malley and I have some important business to discuss."

Harriet seemed to understand that sort of excuse.

"No doubt," she said. She kissed Anna again and started back to the car, casting a last look at O'Malley. "Like she said, some other time, Mr. Lawyer."

As Anna changed and composed herself, O'Malley made himself a quick evil Jack at the ornate bar and wandered around to inspect Anna's very impressive home. There was no question that he could get used to life in these surroundings pretty quickly. The names of the pictures on the walls and the style of the black, lacquered furniture could be learned. What needed no tutoring was that the house had beauty and comfort of a sort only great wealth and relentless attention to detail can provide. Walls of glass opened onto luxuriant gardens and lawns. Inside, beige and black predominated, the effect a fusion of Asian and French. The only thing O'Malley could tell about the vases was that one was more beautiful than the next.

He sat down behind the bar to wait for her. As he did he remembered again the crackling fear in her eyes when she had left the room. He had many things to talk about with Anna tonight, but those eyes told him he would have to go slow.

Anna came out in a floor-length terry cloth robe. She hugged the lapels tight against her neck as if seeking another level of modesty. She was far more beautiful in that robe than in her carefully selected outfit in Baird's office. Her honey blond hair fell loosely over the coarse blue material.

She rubbed the back of her bare neck and sat across the onyx bar from him.

"Beautiful room you've got here," he offered gamely. "I've never seen furniture like that. What's it called?" He figured he'd start with the easy stuff. Who knew what that fireplace was all about. It looked like a mosaic of irregularly cut mirrors.

She turned out of habit and her arm swept the room. "Le Corbusier," she said absently. "René Herbst. The Bakelite lamp is from the thirties. The baroque bronze is interesting, but I'm just not sure about it." She turned back and shook her head. "God, what a time for a visit from an old friend."

"You handled it well."

"Do you think you could make something for me?" she asked.

"Sure, what do you want?"

"Whatever you've got there. Don't put any ice in it."

"A good choice," he told her.

He handed her the brown liquid and watched her shiver as it slid burning down her throat. She made a face and held her glass out for another, which went down the same way. This time she gagged and coughed at the taste. He gave her a glass of water. She sipped and breathed deeply for a few minutes.

That done she started cursing—fine, well thought out, and eminently well-deserved curses. "The bastard, the filthy bastard," she repeated over and over. O'Malley didn't interrupt. When she stopped, O'Malley asked, "Can we talk?" She nodded.

For the next two hours, they talked nonstop. O'Malley knew in his stomach this was his first and best opportunity to learn as much as he could about Anna, about John Bradley, about the whole affair. He didn't want to waste it.

He asked her to start at the beginning, before she married John Bradley. Her mother had died within days of

47

childbirth, she said, and for the most part she had only her father while growing up. Edward Kendall, Jr., czar of Kendall Industries: land, agriculture, munitions, oil and gas, exactly as his father had been. He was a very private man and his one unqualified love was his daughter, Anna, named after his dead wife. Anna grew up in a cloistered, protected environment, surrounded by servants, her father, and a virtually endless supply of young women attracted by her father's wealth.

She grew from a shy, skinny young girl to a shy, voluptuous teenager. She attracted boys like sugar attracts flies. At first she feared betrayal by boys interested only in exploiting her body. Later on the more dangerous kind came, those for whom her beauty was only an insignificant bonus.

Her father had suffered deeply with her through all of these missed affairs, she said. He knew gold diggers of the female variety better then anyone, and suspected—rightly, in the latter days—that every young man interested in Anna was really a young man interested only in Edward Kendall's money.

When John Bradley came along, she was twenty-one years old, just graduating from a college experience that with the exception of a handful of sad encounters was every bit as disappointing as her life before college. John was a relatively dashing young figure, an Air Force officer at the time—although not a pilot, of course. Her father thought he was wonderful. Here was a man not only trained with the discipline of the armed forces, but a man trained to appreciate every nickel, an accountant. A man whose habits were conservative, almost those of the cloth. John Bradley was the farthest thing from a man who would betray her. Or so it seemed at the time.

Anna seemed to sigh a bit when she recounted their early romance. "It was really very nice," she told O'Malley. "We spent a tremendous amount of time together, and I actually think I was quite in love with him then. For one thing, he wasn't threatening like the other boys had been. For another, he seemed genuinely interested in me and my well-being." She paused a little bit and blushed at the memory. "Finally, for all his stodginess on the outside, he was actually quite, uh, appreciative in the . . . in the bedroom."

And so they had moved in together. John was at that time a young studio accountant, as ambitious as it was possible to be. He was devoted to his work, leaving the house at the crack of dawn and staying in the office long after dark. "There were only two things that seemed to interest him back then," Anna reported with a bit of a smile, "work and me."

She clutched the robe around her and walked away from the bar to stare out the window. She spoke into her English garden. "The problems started slowly," she began. "At the beginning, it was just small lies John was telling me. I don't even know what they were about now, but John was such a terrible liar I found out everything he was up to almost immediately."

"You mean other women?"

Anna shrugged. "Not at first, but ultimately, yes, that too. At first it was just petty corruption, most of which wouldn't have made the slightest difference to me were it not for the fact I knew John was lying. He'd tell me about meetings that never took place, about deals he was involved in that didn't make any sense, about raises in pay he was getting at the studio when I knew he wasn't getting any raises at all."

"How could you know that?" O'Malley asked her.

She smiled again. "I am a very rich woman and I am well known at the studio. If I called and asked a question, I usually got an answer. At least back then I did."

The story from that point on was predictable. She told O'Malley how her live-in boyfriend became more and more remote, more and more engrossed in his work. She fought against it, beginning with small revolutions, but soon aban-

49

doned even those. In time, by the suppression of her needs, she fell ill.

"What kind of illness?" O'Malley asked.

"An emotional illness, I believe it's called. I was hospitalized for a brief period." She paused and looked at him, then seemed to reach a decision. "Involuntarily," she said softly.

"I'm sorry," O'Malley said softly.

"Thank you." Her voice was matter of fact. "It was an ironic event. John was the cause of my distress. Yet once in the hospital, I decided to marry him."

"Why?"

She smiled weakly. "Why, indeed. Let's just say I was very much lost in an institution. Very vulnerable. My father had died by that time and I had no one. I was alone and wanted very much to leave. John came out one day and proposed. It seemed a small price at the time."

"And you've been happy ever after?" he asked.

"There's an irony in your voice. You really don't believe I would be happy. But I was content. I felt a control over my life that I hadn't felt since my father died."

"When did that happen?"

"When?" She thought for a moment. "Sometimes I wake and think he's still upstairs. Other times I think he's been dead forever."

O'Malley could think of no response to that. He said nothing and neither did she. Then finally she turned from her garden.

"You know I haven't even thanked you. You were quite brave out there. I think if that man had not had a gun, you would have attacked him."

"We got lucky," O'Malley told her. "Anyway, if I'm on your payroll, the least I can do is prevent you from getting assaulted if it's taking place right in front of me."

"Was he as dangerous as he seemed, then?"

"I don't want to frighten you, but I think so." He told her the story of the man ransacking his room. "I've seen him twice now and I'm more concerned than ever. I think he's the sort that enjoys hurting people."

"What does that mean?"

"Maybe nothing. But the way he looked at you just before he left gave me chills. I think he wanted to stay and have fun for awhile, then thought better of it."

"Why, what have I done to him?"

"Appealed to him, would be my guess."

She looked at him strangely, as though the concept was new to her. From O'Malley's point of view it shouldn't have been. "Do you know him?" he asked. "I mean, have you ever seen him before?"

She shook her head. "No, never."

"What about the briefcase? What was in there?"

"You know, I don't even remember," she said. "I think that case has been sitting in the trunk of the Ferrari for over six months now. My best recollection is there were some of my father's papers in there that the lawyers had gathered for me. Why? Is it important?"

"It was important enough for that fellow to break into your garage, so sure it is." Anna's face registered nothing. Her eyes clouded.

"One more question. Why was Monica blackmailing you?"

She stared at him. "What did you say?"

"I asked why were you paying her money every week?" His voice was soft.

Anna sat down and took a long breath. "The bank, of course. I should have known. . . ." She stiffened slightly. "Mr. O'Malley . . . Ben, please just take my word that it's got nothing to do with John's disappearance. I'm sorry, it's very personal . . . I just can't tell you."

He looked at her for a minute, noticing the strain and tension in her face, and said, "O.K., for now."

Before he could speak again she was on her feet. She took him by the arm.

"Mr. O'Malley, I'm sure you have many more questions, but you'll have to save your inquisition for another day." She led him to the door. "And I'm sure you have many very important things to do. I, however, am now going to call the police and after they leave, quietly break down in private."

There were a number of developing questions in this case that would need serious investigating over time, O'Malley thought as he drove through the Bel Air gates to join the proles on Sunset. Did Brenda have more beautiful green eyes than Anna? Were her legs longer and silkier? Her breasts more womanly? And who was the more passionate? Was Anna enervated by John's dullness or simply hungry for someone with imagination? Was Brenda jaded or simply experienced?

What a lovely debate. O'Malley pulled up to a little telephone booth in a student kiosk on the north side of the UCLA campus and reached for the slip in his wallet with Brenda's number and address. That's when he realized it wasn't there.

He was past concern and into panic by the time he managed to get his fingers to dial "411" for information, and found himself screaming obscenities at the thirty-second recording that told him he could save on his phone bill if he looked up numbers in the white pages. When the operator finally came on she told him the obvious, the number was unlisted. All he could think of were his clothes strewn around the hotel room and the look in the man's eyes as he left Anna's driveway. He jumped back into the Fairmont and sped through the UCLA campus, smashing through the speed bumps like a crazy man.

At the south exit of the campus, he ran smack into the Westwood crush, thousands of moviegoers and college students meandering aimlessly around the streets. The traffic was at a standstill. He searched frantically for a side street or alley. A red light in front of him went from green to red and back to green three times and still he hadn't moved.

He began sounding the horn. Passersby glanced with interest at the noise, but that was the extent of the reaction. Frustration and fear combined to send fat, red flashes through his brain. He jumped out of the car and ran around to stand straight on the rusted blue hood.

Fifty feet south of him an alley branched off Westwood Boulevard. He ran back to the driver's seat, leaned on the horn, and cut out of the traffic flow onto the sidewalk. Moviegoers flattened themselves against the wall while pedestrians headed for the gutter. He affected a wild, crazed look. A cop caught in the traffic saw him, shouted, and turned on his light, but the cop was caught in the same quicksand and didn't move. The alley connected Westwood Boulevard to a relatively untraveled side street. He went down the alley, through a parking lot, down another side street, and was soon on the congested but at least passable Wilshire Boulevard.

He headed east toward Beverly Hills. A half-mile farther down, the first of several blocks of high-rise condominiums began. At Beverly Glen, he parked on the wrong side of the street and jumped out.

Her building was fifteen stories of nondescript steel and looked the same as all the others. The faded glass directory said her unit was on the ninth floor. Her button elicited no response, so he pressed all the buttons of all the units. Angry voices began chattering over the intercom. He kept pressing. A buzzer sounded and he pushed against the door and sprinted in.

The elevator ride seemed to take forever, but soon the number read "9" and the doors magically opened. He walked into an ordinary hallway. Apartment 923 was around the corner. He ran for it.

O'Malley saw it long before he got there, the faint beam of light from an open door casting a fragile glow into the dark hall. The glow played out on a crumpled scrap of studio note paper, laying face up as an indictment in the hall. He bent over and picked up the information that, until a man had rifled his room this evening, had been tucked securely in his wallet.

He walked through the open door. The light in the hall had come from a single naked bulb that lay in the frame of an overturned lamp. The shade was across the room. The living room had been trashed.

He expected to find brutal death. The white ticking of the cool cotton couch was splotched with dark stains. Then he heard the low moans from the bedroom.

O'Malley ran to her. She was curled in a ball, sobbing fitfully. Her clothes hung in shreds from her body. The fashionable dresses in her closet had been dragged out and slashed, and now lay like silken parodies in the middle of the room. O'Malley sat next to her and touched her shoulder lightly. She twisted in fright. "Oh, my God," O'Malley said.

The angelic face was no more. Someone had destroyed it with scientific precision, leaving only swollen eyes, blackened and puffed lips, missing teeth, and a horribly twisted nose. Even that might not be the worst of it. O'Malley could see that the beautifully elevated cheekbones and the lovely line of the jaw were badly bruised and maybe shattered. He wondered whether any doctor, no matter how skilled, could put Humpty Dumpty back together again.

O'Malley took her hand. "Baby, baby, please relax," he said soothingly. "I'm here to help you. It's going to be all right, I promise you. No matter what it takes, I'm taking care of you on this."

She didn't believe him. She turned long enough to speak the accusation through swollen lips, "You gave him the number. You told him where I lived."

"No, no, I didn't," he protested. But she was back to crying.

He left her and went for ice and towels. When he touched her again, she resisted; but he held her firmly, searching gently with his fingers. Her belly, ribs, and arms were discolored. Nevertheless, nothing was broken. Except for her face.

When he washed the blood away she twisted with pain, but he held her head in place. He stayed away from the jaw and cheekbones, areas he knew would require an expert's touch. He breathed easier with the blood out of the way.

"It's not that bad," he lied. "We'll just have to give it time."

She lost it again as the memory returned. Her voice was thick. "He just kept hitting me and hitting me and hitting me," she cried. "He was so calm about it. Like he knew just where he wanted to hit."

"Why did he do it?"

She took a breath and her sobs slowed. "The motherfucker said if I told, he'd come back and get me." She spit out some blood and a piece of tooth. "But I don't care. All I want to do is get them."

O'Malley leaned forward. "Get who?" he asked quietly.

"That fucker Perino," she answered. "Him and John. And Monica. The sons of bitches."

O'Malley's ears were straining. Brenda's voice was weak and slurred. "Why did they do this to you, Brenda?" he asked softly.

When she didn't answer, O'Malley pressed again. "Come on, baby, work with me. We'll get them together. Why?"

She looked at him for a long moment. "To shut me up," she said finally. "And to hit me for talking to you."

"Why? What do you know? Come on, Brenda, speak to me."

She stopped crying. Her voice came out weak and thin. She didn't move, maybe couldn't move, the lips and jaw. "Because I know what they've been doing," she said. "About six months ago John started acting real strange. He'd come in in the morning, shut his door, and be in there on the phone all day long. Then he'd come out all nervous-like. Monica told me to mind my own business. Then one day she came and asked me to come back late to a big party. Said we could both make some money."

"Where? The studio?"

"Yeah. So I didn't push her. That day Perino was in to see John five, six times, and you know a heavy hitter like Perino doesn't screw around with John."

"So why?"

She was starting to relax a little, letting O'Malley quietly and competently fix the cuts and bruises. Her tension was slowly leaving. "It was a French deal," she said finally. "John was buying all sorts of stuff from this company in France, which got it from this other company in Switzerland. Old movies, new movies, equipment, land, all sorts of stuff."

"How do you know all that?"

"Because I'm a secretary. Secretaries know all kinds of shit. Anyway, there was this big buy. Monica and I typed up all the contracts. The French guy was getting millions of dollars up front."

"So what?"

She winced. "How do I know? The only thing I know is what I saw. Perino was in there five, six, seven times; John had his door closed for days on end; and any time this French guy called—Simon Jacoby was his name—you weren't supposed to just go shouting into John's room that Jacoby was on the phone. You had to use another name."

"What do you mean 'another name'?"

"I mean you had to call him something else. Like Mr. Smith or Mr. Jones or something."

"Anything else?"

"Yeah. None of the copies went to the right people."

"Copies of what?"

"Copies of the deal. You know, the contract. Contracts are supposed to go to all sorts of people, the fucking president and the guy in the shipping room and fifty others. You know, the higher-ups so they know what's going on and the flunkies so they get it done."

"How do you know they didn't get distributed?"

"'Cause I did the fucking typing. And 'cause John Bradley himself told me and Monica that nobody got copies except for him and Perino and the guy who had to pay the money. You got it, O'Malley? No one was supposed to know about this."

He got it. "O.K. So what happened then?"

She shrugged. "That was it. That day, I went home at five just like any other day. Then me and Monica changed into working clothes and went back that night. They had this big party in John's office. Perino was there and John was there and Monica and me. We had nice champagne and we called France and talked to Jacoby. Then everybody got looped and Perino took me over on the couch and pulled my pants down. He fucked me and then John fucked Monica. Then we had some more champagne and John came over and tried to fuck me too, but his eyes were bigger than his stomach, if you know what I mean. Perino didn't even try."

"And that was that?"

"Yeah, except they gave us a bunch of money. You know, and told us to keep it buttoned." Her voice began trailing away. Her hand reached for her face. "Hey, man, I don't want to talk any more." Then the tears came again.

O'Malley reached for the bedside telephone. "Let's get an ambulance," he said. He dialed the number, spoke into the phone briefly, and hung up.

He went back to her bruises, leaving the rest of her story for later. She relaxed again. Minutes later they heard the siren and a noisy clattering on the stairs. "Look, Brenda, we'll take care of you, me and Baird. We've got a bunch of money for you now and Baird will get you some more. Anything you need us to do beyond that, we're here for you."

She nodded. "Come on over to the hospital with me?"

"Sure."

"They gonna be able to fix me up?" Her voice was catching again.

"That's right," O'Malley lied. "Just like before."

57

That satisfied her. They didn't say anything more until they heard the men coming through the still-open door.

7

It was 3:00 A.M. before O'Malley got out of Cedars Sinai. At the end, she was sitting up with metal frames around her jaw and bandages on her face. O'Malley left the hospital and dialed Baird's number at 3:30.

Baird's voice was thick with sleep. O'Malley began without pleasantries. "I need to talk to you right away," he said.

Baird didn't object. "Then come over right away."

It took him a half-hour to get there. He drove slowly in an effort to avoid giving vent to the passions he felt. Baird very considerately had coffee brewing in a pot when he got there.

"I've got a lot to talk to you about."

"I figured that." Baird handed him the cup and the pot. "Even you don't call at three A.M. without a reason."

O'Malley talked rapidly, bringing him up to date on the confrontation in the garage, the involvement of David Perino, O'Malley's chat with Anna. Baird sat quietly throughout the whole thing, his eyes becoming more intense as O'Malley talked. His eyes were small red coals when O'Malley told him about Brenda.

Baird got up and walked over to the wall, holding his coffee. There wasn't even a window there. He just stood and stared at the white plaster.

"What do you make of it?" Baird asked.

"Which part? The boxer's got to be working with Perino. He pops up in my room right after we start looking into this thing, then he's in Anna's garage, then he's beating up on Brenda. It's got to be Perino, John, and the boxer."

Baird agreed. "No question about it. Now what are they up to?"

"I don't know," O'Malley said. "Brenda says they were buying a bunch of foreign property from a company in France. That's all I know."

Baird turned around. "Remember what I told you about David Perino? About his background, I mean?"

"Sort of. He worked for the Cappicis in New York and Las Vegas, then came out west to free-lance. So what?"

"Do you know who owns the studio?"

More questions. Why couldn't Baird ever just come out with it? He tried to think. It seemed it had been in all the papers before he had left L. A. He was sure he didn't remember it from the Mendocino *Post*. "Yeah, I remember something. There was this guy from New Mexico or Texas—"

"Arizona," Baird interjected.

"That's right, Arizona. He had a partner in New York and the two of them bought the whole thing." O'Malley looked up, rather pleased with himself. "That's not bad after three years in Gualala."

Baird sniffed. "Correct, but superficial. The studio was purchased three years ago by two men, one of whom is an Arizona real estate developer named Eliot Newsome. Newsome is a nice overweight WASP with a lovely Italian wife." Baird paused to let the dramatic moment grow. "Her name is Angela Newsome. It used to be Angela Cappici."

O'Malley grinned. "That's why I let you hang around me, Baird."

Baird ignored him. "You're also right about the partner in New York," he said, "His name is James Silver and he's technically a fifty percent owner of the studio."

"Let me guess. He married the Cappicis' other daughter, Maria? Maybe he's their son and changed his name?"

"No, Mr. Silver is simply an independent businessman, specializing in the international commodities business."

Whatever that was. "Sorry, but we only had a few of those in Gualala."

"Mr. Silver's company, to keep it simple for your benefit, is involved with taking positions long and short on international commodities exchanges on behalf of a variety of clients. He has offices in New York and Switzerland."

"Sounds very fancy. What does that have to do with the Cappicis? Not to mention John Bradley? Not to mention my previous question of how the hell do you know all this stuff?" O'Malley really didn't need an answer to the last question. Baird had been a walking encyclopedia three years before and things hadn't changed. The man had obviously been doing his homework since Anna became a client.

"The Cappicis must use Silver for investments," Baird answered, "legal and illegal. The papers don't actually say that, but they do charge Silver has quote associations end quote with certain powerful organizations. He was even on some sort of attorney general's list in New York once."

"Fascinating. Let's see if I've got this. Perino has been with the Cappicis for years. Both fifty percent owners are front men for the mob. Perino and John Bradley are on the phone to some guy in France, buying the rights to old movies with a few projectors and a piece of land thrown in for the hell of it." O'Malley shook his head. "I'm going back to Gualala."

"Don't give up so quickly. It's never really as complicated as it sounds." Baird left his wall and walked to a chest, returning with a nice bottle of Courvoisier. He poured a hefty tote into each cup of coffee. "What they were doing, my friend, is stealing from their own company. Self-dealing, if you will."

"What the hell does that mean?"

"It means what I said. Think about Roberts's and Brenda's stories for a second and it all makes sense. They were embezzling. Simon Jacoby is their partner. They pay millions for something worthless and just pocket the profit."

"Why?"

"A lot of possible reasons. One is to transform dirty money into clean money. Remember, the goal of every laundry operation is to scrub money clean so it can be used. So the Cappicis invest in a company they control. That company buys something worthless for millions of dollars from a Swiss company they also control. The Swiss company plunks it down in a Swiss account and it's gone forever."

O'Malley sort of got it, but not really. "Yeah," he said slowly, "maybe. But maybe Perino's just ripping the others off. Maybe the guy in Europe is *his* partner and has nothing to do with the Cappicis. What about that?"

Baird looked pleased. "Not bad, O'Malley. I knew with time you'd contribute something."

O'Malley ignored that. "So which is it?"

Baird shrugged and grinned. "That's what will make this fun, O'Malley."

"Yeah, a ball." He was barely keeping up, but with Baird that was nothing new.

"Why would Bradley be involved?"

"He had to be involved," Baird said. "He was the auditor, the watchdog if you like. He has to sign off on deals like these or the checks don't get issued. Bradley must have known right away the prices were wrong."

"So why did he run away?"

Baird had to think about that one. "That's an interesting question because running away should be the last thing they would want. That just about guarantees an investigation. From what you've told me, Perino had to scramble to squelch this one."

"So why?"

Baird shrugged. "Maybe he was in love."

"With a prostitute who was blackmailing his wife?"

"I didn't say it made sense."

"No you didn't." And it didn't. O'Malley had the sinking feeling he would be running three steps behind everyone on this one.

He was about to ask something more when Baird raised his hand. "Save it for now." Then he grinned unexpectedly. "Tell me more about Brenda."

When O'Malley left, the dawn was still an hour away. He was strangely alert; maybe the horrible thought of going back to his fleabag hotel and crashing in the cardboard sheets was energizing. He needed a distraction, so he pointed the Fairmont west.

To make it from Baird's house to Anna's was a forty-minute trip down the length of Sunset, a careful weave through the drunks. Once into Bel Air, the road was quiet and dark. Nobody out partying, nobody out breaking the law.

He didn't drive the car inside. He parked outside the Swiss guards and left the key in the ignition. He shut the engine and lights off and left the car quiet. Then he walked down the dark driveway.

Anna's black Mercedes stood alone and unattended. He looked around the quiet grounds. There was no sign of life; for a moment, no danger. He sat on Anna's polished fender and stared at the house with his chin cupped in his hands. Upstairs the same pale light glowed. Upstairs, on ordinary days, John Bradley had gone to the bedroom to find his beautiful rich wife waiting for him. And if he grew tired of his wife's voluptuous body, he could amuse himself with her money. Or her fancy cars. Instead, he had run away with nothing. And now Anna slept alone upstairs.

Sour grapes, O'Malley, sour grapes. He hopped off the Mercedes and went back to the Fairmont, a change the significance of which was not lost on him. He drove out of the

Bel Air gates, through the Westwood campus, and back onto the mad, deserted colors of Wilshire. The sun was breaking over the top, and the streetlights were going out. The dawn was always his favorite time of day.

8

O'Malley and Baird learned right away the problems of getting information when no one wants to talk to you. As soon as the quarry learned who they were and what they wanted, all sorts of games began: Calls didn't get answered, emergency meetings popped up in the middle of interviews, long lost friends arrived from out of town. The bits of information picked up from time to time never seemed worth the effort. At best they could say they were learning the territory; at worst they were wasting Anna Bradley's money.

Occasionally they'd have a good day and feel progress was being made. That happened once early, with the pockmarked man's identity. After a ton of phone calls O'Malley found an aging sportswriter at the *Times* who would talk for as long as anybody bought him a drink. The writer's interest in boxing—his name was Sullivan, strangely enough—had ended with Tunney-Dempsey, enjoyed a brief resurrection with Louis-Schmeling, and faded completely with Ali, whom Sullivan still called Clay and accused of participation in Liston's fake knockout in Lewiston. But booze cost money, and money meant work, so Sullivan found himself not only writing nice things about Ali every so often— even Sullivan had to admit Zaire was impressive—but also attending every rummy match put on at the Olympic for the past thirty years. Could Sullivan find the man? The sportswriter looked insulted. Who could forget a white face at the Olympic?

They went back to the paper from the Redwood Room to look the man up in the dead file. It didn't take more than an hour. "A nice fighter," Sullivan recalled, looking at the press photo. "Came in at about one seventy-six and for a year or so was a white hope in light-heavy. Then they moved him up in class too fast and a pair of black hands named Danny Pines used him for target practice for six rounds. The corner wouldn't stop the fight 'cause they wanted a decision, not a knockout. By the time he fell in the sixth, there wasn't much left of him."

The files bore Sullivan's memory out. Larry Reynolds was the name he fought under from 1967 to 1971. He ended up 13-11 with nineteen knockouts—ten going the wrong way. In his early career he was a tiger, winning ten straight fights with a lightning left jab. The files showed Larry fought thirteen more fights after Pines and won three of them; of the ten fights he lost, only one was by decision. His last fight, against a mediocre Mexican moving up from middleweight, lasted less than a round.

"The hands were still O.K., but he just couldn't take the clinching anymore," Sullivan observed. "Pines was always one mean black mother."

O'Malley nodded, remembering Larry had not enjoyed the pounding on the floor of Anna's garage. He also remembered that lightning jab. If he met the man again, it had better not be in an empty room.

The Sullivan lead seemed a gold mine at first. Through Sullivan, O'Malley was introduced to a Latino cop named Medina who ran Larry's sheet, which had him down twice for drunk driving and once for assault in the last year. On the second drunk driving he spent thirty days in the jug after the cops who impounded the car found an unregistered pistol

64

under the seat. The assault—a fight in a bar—was dropped after the victim came out of the hospital and decided not to testify.

High point. An island in a sea of blank stares and rude invitations to leave. A moment leading to an evening of celebration and a month of frustration.

The cops wore the same blank stares, even when they heard about Brenda. In a city that leads the world in homicides, an assault on a part-time hooker simply does not cause the watch commander to funnel all available resources to the case. About a week after the beating a bored uniform showed up to ask a few questions for an hour or so, take O'Malley's statement, take Brenda's statement, and file it all away. The cops weren't heard from after that.

When Anna heard about Brenda, however, she was genuinely shocked. She and O'Malley were sitting in the little patio in back of her house, looking over the peaceful parklike grounds. A maid was serving tea. She had looked up at him intently.

"Whatever they are trying to do, it won't work," she said. "I want this Larry fellow turned over to the police immediately. Let me put it to you very strongly. You have two jobs now. One is to find my husband. The second is to find Larry. Even if we were to find my husband tomorrow, you are to continue on this case until that man is brought to justice."

O'Malley had nodded assent. "All right. But let me ask you one thing. What about your husband? What if Brenda is right and he was stealing?"

She had turned away at that and stirred her tea. Then she looked back at him. "He is my husband and I want him found," she said with calm assurance. "We'll sort the rest out later."

So they left it at that. She didn't care if John was a crook. O'Malley didn't care either. And if O'Malley could find a son of a bitch named Larry Reynolds walking the streets, he could drag him in. All paid for by Anna Bradley at in excess of one hundred dollars per hour. Fair enough.

That left Brenda, the care of whom Anna immediately agreed was a chargeable expense. At first O'Malley tried to spend as much time as he could at the hospital. As time went on, however, Baird began more and more to volunteer to man the evening vigils, suggesting solicitously that O'Malley's difficult days must be tiring him. This commendable concern had not surfaced before, so the rat was not hard to smell, but O'Malley stepped back and let him in anyway. Soon Baird was taking all of the evenings, and sometimes stopping by at lunch for a quick hello as well. O'Malley was used to Baird's reveries—they were as much a part of Baird as his rumpled clothes—it was the queer little smiles on Baird's face when he returned to earth that were new. But not hard to figure.

For some strange reason O'Malley was at the hospital instead of Baird when they wheeled Brenda into her room after the final procedure. It had gone well and the betting was she'd be out in a day. He was about to congratulate her when a nurse came in.

"Is there a Mr. O'Malley here?"

"Yes, that's me."

"There's a fellow named Baird on the phone. He says he has to talk to you right away. We're not supposed to do this but . . . he was terribly insistent."

She plugged the phone into the wall. "Here's the number he's calling from. It's a phone booth. Says it's a matter of life and death."

Baird picked it up on the first ring. "What's the matter?" O'Malley asked him.

"I just came from the D.A.'s office. John Bradley's dead. He was found hanging from a shower rod in a fancy hotel in New York. The D.A.'s on the phone to Anna now."

9

O'Malley leaned back in the plush first-class seat of the 747 and watched the clouds roll by. Thirty-eight thousand feet below the farmlands of western Pennsylvania formed a green checkerboard. In the seat next to him a man who claimed to be a famous director fumbled through some papers. Periodically the man rose and ran back to the coach section to check on a fact with his secretary.

O'Malley felt bad for the secretary, but not everybody can fit in the front, he reasoned. Two nights before, O'Malley would have bet the ranch he'd be in the back of a plane himself, probably some smelly prop heading back to Mendocino. But that wasn't what Anna wanted. O'Malley went over to see her the day after the funeral. She was wearing a fetching yet appropriately somber outfit. O'Malley thought she looked wonderful.

"I'm sorry if I'm disrupting matters," O'Malley said. "I realize we've been unsuccessful in finding your husband. I'm sure Baird's office will settle accounts with you and you can put this behind you."

She shook her head firmly. "Mr. O'Malley, I didn't ask you to come here to fire you, or even settle accounts," she told him. "I want you to continue."

Her tone had surprised him. It was firm, but also warm. There was even a hint of invitation in her voice. What surprised him more was how glad he was to hear it.

He held up his empty glass to the lovely lady who kept pouring Jack Daniels into it, but this time she shook her head with a smile. Apparently, they were landing, although you

67

couldn't tell that from this part of the plane. He took her word for it and leaned back, watching the lights of New York appear as the airship coasted comfortably onto runway sixteen at JFK. It was an impressive sight, and for the first thirty seconds since he left L.A. he took his mind off Anna. The departing passengers from steerage looked at him enviously. He tried to affect the look of a bicoastal big shot who's done it all a million times before.

He walked off the plane to a waiting area where a nicely dressed man in a black cap was holding up a sign with the words "B. O'Malley" in large red letters. O'Malley introduced himself and the man took his grip and baggage checks, leading him wordlessly to a long, black, evil-looking Cadillac parked illegally in a waiting zone. O'Malley settled into a plush seating area the size of a living room while the black cap scurried back for the bags.

The trip into town was so quiet and restful O'Malley wondered if they'd filled in all the potholes since the last time he was here. Or maybe they just had special lanes for the rich on the Van Wyck. The stretch limo was an oddity on the highway and he could feel heads turn to see the celebrity. Fame is fleeting, however. When the black car turned in front of the hotel where John had died, it had to queue up behind three others just like it.

The Park Lane has never been the fanciest or most expensive hotel in New York City. But it is a sturdy, wonderful hotel, now owned by Mr. Helmsley, set smack in the middle of hotel row on Central Park South, looking north longitudinally across the park. The rooms thirty stories up with a park view seem ordinary at first, Hilton-type affairs. All that changes when the bellman pulls open the drapes, a gesture that's usually done with a bit of theatricality. There, spread straight ahead for fifty blocks is the whole of Central Park, an ocean of green that denies the concrete of the city around it. Intricately carved graystone edifices stand vigil on its east and west flanks, quietly but unmistakeably declaring the money within them. It is without doubt one of the most magical sights in the city.

After the bellman did his thing he turned to leave, but O'Malley put a hand on his shoulder. The man looked up quizzically. "Something else?" He was about thirty-six, old enough to have been around the hotel for awhile, young enough to be hungry. O'Malley walked over to the writing table where his wallet was, crooking a finger for the man to follow. At the table O'Malley peeled off three ten dollars bills and placed them side by side neatly.

"There was a death here at the hotel a week ago," O'Malley said. The man said nothing, just raised his eyes. O'Malley placed a fourth ten on the table next to the others.

"Yes, sir. A man hanged himself. Right next door, as a matter of fact."

"What a coincidence. What do you know about it?"

The man shrugged. "It was terrible," he said. "Maid came in to clean and found him. Did it from the shower curtain rod. Scared the shit out of her."

O'Malley looked down at the currency on the table. "Newspapers cost thirty cents."

The man smiled. "I'm going a little slow, just to see where you're going. Ask me something particular and I'll tell you what I can."

"Start at the beginning. When did he check in?"

"Four days before it happened."

"Was he here alone?"

"Not the first two days," the bellman said. "He had a lady with him. After that he was alone."

"What did she look like?"

The man smiled and his voice developed a locker room familiarity. "She looked great. Real great. A little small, maybe five-four, dirty-blond hair, blue eyes, and a body you'd sell out to the Russians for. And always smiling, smiling at everybody. This great big grin about made your heart stop."

"What was her name? Did she call herself Monica? Or Davis? Or Glitzman?"

He shook his head up and down. "She checked in as Mrs. John Bradley, but she told everybody, 'Call me Monica.'"

"Why did she leave?" O'Malley asked.

"Best we can figure they had a fight," he answered with an assurance that said he had thought about it. "Last day she was here that smile wasn't on her face anymore. She was mopin' around, not looking anybody in the eye. I know 'cause I was always trying to look her in the eye."

"Anything else?"

"Yeah," he said. "They had this scene out in front, on Central Park South. They was waiting for a cab. I was leaning up against the desk watching, trying not to be too obvious, you know. She had the most spectacular ass you ever seen in your life. Anyway, they're not talking. He's staring one way and she's staring the other. Then every once in a while, he turns to her and starts trying to talk, but she just turns away. Then one time he grabs her by the arm to turn her around but she spins away and comes running back inside, tears all over her face. He makes like he's going to follow her, then decides against it. She goes into the elevator and he goes out and gets a cab."

"That the night he hung himself?"

The bellman shook his head. "No, he didn't do that until two nights later. But the night of the fight was the night she left. Fifteen, maybe twenty minutes later we get a call to go up and get her bags." He grinned. "I volunteered."

"She say anything when you saw her?"

"No," the man said, "but she didn't seem mad anymore. Just folded up her stuff and put it in her bags. She was even smiling again."

"Any idea where she went?"

"Nope."

O'Malley took two of the tens and put them in the man's

hand. The man looked at them for a moment, then reached down without ceremony and picked up another. Inflation, O'Malley supposed. He put down thirty more to even things out.

"Let's turn to John. When did he die?"

"According to the coroner's official report, John Bradley died at seven thirty-seven P.M." When O'Malley stared at him, the man shrugged. "There was a pool. Everybody was in it," he said slightly embarrassed.

"What did he do the day he died?"

The man shook his head. "That I can't tell you. The word is he had a breakfast tab real early and a drink tab later on, maybe five at night. He was there drinking until six-thirty. Then he went to his room and hung himself." He thought for a second. "Except that wasn't until an hour later. So maybe he watched the news first and got depressed." He laughed a little.

"Did he drink alone?"

"Marcel—that's the bartender—says there was people talking to him. Who it was, I don't know. Maybe Marcel knows."

"How long were the people there?"

He shrugged. "I don't know. Marcel works nights and we don't get to grill him. But I know there was people there."

O'Malley was listening intently, so intently he didn't notice the dark shape appear behind him. The man stood motionless for a time, listening almost politely. Then he moved slightly and O'Malley, sensing rather than seeing the movement, jerked reactively. But on closer inspection the man was not threatening.

"Who the hell are you?" O'Malley asked abruptly. He was unnerved by the man's quiet presence.

The man coughed. "I am Hamilton Brent," he said simply. The voice was orderly. "I was looking for this room, number sixteen twenty-three, and the door was open. I assure you I was not trying to overhear your conversation."

"What the hell do you want?" O'Malley's voice was still more hostile than it needed to have been.

The little man cleared his throat. "Ah, yes, well, I'm looking for a Mr. Benjamin O'Malley in this room. You see I've been sent to meet you by . . ."

Now O'Malley got it. "Mrs. John Bradley," he said.

"Why, yes, that's correct," Brent said. "You see, Mrs. Bradley has asked our firm to . . ."

"Meet me at the room, take me to dinner, supply me with whatever support I need." This was too easy. "Why?"

Hamilton Brent seemed to think the question was odd. "Because that's my job," he said simply.

Of course. O'Malley patted him on the shoulder and turned back to the bellman. "We'll continue this later." The bellman shifted slightly, looking hungrily at the remaining green bills. O'Malley handed him a ten. Then he picked up two more and ran them slowly under the man's nose. "Breathe deeply and you can smell the lady's perfume at the mint. You know what? I've got lots more with that perfume."

The man grinned broadly. "We'll talk later," he said eagerly. "And I'll tell Marcel about you." Then he was gone.

Hamilton Brent watched the bellman go with mild interest, then turned to O'Malley with a questioning look. O'Malley was lost in thought, forgetting at first the man standing in the doorway. Then he reached a decision, a decision that further thinking would be a complete waste of time. He slapped a hearty arm around Hamilton Brent's shoulders. "Mr. Brent, do you enjoy Jack Daniels?"

72

10

Nick Roth sat behind a big, black art deco desk with strange little porcelain objects of art at the corners. The red light of a speakerphone blinked up at him. He had both hands wrapped around a large, unwieldy sandwich that he kept trying to jam into his mouth between sentences. As he talked he sprayed bits of mustard and rye bread at the green box. Occasionally, after a few bites, he'd put down the sandwich, grunt with satisfaction, and grab his enormous belly with both hands, literally yanking the protuberance a few extra inches out of his pants. That done, there was more room for more rye bread.

Baird sat in a chair across from Nick Roth, watching the rye bread go down and listening to the conversations with equal fascination. At some point he expected to have a conference with the man, or at least that was what Roth's secretary had promised when she called to ask him to come in. Yet the wait was not without interest. It was fascinating to watch a man like Roth do business.

ROTH: Hello, Barney, this is Nick. Why are you cutting my balls off on that music deal?

BARNEY: Hello, Nick. I'm trying to be fair. It's just . . .

ROTH: Don't give me fair, you crook. You'd sell your mother for fifty cents. You're knifing me in the back, you crud.

BARNEY: Nick, please, let me . . .

ROTH: If I don't see those contracts by noon I'm going to war. I'm going to rip that fag singer into little

	pieces and throw him to the dogs like they did Samson in the Bible.
BARNEY:	Jezebel. Nick, noon's no good. I'm taking a lunch meeting with my man and . . .
ROTH:	Two o'clock. Then I come hunting.
BARNEY:	O.K. Nick.
ROTH:	I love ya, Barney.
BARNEY:	You too, Nick.

Each call to the enemy was quickly followed by another to the client, magically placed by an unseen hand in another room.

ROTH:	Marvin, Nick. I just got off the phone with Barney. He's screaming like a pig. You've got to stop raping this guy.
MARVIN:	It's just good business, Nick. Don't get excited.
ROTH:	Good business, my ass. If that fairy signs those contracts, the only thing he'll have left is Nigerian jukebox rights. That's in Africa, Marvin.
MARVIN:	What should I do?
ROTH:	I'm taking a meeting with Barney at two. If he comes in with the contracts, sign them, and try not to get saliva all over the pages.
MARVIN:	I understand, Nick.
ROTH:	Later, Marvin.

The calls were incessant and Baird had plenty of time to wander around the office looking at the art, the memorabilia, the photos, and the magnificent north-facing view of the snow-capped San Gabriel and San Bernardino mountains. Roth had obviously led an interesting life. The photos, each elaborately inscribed, showed him with stars and starlets, studio executives, politicians, and famous athletes. At the edges of some of the photos were a few discreet shots of hard-faced unsmiling men who looked to be slightly averting their eyes. These photos weren't signed.

Every once in a while Nick Roth would reach a quiet

harbor and start gesturing to Baird excitedly, as if they were really going to talk about something. "All right, this is what I have to tell you," he would say. "Listen up real close now because it's important." Those two sentences were as far as he ever got. Inevitably by the time he opened his mouth to convey the important information, the phone would ring again.

Yet Baird really didn't care. He already had an instinctive trust of and affection for Roth. He suspected that eventually, when it was important enough, Roth would make the time.

The time came at lunch. As though cut off by a switch, the phone went dead at 12:30. Roth, who had been throwing back food nonstop for two straight hours, leaned back, wrapped his hands around his belly, and announced: "The only way we're going to get anything done is to take a lunch. Someplace quiet."

And so Baird and Nick Roth had taken a lunch. Between his office and the elevator Roth couldn't resist stopping to give detailed instructions to four different people on how they were to spend each moment of the ninety minutes he expected to be out of their lives. In the elevator to the parking lot, he met three people and seemed to make three deals—small deals, but deals nonetheless. "What else you gonna do in an elevator?" he asked Baird. The quiet spot he chose was Chasen's, a Beverly Boulevard hangout where a guy like Roth could do as much business as in his office. Baird began to get concerned that he was never going to get his information.

Roth was true to his word, however, and for the most part walked in a straight line to the quiet room reserved for him and Baird. The hors d'oeuvres were waiting. Roth began on them immediately.

"Been in the business long, son?" he asked between bites.

"About thirty days, actually."

"Got any questions?"

75

"Yeah," Baird said. "Why are people always 'taking a meeting' or 'taking a lunch.' Doesn't anybody just 'have a meeting' or 'go to lunch' anymore?"

Roth stopped the food halfway to his mouth. "Jesus Christ, don't say things like that." He looked around to make sure nobody had overheard. "Let me try an easy one. You know who I am?"

"Of course," Baird told him. "It's why I'm excited to speak with you. I've been told by many people you're very powerful and very honest. It's considered an anomaly in this town because usually people are just one or the other."

Roth thought that was funny. "Not bad, kid." He pointed his fork at Baird. "And that's right, too. I been an agent in this town for thirty years and I get business because people trust me." He again stared at Baird and seemed to want to poke him with the fork. "Christ, you're like those little girls who starve themselves to death. Here, have some mackerel."

"Thanks." Baird accepted the dish. "Why did you contact me?"

Nick Roth looked over with a narrow eye. "Kid, you talk like that people are gonna think you got no class. You're supposed to relax and enjoy yourself, eat some food for a while, observe the amenities. It's a custom," he said simply.

"O.K."

Roth yanked the belly a few more inches out of its prison. "But seeing how's you're new, I'll get down to business right away. I hear you're looking into David Perino. Perino would steal the hot stove his grandmother was making her last meal on."

"That's sort of true," Baird agreed. "But we're actually looking into John Bradley's disappearance. Perino's name has come up from time to time."

"He's in it to his eyeballs, son," Roth told him. "He fucked me and I told him I'd get him for it."

"Could you be more precise?"

76

But nobody moved a raconteur like Nick Roth off his style. "Nobody knows Perino like I know Perino," Roth began, leaning back. "I've watched him for thirty years and I can always spot a David Perino deal. Everybody comes out of the meeting with dollar bills in both hands and dollar bills hanging out of their pants and dollar bills in their teeth. He's got no class, if you know what I mean."

"You mean others steal with more finesse?" Baird asked.

"That's it," Nick Roth said. This time he really did stick the fork in Baird's chest. "There's guys in this town I want to videotape it looks so smooth. With Perino I just come home one day and find the son of a bitch going through my drawers."

"What does all this have to do with John Bradley?"

"It's what I'm trying to tell you, son," Roth said impatiently. "Perino just sent Bradley into the vault and told him to come out with a ton of money."

"How do you know that?"

"Because I'm the one who got fucked by him." Roth jabbed his own chest this time. "I'm the one who was selling those frog flicks first." Roth leaned over and spoke in a conspiratorial tone. "Actually, just between you and me, I'm sort of happy to see the frogs get fucked. They're all crooks, you know."

"All of them? It doesn't seem possible. How did the frogs get fucked, to use your evocative phrase?"

"Those pictures were all dogs," Roth said. "Never seen by a human being in any theater in the world. The value was close to zero. Are you familiar with *They Ate Napoleon's Brain* by chance? That was one of the best."

Baird noted with interest that when Roth began to discuss business seriously his language drifted more to that befitting the top-of-the-line Wharton School graduate he was.

"Maybe Bradley didn't know the value," Baird observed reasonably. "Maybe you're smarter than him."

"That's beside the point," Roth said. "Bradley and Perino sure as hell knew because I went to Perino and tried to sell to him. He asked me how much I wanted and I told him. Then he calls me back with Bradley and says no. I figured what the fuck and forgot it. Next thing I get a call from Simon Jacoby. He says he'll meet my price. No negotiation, nothing, and he's got to know there's water in there. I say great, and we run the deal through one of Jacoby's dummy Swiss companies."

"So what's your problem? You got paid a hundred cents on the dollar. Maybe a hundred and fifty cents."

"My problem, son," Nick Roth said, "is two weeks after I made my deal with Jacoby, he turned around and sold them to Perino and Bradley for twenty times what I got. You hear me, son? Twenty times! And the fucking thieves already turned me down!" The last was shouted. People at adjoining tables began turning toward the noise.

"I hear you," Baird said soothingly. "What did you do when you found out?"

"I screamed like a man who got stabbed. I put in a call to Perino every day for a month." Roth shrugged, resigned again. "He ain't talkin' to me. I also wrote him a bunch of letters calling him a filthy pig in nice language. He hasn't answered those either." Roth shook his head. "That son of a bitch would steal a hot stove."

"How much money are we talking about?"

"Let's just use round numbers," Roth said, "so you don't get confused. I'm talking millions. Lots of millions."

"Any idea why John Bradley died?" Baird asked.

"Yeah, I got an idea. I got an idea he died because Perino wanted him to die. You see Perino is sort of well connected in certain unsavory circles."

"So are you."

Roth grinned and picked some chopped liver from his teeth. "You don't know what you're talking about, son. Jews are businessmen. It's them Italians got all the unsavory connections." Then he laughed heartily at his own joke.

"But that doesn't matter," Baird said. "What you're telling me is it was easy for Perino to have it done, and you think he did it."

Roth shrugged. "What the fuck do I know? I'm sitting out here in California with my thumb up my ass while Perino fucks me. Some miscellaneous character turns up dead in a New York hotel. I'm just looking at it like a sensible man."

"Anything else?"

"Yeah," Nick Roth said. "In my opinion, the chances of you two fellows remaining on this planet with the rest of us much longer are sort of dropping every day."

11

Baird went back to his office to let it all sink in. He never got the chance. As he opened the door they were there waiting for him, every one of the members of the board of directors of the Sunset Investment Company. All three had a sour look. The secretary/treasurer looked the most down in the dumps, so Baird started there first.

"Lisa, you get busted again today?" he asked.

The blond looked up quickly. "No, I didn't even work today. I had a cold. That's what we're here to talk about. With all this fancy stuff you got us into, I can't even buy decent clothes. None of us has any money anymore. We want to cash out."

So that's what it was about. He shook his head resolutely. "That can't happen," he told her. "I told you ladies at the beginning once you put your money into the corporation we'd have to wait. This isn't the time to get panicky. The market will turn around. Matter of fact we should probably be buying on the way down."

The vice-president and chairman of the management committee wasn't convinced. Besides, there were more important things than an uptick. "It's getting so I can't hold my head up on the Strip," she complained. "The other girls have tons of cash. Christ, that's what this business is all about. Cash—lots of green bills, you know? Instead of that, you got us into these, whatever it is"—she held up a piece of paper and squinted at it—"trusts and pension plans and money market funds and all the rest of this crap. What the fuck is a tax-free mutual fund anyway?" She threw down the paper in a huff. "I don't understand any of it. All I know is every time I go out to eat I'm scrounging in the bottom of my purse."

Baird just continued to shake his head. As counsel to the board of directors he had to be firm. It was up to the president and chairman of the board to make the final pitch. She was clearly Baird's favorite. "Jerry," she began, "it's very important to me I get some money. You might even say it's a matter of life and death." Then she managed to cause a small tear to come glistening down the side of her cheek.

It was a totally unethical ploy. Baird felt himself wavering. "What do you need the money for?" he asked firmly. "The truth now."

"My grandmother has to have this brain operation," the woman said. "It's real expensive."

"Kimberly," Baird warned.

The president raised her arms in exasperation. "I want what everyone wants. You know, trips, clothes, jewelry, the usual stuff."

"I thought so. Kim, I told you and the others at the beginning, the whole reason for doing this was to build up a nest egg. You want to end up like some old bag lady? You want to do something legitimate, buy a house, whatever, we can arrange a loan from the pension fund. But I don't want you taking money out just to blow it. Use your own money for that."

"But it *is* my money." she protested.

"No, it's not," Baird told her. "It belongs to the pension fund set up by your corporation. It's no more your money than the Clifford trusts for your kids."

Kim began crying. "I was better off with a stash in the closet."

Game, set, match. "All right, all right, maybe we'll get the pension fund to make a small loan," Baird grumbled.

Kim brightened. "You mean, I can lend myself my own money?"

Baird nodded affirmatively. "And the interest you pay yourself is deductible."

Kimberly ran to him, wrapping her arms around him with appreciation. At the beginning of his unusual practice, Baird found these affectionate gestures uncomfortable. He was now getting used to it, but still didn't want them to think he could be moved by a little schmoozing. "O.K. that's enough," he told her, unwrapping himself. "Just remember, you have to pay back every penny to the fund."

"I promise," Kim told him. She turned solemnly to Lisa, a newcomer watching the whole thing with undisguised amazement. "You just listen to him and you'll be O.K. too," Kim instructed.

"Never mind that for now," Baird told them. "I want to ask you something. It's sort of a game, a mystery." They looked up curiously.

He walked to the other side of the room with his hands behind his back, thinking hard. He spoke without looking at the women. "The name of the game is 'The Case of the Missing Accountant,'" he said, "actually controller, but accountant is good enough for now. Once upon a time there was a young accountant named John Bradley. He was married to a very wealthy woman named Anna and his job was to make sure nobody stole anything from the company.

"One day, John got a call from a very important man, a friend of the owners of the company, who are real big men around town and have lots of money. The man says, 'John, about that French deal, let's buy some pictures for a few million bucks from this real good friend of mine.' John knows those movies are worth about as much as Chicago Cub tickets in September but he goes along with it anyway, because any friend of the big boss is a good friend of his."

Baird was walking in tight circles now, faster and faster. "So they go ahead and do it and John signs some papers saying it's the best deal the company could ever hope for."

Baird turned and pointed a finger at Lisa. "Then one day John disappears." Lisa sat upright. "The company starts to investigate, but the friend of the owners stops that quick. If it could have gone on, the investigation would have turned up everything rotten about this deal and a lot of other sweet deals as well. By the way, John splits with his longtime secretary, a lady named Monica, who is a colleague of yours."

Lisa didn't know what a colleague was but she got the drift. She nodded in understanding. "Mrs. Bradley, that's the wife, is so distraught at her husband's disappearance she hires two nobodies to find out what happened to him, people who have absolutely no clout and couldn't find John Bradley if he was sleeping in their bed. Nevertheless, sometimes people stumbling around can be dangerous, even nobodies."

Baird was absolutely racing around his circles now. The girls were leaning forward. "Then the accountant, John Bradley, turns up dead, hanged like a side of beef in a fancy hotel room in New York. Nobody knows whether he did it himself or somebody did it for him. Monica is nowhere to be found."

Baird stopped his pacing and turned to them. "So, ladies, tell me. Who done it?"

They hesitated for a second, each embarrassed to speak first. They turned to each other and grinned. The shout came simultaneously. "The big man!"

Baird shrugged and smiled.

12

Baird squirmed grumpily on David Perino's pink and mauve couch, trying as unsuccessfully as he had for the last three hours to find a comfortable position. He was as bored as he was uncomfortable. The art on the walls was too obvious to be interesting and he had long since worn out any potential conversation with the pretty, nineteen-year-old receptionist. He now knew she was nineteen as well as everything else about her life: high-school graduate two years earlier; ninth in the Rose Queen competition; rejected academically by UCLA; six months at a junior college in the valley, quit college to do some "temping" as a receptionist "with a little modeling on the side." No surprises whatsoever. Nor was it really a surprise that David Perino, after finally agreeing to this meeting, had now decided to let him cool his heels with Cheryl the receptionist for three solid hours.

Baird thought about leaving a few times. That would have massaged his ego and accomplished nothing. He would still want to see Perino and the next time he'd be left with pretty Cheryl for a week.

So he waited. And chatted with Cheryl about her career. And didn't act the least bit surprised when a nice matronly lady finally led him without a word of apology into an anteroom outside Perino's office.

The second wait was only a half-hour and this time he had company. A trio of men in suits sat nervously with him, each apparently with some sort of business to negotiate with David Perino. One at a time they were tapped by the matronly lady to go in and be screamed at by the great man before Baird's number was called. The third one seemed almost dead by the time his turn came.

When all that nonsense was over, the nice lady finally came back and tapped Baird. He walked into an empty office, Perino apparently having escaped to his private conveniences for a moment of preparation before the next beheading. Baird amused himself by reading the man's mail.

Perino came out screaming and cursing and zipping. It wasn't clear what the curses were directed at. Baird listened for a while without speaking. Finally Perino raised his hand.

"What? What the fuck do you want?"

"A great many things, actually. But first of all I was curious why you shout so much. It's quite rude."

Perino pointed a finger at him. "It's because I goddam well like to shout," he shouted. "And I especially like to shout at punks like you and your friend."

"That would be Mr. O'Malley. I understand you two have met, although I also understand you have not become friends."

"Friends! I'll have that punk thrown in jail, and you can follow him."

"And why would you do that?" Baird asked reasonably.

"Just let me ask the questions," Perino barked. "I let you come because I want answers, not questions. Understand?"

"I understand with great clarity you would prefer not to answer any questions."

"I'm going to forget you said that," Perino told him, pointing his finger again. "You two are playing way out of your league, and a smart mouth isn't going to help you. Let's just start from the top. How the hell did Anna Bradley ever wind up in a deal with you two bums?"

"I don't mind answering that," Baird said. "O'Malley and I are both attorneys, formerly with Jenkins and Dorman. As to how Anna found me, it was probably through J and D. Anna called, we chatted, and I agreed to help convince the police to take her husband's disappearance seriously. She said she wanted more than that, a full-scale investigation, and money was no object. I asked her permission to engage Mr. O'Malley's services and she assented to that additional expense."

The name of the great law firm brought Perino up short. The irony was that Perino seemed to think more of the place than Baird did. And certainly more than O'Malley ever had.

"J and D, huh. When did you leave?" he asked quietly.

"Three years ago, maybe three and one-half now."

"Why? They throw you bums out?"

Baird shook his head. "Not both of us. They threw Mr. O'Malley out, to use your phrase. I left voluntarily."

Perino almost shivered with delight. "Why did they throw O'Malley out?"

"Because Mr. O'Malley had been indicted by a federal grand jury for securities fraud and by a state grand jury for embezzlement," Baird said evenly. Perino's eyes grew wide and his mouth contorted with happiness. "J and D was at that time representing the corporation that Mr. O'Malley was accused of defrauding," Baird continued. "It was decided, without great debate, it would be better for Mr. O'Malley to leave under the circumstances."

"I knew it," Perino shouted. "So why did you leave?"

"I left to represent Mr. O'Malley in the criminal proceedings and the disbarment proceedings," Baird said simply.

"So the son of a bitch got disbarred too. This is going to be great." He reached for a phone.

Baird interrupted. "Mr. Perino, perhaps we can focus this conversation. The company involved was Associated Computer Research." The grin left Perino's face as quickly as his hand left the phone. He might not have remembered O'Malley's name, but he certainly remembered the ACR scandal of three years previously. It had begun with the discovery of fifty-three million dollars in embezzled funds, continued through O'Malley's indictment and the violent deaths of the president and board chairman of ACR, and culminated in some very successful people winding up in jail. Except O'Malley wasn't one of them."

"He was the kid they first tapped?"

"That's right," Baird said. "Did you happen to know Randall Elliott Marks by chance?"

Perino stared at Baird this time, licking his lips nervously. "I know everybody that's worth knowing, son. Marks was sure as hell worth knowing. Before he went down, that is." Perino was no longer shouting.

Baird decided to jump into the breach. "If it's all right with you, I'd like to ask you a few questions now, if I may."

Perino stopped staring absently and looked at Baird's face. Then he leaned back. "Sure, go ahead."

"I'd like to begin with Simon Jacoby." Perino's eyes flattened. "He's a French broker," Baird told him.

"I know who the fuck Simon Jacoby is," Perino screamed. "What on earth does my relationship with Simon Jacoby have to do with John Bradley?"

"I don't know," Baird said. "I do know one of Jacoby's funny companies sold a bunch of property to the studio; rights to films, real estate, equipment, the works. John Bradley approved the transaction. I also understand the studio paid a lot more than it had to."

"For all your pretty talk you're still a funking punk," Perino told him. "You been talking to Nick Roth. Nick Roth got beat out of a deal. So now he's making accusations. Nick's getting a little old now and I suppose he's desperate for money. Maybe that's the explanation."

"The rumor is this deal is only the biggest of a lot of sweet deals that went down when John Bradley was around."

"That's what Roth told you, huh?"

"No comment."

"All right, son," Perino said, "suppose I prove to you Bradley was a wonderful guy, kind to animals and all the rest. A regular priest. Would that make you go away?"

86

Baird shrugged. "Not go away, but certainly rethink things."

"Smart ass. But you're telling me the same thing. If you can't blame me and Bradley for this deal, you got no place to go. Right?"

"Yes."

Perino reached in back of him and yanked out a folder. He flipped it in front of Baird. It slid across the table and dropped at Baird's feet.

Baird felt his stomach sink. Perino was not the sort of man to make dramatic gestures that did not work dramatically to his advantage. He picked up the folder and opened it.

There was only a single sheet of paper inside the folder. It was a copy of a studio memorandum to the management committee from John Bradley, labeled "Purchase of French Theater Property." Baird read the memorandum to himself.

This is to advise you we received two competing proposals for the purchase of a foreign package for use in Western Europe by our Netherlands subsidiary.

One of the offers came in through Nick Roth. Our cost is 180,000 francs per title. This equates to 30,000 in U.S. dollars given the current exchange rate. It is a very tempting offer brought in by a reputable agent.

The second offer is from a Swiss corporation we believe is controlled by Simon Jacoby. This is for the same group of films but is less attractive. In addition to films we would be required to purchase a number of unnecessary items at inflated prices, such as theater leases and equipment. The cost increase to us is 25 percent. Jacoby apparently intends to act as a middleman between Roth's client and ourselves. Jacoby is a relatively reputable figure, however some people have raised questions concerning his method of doing business.

Each of the respective deal memoranda are attached hereto, with the recommendation of the director of international sales.

I concur with the recommendation of sales. The deal from Nick Roth is an especially attractive one. I strongly recommend acceptance.

Please advise if I should instruct sales to contact Roth and close this.

Baird sat stunned, staring at the paper as if it were alive and moving. The date was right after the meeting between Roth, Perino, and Bradley, when Roth said Bradley was already working with Perino. But if Bradley was Perino's partner, what was he doing recommending Roth's deal? And, more importantly, how did Roth's deal ever get rejected? The conclusion was inescapable that if someone had his hand in the till, that someone was not John Bradley.

Baird heard Perino cackling in the background. He ignored him, concentrating on the sheet before him, on every line, every detail. He studied the stationery, the signature over Bradley's name, the typeface and the margins. He even studied the phrasing, the spelling, the terminology. Then he caught it, a series of initials sitting lonely and alone in the left-hand corner. It read: "JLB/md." Baird looked again at the date to be sure and then chuckled, flipping the folder back at Perino.

"You've blown it."

"How so?"

"Those initials at the bottom."

Perino grabbed the paper back and looked at it. "So what?" he said. "John Bradley wrote it and that slut he ran away with typed it. Probably the only thing she ever typed. What's your problem?"

"The secretary. She calls herself Monica Davis now but she didn't back then. This document is a phony. If it's in the studio files now, it will hang all of you."

Perino looked harsh for a moment, then leaned back and grinned. He looked at Baird as though seeing him for the first time. "Not bad, son," he admitted. He had the paper in his hand and looked at it again. "Who can figure it all," he muttered. He crushed the paper and jammed it in a drawer. "End of problem," he said, smiling.

"Sort of," Baird said. "I know about it."

"That's not something that's going to cause me to lose a lot of sleep, friend." Perino stared at Baird for a moment, then began playing with his pen, twirling it around in little circles. "But let's not play games. This piece of paper will be gone from the files by lunch and your word isn't worth spit. Let's get down to the only thing that interests either of us. How much is Anna paying you?"

There wasn't much doubt where this conversation was going. He decided to play along. "Basic legal fees for me and O'Malley. Plus expenses."

"I'll triple it," Perino said. "And guarantee you a year. Two years if you want."

"That's very generous. What am I supposed to do?"

Perino shrugged. "Same as you're doing. Except make sure you don't do it too well. Not that you're doing it too well now, of course. Matter of fact, you can just keep investigating about the same as you're doing." He hesitated. "Just check in with me from time to time. Let me know what's going on."

"Why?"

"Why is my business. Your business is to give me a telephone call every few weeks and cash my checks."

"In other words breach my duty to my client?" Baird asked sweetly.

"That's a terrible thing to say. I'm shocked. It's probably going to spoil my dinner." Perino stopped twirling the pen and held it aloft, then fished a checkbook out of a drawer. "Shall we say ten thousand on retainer?" Perino asked.

What a nice round number, Baird thought. He had to clear his throat to get the words out. "No, thanks," he said hoarsely.

He was about to say something else when the large door in back of him opened with a whoosh.

*   *   *

Baird walked from the bank building into the chaos of Century Park East. For the first time in a long time he felt good. This was a morning even O'Malley would be proud of: a confrontation, a refusal to be intimidated, a demonstration to the enemy that he could not be corrupted. So what if Perino could correct the problem with the initials, he could have done that anyway, cooked up some sort of excuse. The point was Baird had proven to the man there would be no easy cover-ups. And that was something that should at least make them nervous.

He entered the plaza elevator to the subterranean parking lots. Because of the enormous value of above-ground Century City land, nobody, ever, is permitted to park a car on the street. All the parking lots are in enormous labyrinthine below-ground complexes; extensive, expensive, brooding, gloomy, concrete tunnels supporting the glass and steel towers above. Baird had never come to Century City without getting lost in these caverns and to solve that problem had taken to scribbling codes on the back of his ticket such as, "C-l-Green-ll (A)." He squinted at his ticket as the glass elevator left the sun and took him alone down into the depths. It was very gloomy and quiet by the time the doors opened slowly at the bottom.

Baird wrote off his vague anxiety to the endless walls of dank concrete. He wondered if the women in the building had the same anxiety when they came down in the evening for their cars. Like that amiable replacement for Cheryl, the one sitting at the reception desk at Perino's office when he left, an older and more mature woman, the one who so carefully validated his ticket by affixing the small stickers on the back. Baird stopped dead. The realization hit him as a quick chill. The one who so carefully wrote down all the numbers and letters on the back of his ticket.

He peered into the dimness but the crypt was death-quiet. Why the hell would she do that? The elevator and escalators were now far away, as was the road leading back up the maze to the exit. His car was in a corner, next to a beam, inconspicuous, lit only by dancing shards of light from far away. Probably the worst place in the complex for it.

He breathed easier when he drew close to the car. He had his keys in his hands, ready to open the door quickly. Then he heard the click of leather heels behind him.

The chills came back. He didn't want to turn but the noise forced him to. A man in a dark suit was walking with purposeful strides toward Baird's car.

It didn't take the man long to get there. Baird tried to open the door quickly and get in, but the man put his hand on the window, stopping the door half open. Baird looked back at him with a look of outrage. The man smiled, unaffected, then suddenly pushed the door hard. Baird's fingers escaped the pinching metal a split second before the door slammed shut.

Baird looked up at the man without speaking. It was exactly what he had expected: the face bloated and pockmarked, the hair thick and dirty blond, a small but vicious scar just over the left eyebrow. O'Malley had described this man with great precision.

The man spoke. "Don't leave so soon, friend. The party's just starting."

Baird forced his voice to speak. "Look, I don't know what you want. If you're here to rob me, let's get it over with." He reached for his wallet.

The man smiled, spread his feet wide and stood directly in front of Baird. Baird tried to look away. The man taunted him. "Come on, come on, look over here. Come on, baby. Look at me." He said it soft and low, as if he was talking to a lover. The tone inspired terror. Then the man began using his hands, straightening Baird's lapels, fumbling with his tie, patting him lightly on the cheek, reaching for Baird's groin and laughing as Baird flinched. All the while he kept up his

91

soft, taunting banter. "Come on"—pat, pat—"look at me now, honey, don't look away, what are you afraid of? Come on, sweetie, let's have a little talk. You and me, hon."

Baird's hands clenched and he could feel tears of rage welling. He was sure he had never in his life been imprudent enough to allow his gawky body to get into a fight. Maybe in the second grade against that fat kid. That one hadn't turned out well either. He forced himself to look in the man's eyes. The man smiled, patted Baird twice on the cheek, turned, and slapped him hard across the face, backhand, a blow that split Baird's lower lip like a grape.

Baird staggered backward. He reached up and felt the blood on his fingers.

The man moved in again. Baird struggled but the man grabbed the tie and twisted, choking off the air supply. "I want you to tell your friend about this," the man growled. Great, Baird thought, I'm getting beat up for O'Malley.

The man had his orders. The open hand moved back and forth with mechanical precision. With each blow Baird's anger grew, an anger that quickly extinguished fear and pain. The iron hand came hard again across the side of Baird's head. Baird fell heavily to the ground.

"Come on, honey," the man said, "I'm having fun batting you around. Stand up and we'll have another big kiss."

"Sure," Baird said. Then he stood, looked through swollen eyes, and spat with precision right between the man's narrow eyes.

Larry roared with anger, coming at Baird with fists closed this time. Baird swung wildly, a weak ineffectual blow that Larry just stepped around, giving him room to work at sort of half speed to the body. Larry's blows hurt, but Baird was now resigned to getting beaten. He kept striking back with fists that had never before struck another human being. Twice, however, he actually managed to hit Larry in the head, blows that did nothing but send shafts of pain up his arm and pride to his heart.

When Larry finally stopped, Baird's face was flushed and cut. He was bent double from the beating. He had to gulp for the air to speak. "What's the matter," he gasped. "Lose your nerve?"

"Jesus Christ." Larry shook his head in exasperation. "Listen, fuckhead, this is just a taste of what you get you keep fucking with our business. And tell your friend, next time I see him I break him. Break him hard."

"We are not intimidated, sir," Baird told him. He fought through the pain to straighten. "So you may take your simian brutality and go elsewhere. We are not impressed." At the end he was actually sticking out his skinny chest.

Larry stared with disbelief. "You are exactly, I mean fucking exactly, like my first wife. The more I smacked that woman around, the more her lips flapped. There was a broad didn't know what it meant to just shut the fuck up for five minutes."

"Why did you do this to me?"

Larry grinned. Up close his teeth were as bad as his complexion. "'Cause I'm delivering a message," Larry said. "Like Western Union. Get lost. Disappear. Evaporate. You got that?"

Baird nodded. Even nodding hurt. "Perino told you to do this to me, didn't he?"

Larry's face took on a flat, dark look. "You can go fuck yourself with questions like that. I ain't stupid. I ain't telling you who told me what."

"You've got me there. But how the hell did you get down here so fast?"

Larry patted his flat stomach. "Staying in shape," he said proudly.

For all the pain, Baird was feeling better than ever. Now he had not only fought a battle of wits with Perino but a real battle with the famous Larry Reynolds. He had even

93

gotten in two healthy blows—"shots" O'Malley would call them, a nice term, shots—blows that increased in effectiveness as Baird replayed them in his mind. Within fifteen minutes he envisioned Perino recoiling in fear at his cleverness and Larry in pain at the "shots."

Baird needed a soul mate, someone to share his moment of triumph. O'Malley was still in New York, but Brenda was now at home. What a great idea. He headed down Beverly Glen toward Westwood.

When he reached her building he felt suddenly anxious, a strange feeling of excitement that he wrote off as a hangover from the fight. She was on the ninth floor, according to the directory. When she answered the bell her voice was warm.

"Who is it?"

"Hi. This is Baird," he began, unexpectedly stammering slightly. "I was, uh, happening by the neighborhood and I have an interesting piece of news to give you if you have a moment." Strangely, his hand had trembled on the bell.

"Sure, Jerry," she said easily. "Come on up."

Halfway to the ninth floor the butterflies took wing. He was startled at the sensation and told himself not to be a fool. What was the big deal? What was he afraid of? Brenda was a straightforward, twenty-three-year-old girl, a bit flashy perhaps, a bit worldly perhaps, but fundamentally uncomplicated. What was the problem? He reached her door and knocked softly.

She waited a minute before answering. When the door opened he saw only dim light behind her. Her face was still swollen in spots and bandages covered her right cheekbone. Yet even in the soft light he could also see her hair was full and rich, her jeans tight and tucked into jaunty calf-high brown boots. Her lovely pale blue silk blouse had the first three buttons open.

"Hi."

Beads of sweat broke through the pores of his forehead,

but now there was no place to run. "Hello there," he responded gamely.

She came out into the light and ran a cool hand over his cheek. "What happened to you?"

Baird's chest expanded. "I've been in a fight," he explained. "I think it was the same fellow who beat you, actually."

Brenda's eyes widened. "No," she said loudly. "Did he hurt you? Are you all right?"

"Yes, I'm all right. I don't know what his condition is."

"Oh, my God, you poor thing. Come in here immediately and I'll clean you up."

Baird followed her in to what was once more an impeccable apartment. She sat him down in a chair, gave him a lovely rich glass of Merlot, and brought some ice and towels for his cuts. "You know your friend O'Malley did this for me," she told him as she washed away the blood. "He was so gentle and kind, going over the parts that hurt so carefully. He's really a great guy."

Baird was already falling into a lovely reverie. "Yes, he's a prince," he agreed. "He's now in New York, and apt to stay there for some time."

"I know. He sends me checks too." She grinned. "You guys are the best thing that ever happened to me." Her hands moved easily. When she was done, she stepped back, then laughed gaily. "Come here, you've got to see this."

She led him to a full-length mirror. They looked into it and then they both laughed. The glass reflected the strangest collection of swollen eyes, puffed lips, twisted noses, lumps, and bandages that had ever been assembled on two heads. She took his hand and shook it. "We're a team," Brenda said. "Broken up by the same dude."

Baird felt warmth replace his anxiety. Before he could respond she touched his arm. "Let's go into the living room," she offered.

They sat on the couch together. She poured him an-

95

other glass of wine and watched with interest while he sipped it. It was after dusk and the Wilshire lights came pale through the living room. She rose. "Let's look at the lights for awhile," she said softly.

She snapped switches, leaving only a small table lamp. She knelt on the couch next to him. "Do you feel strange getting banged up like that?" she asked suddenly. It sounded like a question she had been thinking about for awhile.

"What do you mean?"

"I don't know. I used to feel good about myself, about the way I looked. I used to trust people, too, as weird as that sounds. When that guy beat me up it was like he took something away. My face will get better, sort of, but I know it'll never be the same. But more than that I'm always afraid now. And I never was afraid before." Brenda's voice didn't quaver. Nevertheless, Baird was moved.

"As for your face, I can only talk about it now, because I never saw you before you were hurt," he told her. "To me, right now, this moment, you are as lovely as any woman I've ever seen."

Baird heard the words and flushed. He expected her to laugh. Instead she smiled.

"That's an awfully nice thing to say, Jerry. Do people call you Jerry?"

"Most people call me Baird."

"Then I'll call you Jerry. That way I'll be different than everybody else, O.K.?"

"That's fine," he said quickly.

The wine was warm and red and they drank some more. Brenda moved closer to him. Her half-open blouse followed precisely the curve of her breasts. She spoke softly. "You know, we could have fun together. You could teach me about all those things I don't know anything about. Maybe I can show you some things you haven't thought about either."

When Baird didn't answer, she leaned over suddenly and gave him a soft gentle kiss on the lips, a kiss that barely touched the skin. She kissed him twice more with the same soft brush kisses. He felt his mind short-circuiting. Then she leaned back. "Would you like to unbutton my blouse?"

This is it, all systems go. Try not to blow it, Baird. His hands shook but she didn't seem to mind. He fumbled but the soft fabric soon fell away. Brenda spread the material for him. His eyes grew wide.

"Put your hands here," she suggested softly. Baird did as he was told. Her skin was warm. Her breasts were warm. Everything was warm. He ran his hands over her with a tenderness born of his complete disbelief that he was actually doing this. He couldn't wait to feel all of her.

"You're picking this up very well," Brenda told him. The tips of her breasts rose. She reached for the back of his head and brought him close.

"Yes, that's right," she murmured. "Just like that. You're doing just fine, Jerry." Her voice seemed to come from far away.

She put her mouth near his ear, kissing lightly, unbuttoning his shirt with her right hand. Her voice had a practiced seductiveness. "I know your fantasies must involve a girl who is naked," she whispered. "Stark naked. Without a stitch of clothes on for you to do whatever it is you want. Is that what you'd like?" Baird's head jerked up and down spasmodically. He remembered every comic book he had ever read where the nerd meets the beautiful girl and his glasses fog up. He found it doesn't happen quite like that in real life. What does happen is a tremendous amount of sweat immediately builds up under the glasses and causes chafing. Still the sign of a nerd.

But Brenda didn't seem to mind. "Jerry, it's gonna be so great when you take me to bed," she told him. "I can just feel it."

Baird had a cup of water underneath his glasses. He decided to leave hesitancy to the nerds. "Let's go," he said.

He ran into the bedroom, ripped off his clothes, ripped

off hers, pushed her back, fell upon her, and kissed everything he could find without a bruise. He entered her within ninety seconds and exploded at the two-minute mark. He ignored the interruption and continued on, his glasses banging so vigorously against the pillow they finally just fell away. Soon he felt himself stiffen within her again and exploded anew. He was going for the hat trick ten minutes later when she begged him to stop with giggled entreaties.

He came to rest slowly, still kissing her eyes, her mouth, her hair. She held him close. He began leaning over her again.

"Jerry, please," she laughed. "Give me just a moment. I wasn't quite prepared for this."

"I'm sorry," he said reflexively.

She half shut her eyes as small aftershocks took her. "Oh, don't be sorry. Don't be sorry at all."

Baird didn't say anything. Soon she opened her eyes and just looked at him.

"It's true, just like I figured," she said. "You are different. I knew you'd be good for me."

"I will. I promise." He would have promised anything as long as she would let him stay.

She laughed at that and slid into his arms. "You know, I've been hoping you'd be coming up here for a long time now, Jerry Baird. I remember you so well from that first time at the hospital. You were so shy, you even wanted to put blankets over me. Your friend O'Malley would have been just as happy for the quick thrill. Then I heard you talking to the doctor and in five minutes you knew more about me than he did. To tell you the truth, I sort of paid attention after that."

Baird was cooling down now, at least enough to think about things. All this romance and sweet talk was fine as long as they had a clear understanding on a fundamental issue. "I want you to give up the business," he said, "if you're serious about spending time with me, that is."

He expected her to balk but she didn't.

"Yes, Jerry," she said. Her voice was serious, as though it were very important she accommodate her man the first time he asked for something. Baird fought hard against a smile.

"Good," he said. Then he gently pushed her back on the bed. His hands moved with a new confidence. He put his mouth near her ear. "Now let me tell you what I've really been thinking about."

13

Twenty-seven hours after Baird's meeting with David Perino, O'Malley walked out of the Park Lane with Hamilton Brent.

"New York is such a wonderful city," Brent began as they meandered past the fancy store fronts, "especially when it comes to food. The number of first-class restaurants is really without compare anywhere in the world. Why, within ten blocks of where we stand, there are probably twenty magnificent, world-class establishments."

O'Malley wasn't going to let some stranger slide by with generalities. "Like what?" he challenged.

Brent just gestured. "You have your choice," he said amiably. "On East Fifty-fourth Le Cygne is excellent, quiet and elegant with a magnificent wine list and a sublime raspberry soufflé. I recommend it highly. A bit more trendy is La Côte Basque a block away on Fifty-fifth, which has a mousseline de poisson with lobster sauce I've never seen equaled."

O'Malley knew he was in over his head. "Well, both of those sound nice," he offered.

"Quite," Brent agreed. "Now in the same neighborhood down on Fifty-second is La Grenouille, where I know the captain very well and can almost guarantee he'll accommodate us with the perles noires de la Volga and iced Vodka he keeps for special guests. Otherwise I'm afraid we'll have to do with the menu."

"Oh, God," O'Malley said.

"I see your point. There is a risk. Well, we could stroll a few blocks over and try Lutèce. The difficulty, of course, is we may not be able to resist the ris de veau financière, which is a bit leaden if Robert is not in the kitchen." The dilemma seemed to confound Brent, and soon he began having a little conversation with himelf, nodding his head at the pros, making a small face at the cons. As most of the chat was in French, O'Malley felt no need even to feign participation. As he walked his mind wandered, Hamilton Brent's mumblings alongside becoming simply a background hum, the decision made that whoever or whatever Brent was, at least O'Malley was going to get a nice meal out of it. The staff at the hotel would be a marvelous resource, all those eyes and ears available to question. And at a relatively low price by Anna's standards. None of them was privy to the actual moment of John's death but that wasn't important; very important would be their description of John, of Monica, of how they spent their final days. And above all who they were seen with. What a delicious piece of information that would be. Who knows, maybe an old, distinguished fellow named Perino was hanging around. What a break! Maybe even . . .

His train of thought was broken by a tugging at his sleeve. Hamilton Brent was speaking to him. "Chez Pascal," he said excitedly. "Shall we chance it?"

"You're an impulsive man, Mr. Brent," O'Malley told him. "Lead the way."

But even the good life has to come to an end sooner or later. It was after 11:00 when the waiter brought the cigars and brandy. They both leaned back in well-upholstered chairs and took long, satisfied puffs.

O'Malley inspected the end of his cigar, then blew on it like every fat cat he had ever seen in a movie. "This is great," he said. "A few months of this and I'd look like a circle. My blood would have to use blasting caps to fight its way through the veins. But so what. A quick heart attack and it's lights out. Who wants a lingering life with your nose pressed up against the window?"

Hamilton Brent agreed. "I must confess this is unusual for me. I'm typically a bit like a restaurant critic, sampling just a touch of this and a touch of that, but never a full meal. It's quite frustrating sometimes only to take a single glass of Bordeaux, only a sip of the truffle soup."

"Well, war is hell, Brent. Just keep remembering it's for a good cause." O'Malley clicked his glass against Brent's in sympathy.

Brent signed for the check, and they hit the bricks. Before dinner, Brent had displayed some beginner potential with Jack Daniels and wanted to continue. Around midnight they slid onto stools at the Hunt Bar of the Helmsley Palace. At 1:00 A.M., they hit the wall together. "This is terrible," Hamilton Brent said. "I fear we've overindulged."

That was entirely possible. "Think of it as training, Brent," O'Malley told him. "No gain without pain and all that."

"Quite."

Brent took another small sip and said, "By the way, I haven't asked you what you do for Anna. If it's all right for you to talk about it, I mean."

O'Malley said, "It's no secret. I'm trying to help her find out how and why her husband died. That and a small side assignment."

"What's that?"

"Trying to find a man named Larry. He beat up a woman in Los Angeles and Anna feels responsible."

Brent said, "I know about Anna's husband, of course. It's a terrible thing. Why do you think he died?"

O'Malley shrugged. "I don't know. We've got a few angles we're working, but right now it's very early in the game. My best guess is it's somehow involved with John's work."

"Really? How so?"

"I think John was a crook," O'Malley said simply.

"I see." Hamilton Brent sipped again, then said, "How did you find out the other fellow's name? Larry, I mean."

O'Malley just stared straight ahead. What a perceptive question. "Let's take a walk," he suggested.

They left the glorious bar, then walked through the Gold Room and down the long staircase—white marble glistening in the glow of Tiffany chandeliers. A red and gold bedecked doorman ushered them into the blackness of the New York night.

Brent led them up Madison. Within two blocks the lights of the hotel were gone. He then turned down a side street, a shortcut, he said. The street was lit by tall, thin street lights and the flash of passing cars. Once a large American car slowed briefly before continuing on.

O'Malley was paying careful attention to the sights and sounds around him. He was also listening to Hamilton Brent's voice, amiably chattering along beside him. The voice had an even ring to it. It was not the voice of a man suffering the effects of a long night.

Six blocks from the hotel even the street lights seemed dim. The traffic was irregular. They reached a large construction site abutting a wide alley. Brent stopped. "Let's walk through here," he suggested. "It's quicker."

That it would be. O'Malley studied the man, who was again smiling at him. Brent was about five-foot-four and looked to weigh about 130 pounds. What the fuck did this squirt think he was doing. "Who are you working for?" O'Malley asked flatly.

The smile on Brent's face quivered a bit but he recovered. He wordlessly gestured toward the alley again.

O'Malley had had about enough. He put a large hand underneath Brent's chin and drove the little man back up against the chain link fence that surrounded the construction site. There was a harsh clinking sound as the man's head bounced against the metal. With his free hand O'Malley patted underneath Brent's jacket. Strapped under the arm was a blue-black .38.

O'Malley jammed the gun under his belt. "Who are you working for?"

Brent licked his lips. He gestured to the alley. "Let's go find out."

O'Malley considered it. He was now armed. Brent was harmless. The alley was sinister, but at least it opened at each end. He pushed Brent in front of him. "Let's go," he said.

They walked slowly down the black corridor. Brent began chattering again. "Make it easy on yourself," he suggested. "All he wants is a little information. Toss the gun away and nobody will be hurt."

"Shut the fuck up," O'Malley ordered. He pushed him roughly forward another few feet.

Brent grinned good-naturedly. "Have it your way," he said. "I just want to get out of here and let you two resolve this between yourselves."

"And just how do you propose to do that?" O'Malley asked.

For the first time Brent's eyes showed fear. He turned around and his voice had panic in it. "Hey, wait, I don't want anything to do with this." O'Malley pushed him forward again.

They were halfway down the alley and still nothing appeared. Suddenly from the far end a pair of bright beams bounced low into a pothole, then rose high, casting an eerie glow on the red brick of the adjacent buildings. The beams fell to level again and an engine roared. Gravel spewed in all directions. The car stopped a hundred feet from O'Malley.

A dark shape exited the car and stood protected behind

the open door on the driver's side. The engine was still running and the high beams on. O'Malley put his hand on Brent's neck and squeezed softly. He took the gun out of his belt.

"Shut the lights off," he shouted.

The man ignored him. It was impossible to see the man's face, but O'Malley didn't really need to. There was a carriage, a bearing about the silhouette that was unmistakable.

O'Malley repeated his order, this time louder. He flashed the .38 behind Brent's ear. The man behind the car door reached under his jacket with his right hand. O'Malley didn't need to see the gun any more than he needed to see Larry's face.

"We got a standoff," O'Malley hollered. "Back out and we'll forget the whole thing."

Larry raised his hands. "Watch out," O'Malley screamed. Three flashes spurted from the dark silhouette. Brent gave a low surprised moan and knelt down, then crumbled into a ball of pain. He held his stomach as the red began welling through his fingers. O'Malley dove into the debris of the construction just as fire spurted from Larry's hands again.

O'Malley heard rather than saw masonry shatter above his head. He crawled into the relative safety of crushed rock and twisted, discarded metal rods. Except for a small aperture at the bottom of the rubbish, the light from Larry's car was completely blocked by the building waste. A wonderful bunker for firing. O'Malley grabbed the .38 with both hands and pointed.

Larry's door was visible through the small hole. O'Malley pulled the trigger twice, delighted Brent had carried such a lovely powerful weapon. He was rewarded by the sounds of tearing metal, shattered glass, and a loud curse. O'Malley squeezed twice more and again saw the bullets rip gaping holes in the steel door behind which Larry hid. In seconds the door slammed shut, the engine of the large American car exploded once again, and the tires squealed painfully down the narrow alley.

O'Malley lay quietly for what seemed a long time. With the danger gone he felt cold and alone in the harsh rubble. He breathed fitfully. He stirred from his daze only when he heard the low moan from the alley.

O'Malley walked to Brent's side. The young man's skin was ashen. What seemed to be quarts of blood formed pools around Brent's stomach.

"Just try to relax," he told him. "I'll see what I can do."

Brent looked at him, then started crying. He was still crying thirty seconds later when O'Malley heard the death rattle in the man's throat. Soon the alley was quiet and black again.

14

O'Malley woke long after the sun had passed over the top of the Park Lane. Without thinking he reached for the phone and ordered up a pot of black coffee, washed down three Excedrins with two Alka Seltzers, and stepped into an alternately steaming hot, biting cold shower. Thirty minutes later he felt as bad as he had waking up.

He dialed Anna in Los Angeles and got no answer. He still felt the harsh aftershocks of Hamilton Brent's murder. The cold-blooded destruction of Brent, a man presumably working for them, was terrifying in its senselessness. He had no illusions any more of what Perino would do to anyone he perceived as a danger.

He dialed Baird. Baird came to the phone sounding as chipper as O'Malley had ever heard him. Sated even. His friend's tone cheered him momentarily.

"What are you so happy about? Did the inheritance come through?"

"Money again. O'Malley, is that all you think of, money? There are many things in life more important than cash."

"You mean like bonds? Because you get interest?"

"O'Malley, you're a Philistine. I'm talking about love. I'm talking about combat."

"Is that two things or the same thing?"

"I am talking about an event that demonstrates you are not the only person on this team capable of responding to physical violence."

O'Malley's glee faded. "Who?"

"Larry. The one and only Larry." Baird talked like he was announcing receipt of a letter from the Nobel committee.

O'Malley's voice was crisp. "When and where, Baird. Tell me the whole thing."

Baird repeated the tale of his meeting with Perino and the confrontation in the garage. "I really don't like to blow my own horn," he concluded, "but it was a relatively short battle. I struck him repeatedly, and he retreated."

O'Malley nodded to himself. Who cared what the truth was? At least Baird was still breathing. "Good work," he said. "But there's something you ought to know for the next time." O'Malley talked for ten minutes straight. When he stopped there was silence on the line.

"You still there?" he asked.

He heard a cough. "Yes."

"What do you think?"

Another cough. "I think we're in pretty good shape."

O'Malley stared at the phone. "How do you figure that?"

106

"We're alive."

"We're lucky."

"You're right," Baird admitted. He didn't sound as happy anymore.

"Anyway, tell me about the other," O'Malley said. "Something about love."

"Yes, this is the harder part." There was a long pause. "I'm afraid I've taken Brenda from you."

Surprise. Surprise. "That's quite all right," O'Malley said. "But you're sure Brenda is not a bit, uh, fast for your tastes?"

"Not a bit," Baird told him confidently. "We've each agreed to make accommodations. She is becoming somewhat more restrained in her, uh, affections, and I on the other hand am endeavoring to become more eclectic in my tastes."

"Yes, that will be necessary. But this is certainly good news. And I want to extend my very best wishes."

"Thank you. Now is there anything else?" Baird sounded like a man who had to get back to something.

"Just one thing. At dinner Brent said something about a trial. He said it like it was something he thought I knew about."

"A trial between whom?"

"I don't know, but I think Anna was involved. As soon as he figured out I didn't know about it he shut up. But it sounded like it could be important."

"I'll check it out. Anything else?"

"Yes. Be careful, please," O'Malley said.

15

The elevator opened with a grand flourish on the second floor of the hotel. Before him was the lovely breakfast room set at eye level with the tops of the trees in the park. Thick burgundy drapes two stories high with gold, braided cords were dramatically pulled back. The green trees lining Central Park South filled the windows. A fat gratuity discreetly transmitted to the headwaiter ensured a prime table next to the squeaky clean glass. The fat gratuity never failed.

O'Malley walked past the elegant eating room and turned right into the dark, wood-dominated bar. The bar was set in the back, without view or particular charm. The bartender was slowly and without great effort buffing a glass with a white rag. A man like that on an average afternoon would probably notice most of what was going on in great detail.

The man came over and buffed his glass in front of O'Malley, his only customer. "Not much action in the afternoon, huh?"

The man shrugged. "My theory is the rich don't drink in public. Now once I worked a Hilton, and let me tell you that's a different crowd. Morning, noon, or night, it don't make no difference. Here they got to sneak it."

"What time's it pick up here?" O'Malley asked.

"We get the predinner crowd, about six-thirty," the man said. "Before that just the odd guy here and there."

"You work this shift every day, do you?"

The man's head leaned back a touch, and his hands

rubbed the glass less vigorously. "What an inquisitive fellow. You know, George told me there was a big guy up on sixteen who was also an inquisitive fellow." He went back to regular buffing. "But that's probably not you, 'cause George said this guy was real generous."

"Whatever happened to man helping his fellow man just for the pure love of it?"

"Oh, that's still around," the man agreed. "You see it around Christmas in all those fancy stores on Fifth Avenue."

There was no hope of winning that debate. O'Malley took out his wallet and placed it next to his beer glass. The man looked down at it. "I ain't Superman, you know. I ain't got no X-ray vision."

O'Malley reached inside and pulled out three tens, exactly as he had with George. The man looked at the bills and then looked back at O'Malley. "George told me it's probably fifty just for telling my name."

"Well, George is wrong, Marcel. I know your name. It's fifty for telling me what I want to know."

The man smiled. "Deal." He scooped up the tens like a croupier. "I'll talk while you fish."

The bartender leaned over on his elbows. He spoke in a conspiratorial tone. "It was right before he died," he began, "the night before, two nights before, I don't remember. He came in about five-thirty all agitated like. You know how people get. Fidgeting, looking around, running his hands over his tie. Even asked me if I had any cigarettes behind the bar, and when I gave him one, he smoked it like he never seen one before. What I'm saying is the guy was shook."

"Anybody with him?"

"Not at first. He just sat there alone looking messed up. So I gave him a drink to calm him down. After that, the other guy showed up."

"What time did Bradley arrive?"

"About five-thirty," the man said impatiently. "Try to pay attention. The other guy showed up maybe twenty minutes later. Bradley was on his third round already."

"Describe the other guy," O'Malley ordered.

"About six-two and beefy. Hair kind of light brown, maybe dirty blond. A sport jacket and no tie, kind of brown plaid it was. Canadian Club straight up. Looked like he was trying hard not to order a beer chaser in a class place."

"And I bet you're also gonna tell me he had a funny face."

"Yeah," Marcel said. "Like I had in high school."

How interesting. John and Larry having a drink together. Maybe talking about the Knicks.

"So what happened?" O'Malley asked. "What did they talk about? How did they act?"

"I'll tell you what I know. The big guy comes in, walks up and taps Bradley. Bradley about jumps over the bar. The big guy sits down and talks real quiet to him, like he's trying to talk him into something Bradley don't want no part of. Bradley is shaking his head and saying, 'No, goddam it, I'm not going to do it.' I'm making believe I'm wiping the glasses, you know, but I'm listening 'cause it looks intense."

"But ultimately Larry ordered a drink?"

"Is that his name, Larry? He looked like a Larry. But that's right. Larry gets a drink and tries to get Bradley to toast something. Bradley don't want no part of it. Then Larry gets a little rough."

"What do you mean?"

"He got pissed off about something," the man said. "All of a sudden, he throws back the CC and bangs on the bar for another one. Then he tries to make Bradley drink a toast again. Only this time Larry grabs the back of Bradley's neck and puts the drink up to his lips. Bradley tries to squirm away and he's spilling the drink all over, all over his clothes and all over the bar. I look at his face and it looks like he's gonna cry he's so mad. But Larry still keeps the drink up to his face."

That angered O'Malley. "What the hell were you doing all this time? They pay you money to polish glasses or make sure nobody breaks up your bar?"

"Don't you worry about me, pal. This may be where the rich people hang out, but I got a sap under the bar just in case anybody comes in who don't belong. I was over there as soon as I saw it start getting heavy."

"So what happened?"

"Nothing. This guy Larry, he leans up and gives me a pat on the cheek and tells me everything's okay. I tell him he touches me with his hands again, he's gonna lose one of 'em, although to tell you the truth I was just as happy he didn't take me up. Anyway, I turn to this guy Bradley and ask him if everything's okay. He clears his throat, takes a drink with those shaking hands, and asks me for another cigarette. Never even answers my question. I ask him again, and he gets all pissed off, tells me to mind my own business and just get him a cigarette. I figure, what the fuck, and go do what the man says."

"It didn't occur to you he was in trouble?"

The bartender shrugged. "What was he gonna do, kill somebody in my bar? That wasn't gonna happen. So I stuck my nose in to make sure everything got cool, then butted out, just like Bradley said."

"When did they leave?"

"That was the funny part. After that scene, they almost started to get friendly. Larry had a couple more Canadian Clubs, Bradley had a few more Scotches, and even the lady had a few."

"What lady?"

"The sweetest piece of ass you're likely to see in your lifetime," the man said. "I mean this lady was built, with just the cutest little tits and the nicest smile I ever saw. I tell you, if me and that lady were out someplace, I would . . ."

When O'Malley cut him off his voice was sharp. "Spare me the gory details. What did they say?"

The bartender turned away and went back to wiping his glasses. "O.K., but it's your loss. The lady told him something he didn't like. He started crying in his beer. Then they left and he went and got hung."

"Did you hear anything at all?"

The man shook his head from side to side. "Not after his lady came. Only thing I can say is she did the talking. He sort of forgot about Larry sitting there. Larry leaned over a couple times trying to horn in but they didn't pay no attention."

"Then what?"

"Then they left. Larry dropped a bunch of cash on the bar and they was gone."

"They left together, then?" The man nodded affirmatively.

"How did Bradley look when he left?"

"Like shit."

So that was that. Larry and Monica working on Bradley the day or two before his death. Maybe asking him to do something he didn't want to do. And when they couldn't talk him into it, Larry dealing with the situation as efficiently as he later dealt with Hamilton Brent. Maybe. The man behind the bar cleared his throat, wondering if O'Malley was through. The sound broke his concentration. O'Malley looked at the man once, then finished the beer with a gulp. He gave the man his money, picked up his wallet, and left.

16

When O'Malley got back to his room the red light was flashing on his phone. He ignored it, closed the drapes, and slept like a stone for four more hours. When he awoke he had the desk read the message to him. It was from Anna. It read: "Good afternoon, Mr. O'Malley. I expect to arrive at the Carlyle at six tonight. May we meet and discuss matters? If convenient, please come for drinks at 7:30. Anna."

O'Malley checked his watch, jumped in and out of a shower, and ran out to Central Park South waving for a cab.

The cab took no more than ten minutes to reach the Carlyle, a quick ride up the east side of the park. He thought of Anna the whole way. For five of the minutes his thoughts were warm and soothing, a growing feeling that even when she wasn't there the woman was enveloping him, blocking all else from his mind. For the other five he had his hand on his wallet, reminding himself that Mrs. O'Malley didn't raise stupid kids. It was in this frame of mind that he left the cab.

O'Malley asked for Anna's room at the desk, then rode the elevator grim-faced to the fourth floor. Now the pleasant thoughts of Anna were completely blocked out by the horror of the night before. Again he saw Hamilton Brent lean forward in a futile effort to hold his stomach together. He again heard the crack of the bullets, the squeal of Larry's tires, the sound of death. O'Malley didn't want his mind cluttered with these visions anymore. He wanted answers.

He knocked hard on the oak door. She didn't answer immediately, so he knocked hard again, his irritation much too obvious. When she appeared, her eyes were apprehensive. He gave her only a passing glance as he walked into the room.

The quarters were as palatial as he had expected. Room 419 was actually a suite, four rooms jammed with gaudy French antiques. A grand piano dominated the spacious living room. At least forty feet of glass looked out onto Seventy-third Street.

Off to the left of the sofa was a wet bar. He walked behind it and found the ice and Jack Daniels in seconds. He poured himself an unusually large one and took an unusually large gulp. Then he leaned on his elbows on the leather bar and looked at her.

Anna closed the door and moved into the room. She stood in back of a chair with both hands on it. Her eyes were fearful. For the first time since he arrived in the room, O'Malley took the time to look at her closely, and he had to admit, in spite of all his efforts to prevent it, that he no longer had any chance with this woman. She was dressed in a black cocktail dress which exposed her white shoulders. Her yellow hair was loose. The gown was flimsy and draped; beyond that he couldn't tell a thing. It wasn't as if he had seen a lot of them lying around in stores.

"Going somewhere?" he asked abruptly.

When she didn't answer, he said it again. His tone was rude.

Anna tried to maintain a certain dignity, but tears soon betrayed her. She kept her hands on the chair and at first refused to wipe the wet away. Then lots of tears followed muffled sobs.

"That's very good. I bet between tennis games you're taking acting lessons. I always wondered how a good actress makes tears come on demand. Do you pinch yourself, or something?"

Her head whipped back to him. The eyes were, indeed, gray and puffy. "Why are you talking to me like this?" she demanded.

"Oh, I don't know," O'Malley said evenly. "Maybe I'm tired. More likely I'm still thinking about a little worm I watched die last night."

"What does that mean?"

O'Malley told her and watched her eyes grow wide at the tale. When he stopped her face had lost its blood.

"You mean he killed him?"

"Dead as John Brown." O'Malley could have been even crueler. "By now they've swept him up. Assuming they haven't lost him, there may even be an investigation beginning."

She looked back up at him, her breathing becoming

more normal. "It's a horrible story. But it still doesn't explain your attitude toward me."

"Doesn't it? Well, let me try to explain. I smell a rat, lady. There're little hairs twitching on the back of my neck telling me to watch out. And the first thing I'm going to watch out for are gorgeous, rich widows who don't tell me everything. Who maybe are using me for something." When she didn't answer, his voice snapped again. "Who is he? *Was* he, I mean."

"I don't know."

"He said you sent him. He knew a lot about you."

"So what."

"So maybe you sent him. Maybe you know who he is."

"For what possible purpose?" she asked.

"To keep an eye on me. Make sure my nose stayed pointed in the wrong direction."

She seemed to relax at that. She put her hands on her hips and smiled at him. "Mr. O'Malley—Benjamin—I have no need for your nose to be pointed in the wrong direction." Her voice was insistent. "You are my only hope in this. If there is anything that makes you doubt that, please, please tell me what it is."

"Okay. Why was Monica blackmailing you?"

The smile fell from her face, the hands from her hips. She didn't answer.

O'Malley brought his glass down hard on the bar. "Christ, Anna, stop playing games with me."

She still didn't answer at first, didn't cry, didn't object, didn't do anything. Then she walked to the bar and sat across from him. In spite of his anger he felt his mood soften; maybe sympathy, more likely the proximity of honey hair and white shoulders. She pointed to his glass and said, "Mr. O'Malley, play bartender again and I'll tell you the story of Monica's money."

He did and she began talking. As she talked O'Malley's last remaining bit of irritation became concentration.

"It all involves my emotional problems, which, as I told you, began right before I married John," she said. "It was a very difficult time of my life, that year. My father was dead. All of a sudden I had an uncontrollable urge to break out of the mold I had been in for twenty years. I did some very stupid things."

"Like what?"

She shrugged. "Probably nothing more than any girl does when it's her time to be rebellious. Except I did it in a lot bigger way and in a lot shorter period of time." She spread her hands as if in apology. "I went into bars on a whim, bars I passed on the street in Hollywood. I went out with rather strange and, I suppose, unsavory men. I experimented with drugs." She smiled. "To today's young girl maybe none of that is strange. To me, to those around me, it meant mental illness."

Her head dropped to her drink; she stirred it with a finger. Her voice was so soft O'Malley could barely hear it. "And that's the way it seemed to the court too."

"What do you mean the court?"

"I mean those responsible for my affairs became concerned. There was an elaborate hearing, really a trial—conducted in a very hush-hush way, of course—and at the end it was determined I needed to be hospitalized. I was sent away for a period of ninety days to a very exclusive rest home." O'Malley could see the wet form around her cheeks. "Then it was over," she said simply.

"So how does Monica fit in?" he asked her. "If it was a public hearing, what did she have on you?"

Anna shook her head vigorously. "It wasn't a public hearing. All the lawyers and the judge agreed that it would do me no good to have these matters sensationalized. Later on . . ." She stopped the tale and smiled. "When Monica became a confidante of John, she learned about the whole mess."

"And then she put the bite on you?"

Anna nodded. "We had lunch one day and she told me what she knew. She asked in a very ordinary way whether I might have some use for her secretarial services when she wasn't working at the studio. I knew what she was asking for." Anna smiled. "She hasn't done any typing for me yet."

O'Malley remembered the trial Brent had talked about. It made sense. He shook his head. "You could have told me when I first asked," he told her. "First of all, it might have helped find John, although I doubt it. But beyond that it's just something . . . something I should have known."

His tone made her smile. "And why is that, Mr. O'Malley?"

Why indeed. He didn't say anything in response.

They looked at each other with interest. O'Malley was beginning to want this woman a great deal. Her pain had transformed her from a caricature of a woman to a real one. But first another question. "How did your father die?" he asked quietly.

Her gaze didn't falter. "He was murdered," she answered just as quietly.

17

Brenda came out of the shower with a large white towel wrapped around her. She called for Baird and was almost relieved when he didn't answer. She moved quickly around the hotel room, picking up articles of clothing wherever they lay. She worked efficiently, as she always did whenever Baird went upstairs for one of his strange meetings. This was her one chance to lend a little order to their lives. With Baird in the room, there just never was the chance.

It was pretty much the same at home, she realized. For a guy who claimed to have been something of a prude, not to mention a rookie, Baird had taken to Brenda's body the way a convert to Catholicism takes to midnight mass. He never got enough of it. And although Brenda was as liberal as the next girl, some of his ideas were enough to turn anyone pink around the cheeks. Not that she was complaining. But it did make it hard to keep things neat.

They had been in Las Vegas for a day and a half now. Brenda had no idea what the hell was going on, except Jerry was trying awfully hard to get a meeting with some big shot. The morning before, he'd gotten up at six, put on his best suit, and left the hotel room at eight. He'd spent the day upstairs on the top floor of the hotel where the suites of offices were. Then at four he'd returned with a long look on his face. This morning he was at it again.

The few times they talked about it, Baird would only say it was important and would help him find out what the hell happened to poor John Bradley. Brenda had no idea what that meant either, so she contented herself with having a great vacation and doing what she could to entertain Baird when he wasn't working. She even acted surprised at the sights, although the fact was she knew Vegas far better than any good girl had a right to. But she stayed away from the old haunts and thus far hadn't had the bad luck to bump into any old friends. What that left was lounging by the hotel pool in her pink bikini, the safest place of all. Things had certainly been worse.

The top floor of the hotel was a long way from the one-armed bandits on the first floor, eighty stories in fact. On this floor were soft couches and soft voices, receptionists and secretaries, thick carpets and paneled offices. The muted ringing of telephones and the unglamorous clicking of typewriters were the only sounds. There was no reason to suspect this area existed only to record, more or less accurately, the hundreds of millions being made in the chaotic pits below.

Baird had begun the process in Los Angeles with a simple telegram he had thrown into the wind just to see if it blew back at him. It was devastating in its understatement and effect.

Dear Mr. Newsome:

I represent Mrs. Anna Bradley in connection with an investigation into the disappearance of her husband, John Bradley. John Bradley was formerly a studio accountant in your employ.

In the course of our investigation we have come upon evidence that John Bradley was intimately familiar with the details of a series of transactions which may interest you. Mr. Bradley, as you may or may not be aware, has recently died in an unpleasant manner in the Park Lane Hotel in New York City.

We also believe, on the basis of our investigation to date, that Mr. David Perino is familiar with the details of these transactions.

I would welcome the opportunity to discuss the foregoing with you at your earliest convenience. I suggest such a discussion will prove useful to you and, ultimately, to the company's other shareholder.

Sincerely,
Jerome Baird
Attorney for Anna Bradley

The wire must have hit Vegas like a bombshell. Within hours, Baird's phone was ringing off the hook. Newsome's minions offered him the finest suites, first-class air fare, the most deluxe accommodations. For him and a guest, of course. Nobody promised him a meeting with Newsome, but everybody seemed to want to hear what he had to say.

For all practical purposes, however, the Las Vegas trip was a complete waste of time. He was getting hoarse asking the same bland question of every person he met: "When can I see Eliot Newsome?" He was also getting tired of the party line response, inevitably a long monologue about Mr. Newsome's schedule, the history of the company, whether Baird was liking Las Vegas, whether he had gotten out to see the Hoover Dam (wasn't it a shame, he really ought to get out there), whether he liked blackjack or craps (craps had better odds, it was said, although harder to learn) and on through fifty other topics including the wine in his glass and the art on the walls. When it was over, Baird would smile politely and say: "When can I see Eliot Newsome?"

And now it was thirty-six hours later and he was sitting on a couch in front of another receptionist. This one was as kind as all the others. He spent another forty minutes paging through magazines and then decided to ask his favorite question again. He walked up and asked very politely, "Do you know when I might see Eliot Newsome?"

She looked up. "Mr. Newsome? Why, of course, Mr. Baird. You can go right in."

He thought it was a joke. He stared at her. She gestured with her hand. Baird walked backward in a daze through the double oak door she indicated.

He entered an anteroom. An unsmiling man sat at a small metal desk. This man didn't offer pleasantries. He stood and patted Baird from head to toe, feeling under his belt and in back of his tie. Then he stepped back and pointed wordlessly. Straight ahead were unmarked double doors.

Newsome's desk was set seventy-five feet from the entrance at the opposite end of a wide expanse of oriental rug. Along the walls were comfortable couches and adjoining chairs for small conversations. The walls were dotted with ordinary oils depicting the Nevada landscape. Well-cared-for plants sat in nice vases. A wall of glass in back of Newsome's desk let in the lights of the city of Las Vegas far below.

Newsome rose and shook hands with a soft touch. He was a heavy, sloppy man dressed correctly in a conservative business suit, two pieces of gray material set off by a blue shirt and oxford tie. On either side of him stood a similarly dressed man holding a tan folder.

Newsome's voice was as friendly as summer rain. He motioned Baird to the conversation area near the couches, and the four of them sat down.

"Mr. Baird, before we begin I'd like to introduce these two gentlemen." He gestured to his right. "This is Stephen Karshan. Mr. Karshan is the general counsel of Nevada Holding Company and a member of the Illinois bar." Baird didn't want to ask where in Illinois. "On my left is Mr. Allen Jeffreys, who is the controller, and I suppose you'd say, principal auditor, for Nevada."

Baird's spirits were immediately raised. The Nevada Holding Company had overall control of all Newsome's holdings, of which the studio was just a plaything. There was also a rumor around that the Cappicis had a big piece of Nevada, which explained why they sent Karshan in. He shook hands all around. "I'm delighted to meet you," he said. "I'm particularly glad you've involved this gentleman in our discussions." He gestured to Karshan. Karshan returned the nod wordlessly.

Newsome was civil enough to embark on a small sidebar, a vignette about Las Vegas and a quaint memorable experience. For all his ominous appearance and reputation, Newsome was approaching this meeting with traditional business protocol. After five minutes, however, he cleared his throat as a signal to get down to business.

"Well, Mr. Baird, I'm pleased you enjoy the city and I'm happy to extend the warm hand of the hotel staff during your visit. However, I'm sure you're eager to get back to your lovely companion."

Baird had not mentioned Brenda. He accepted Newsome's quiet reminder that these men were well informed.

121

"So perhaps the best way to speed this along would be to turn directly to the matters set forth in your telegram," Newsome said.

Stephen Karshan reached into a tan folder and fished out several copies of Baird's wire, handing one to Newsome and one to Baird. "Let's begin at the top," Newsome said. "What sort of investigation are you conducting for Anna Bradley?"

"Originally it was just to look into her husband's disappearance," Baird began. "You see he was the studio controller . . ."

"Yes, we know who Mr. Bradley was," Jeffreys said.

"Well, then you probably also know he disappeared inexplicably with his secretary. As a matter of fact, an internal investigation . . ."

"Yes, we're familiar with the investigation," Stephen Karshan said.

Baird shifted slightly in his chair. "One of the things the investigation looked into was a number of transactions which are . . . well, suspect."

This time Newsome spoke. Again the voice was as mild as May. "Yes, that is what your wire made mention of. That is what we are interested in learning about."

Baird listened to the voices and had a sudden realization of how young he was. Among the conceits of youth is the notion that an understanding of a problem is the functional equivalent of being able to deal with it. Baird thought he understood just about everything there was to know about John Bradley, David Perino, and how they fit together. But he still didn't belong in a room with these people.

"I'd like to tell you straight out that I'm not here to trick you," he said quickly. "I'm going to tell you what I know in as truthful a manner as I can."

The three smiled indulgently. "That would be fine," Stephen Karshan said.

Baird decided to cut through the nonsense. "I've had

conversations with Nick Roth," he said quickly.

The three Nevada people looked at each other hurriedly, a sign of concern they really shouldn't have revealed. What was this clown doing talking to Nick Roth? "Mr. Roth told me he had a client prepared to sell product for considerably less money than the company wound up paying for it," Baird went on. "The difference amounts to several million dollars. He also said he offered the deal to Perino and Bradley and was turned down. Later on the same property was purchased for twenty times Roth's price through a company controlled by Simon Jacoby."

The three of them didn't make the mistake of looking at each other this time. They kept their eyes on Baird. Stephen Karshan spoke. "When were Roth's offers made?"

"Before the deals with Jacoby were signed, of course."

"What else did Roth tell you?"

Baird spoke quickly, detailing as much as he could remember of his lunch with Nick Roth. The three listened intently.

When he was done, Newsome spoke. "Do you have any information about these transactions other than from Nick Roth?"

"All I know is what we've been able to find out during our investigation," Baird said. "When Perino and Bradley purchased the property from Jacoby's company, there were a number of strange things going on at the studio. The clerks and secretaries there at the time can describe them best for you. If you care to ask, that is."

The last remark came out sharper than Baird had intended. Newsome smiled, not a smile of mirth. "What exactly does that mean?"

Baird cleared his throat, then plunged ahead.

"It means this entire conversation may be nothing more than my telling you things you already know."

Newsome and Jeffreys snorted, a small laugh through the nose. They turned to Stephen Karshan for assurance.

But the lawyer from Chicago wasn't smiling.

"Where will you be staying for the next few days, Mr. Baird?" Karshan asked.

"I don't know."

"Would you like to remain here?"

"Only if you think it would be useful."

"Fine," the lawyer said. "You will remain. While you are here your every request is to be immediately satisfied. Is that understood?" He never moved his head when he said it, never looked at the two men on his left. They both nodded affirmatively.

"Will we talk again, sir?"

"Yes," Stephen Karshan said.

18

Anna had a car waiting for them outside the Carlyle. It was a long, black affair that sat at curbside with a uniformed driver huddled inside. The driver jumped out and opened the door for the two of them, then got in and pushed a button. A glass panel slid down.

O'Malley was reasonably certain that this was now his second ride in the back of a limousine, and he decided it was, like all things in Anna's life, something he could get used to right away. There was at least four feet of space between the rear seat and the driver's area. That space was filled with toys: an inlaid television set, an elaborate stereo system, a wet bar. O'Malley made himself a quick Jack Daniels and stretched his legs.

"Park Lane, please," he told the driver through an intercom. "But first drive around the park for a while."

Anna smiled at the suggestion. She sat back and crossed her long legs, holding up a white cigarette. He lit it and watched her suck the smoke. She looked like an ad in a magazine.

O'Malley had questioned Anna extensively about her father's death. It was an event that explained a great deal about Anna, a gruesome murder carried out while she was in the house. She was nineteen years old at the time and had been awakened in the night by the sound of squealing tires in the driveway. She had run to her father's room in terror. She opened his door, turned on the bedroom light, and found the man who meant everything to her face down with an ice pick embedded in his brain.

When her tears came at the memory, O'Malley had comforted her. The story did much more than stir him; if she had wanted a champion she had one now. He wouldn't let them touch her. When her crying slowed, she had looked up at him with a stained face. Her voice was strong.

"It's wonderful to have you here with me at a time like this."

"I'm glad."

She had smiled at that. "Are you, Mr. O'Malley? Benjamin? Would you like to be strong for me? To protect me?"

Very much so. "Yes," he had answered.

This time she hadn't smiled. He had leaned forward, only a hair it seemed in retrospect, and her face was there to be kissed. It was hot and wet from her tears. He had held her loosely, letting his fingers trail along the pale skin of her shoulders and back. His fingers touched the zipper of her gown. He didn't pursue the moment.

She had broken the kiss. Her eyes were glazed. "Don't hesitate, Benjamin," she said huskily. She had turned and held her yellow hair high. "What shall I say? Help yourself?"

He had laughed at that and walked behind her. He kissed her white neck and soft shoulders. He could never remember wanting to do anything as much as he wanted to slide that zipper down its track. The dress would unfold like a flower and Anna's pale white skin would be revealed. He would turn her to him, pushing her hands away from her bare breasts, running his hands insolently over her skin. Then he would take her to bed. They'd stay in bed for a week.

He didn't touch the zipper.

After a moment she had let her hair drop. "Is this a rejection?"

That it was not. "No," he told her. "Just a bit of confusion right now."

She understood confusion. "Maybe I've got an idea that will take care of your doubts. I'm scheduled to go to a party this evening. Take me. Think about me. Then at the end of the evening, if things seem clearer, you can take me back here as well."

"All right."

After a time, O'Malley leaned forward and tapped twice. The driver nodded, then headed south toward the Park Lane. At the hotel entrance, a doorman in a red uniform opened the door for them. Anna hesitated. "You go ahead, I'll wait in the car."

O'Malley shook his head. "Don't be silly. I promise you'll be safe."

Anna began, "That's not . . .," then stopped. She permitted the doorman to help her from the car.

On the nightstand next to the bed were six messages from the night staff, each claiming special knowledge of the "tragedy." Anna had draped her shawl over an armchair. She walked over to the window and looked out. Ahead of her was fifty blocks of park. "I love New York at night," she said. "More than any other city I've ever been in, I feel comfortable here. There is a rhythm to the night of this city that appeals to me on an elemental level. It's very . . . very savage."

There was no doubt about that. "If you listen hard, you can hear the screams of the savages' victims," O'Malley told her as he read the messages. "But why don't you go ahead and relax. I'll just be a minute."

While he was in the shower, Anna called room service and had a magnum of French champagne delivered in a gleaming silver ice bucket. More of the good life, he supposed. She brought him in an ice cold glass of the bubbly liquid while he shaved, then leaned against the door and watched him. "Do you mind?" she asked. "Hell, no," he answered quickly. But nevertheless, for whatever reason, he tightened the towel around his waist. Later, he came out in his pinstripe and they toasted the city together. Anna looked sad and altogether beautiful. Her dress was sleek and fetching, her hair long and full, her face mysterious and captivating. But the eyes were expressionless and the smiles only half smiles. In many ways, she seemed to be going through the motions of living.

As they sipped quietly, she remarked on the obvious. "You know, I'm aware this is the hotel where John died." She looked up. "Do you know which room it was?"

"Right next door."

Anna nodded and looked out at miles of light framing the black park. She sipped for a moment and then suddenly, inexplicably, dropped her head and began to sob.

O'Malley let her cry, cynically hoping a revelation would follow her tears. There was none. He heard only a widow's wails. He thought of leaving, but as he turned to go, she reached for him and held his arm tightly. She said in a cracked voice, "It's the unspeakable horror of it. Just the thought of his death and how terrible it must have been for him. I feel the loss more than ever before. I'm really all alone now." She said it so softly O'Malley had to strain to hear the words.

"Not alone," O'Malley told her firmly.

They walked arm in arm down a set of marble steps into the ballroom of the Sherry-Netherlands. At the bottom of the stairs a hundred and fifty extraordinarily well-dressed and attractive young men and women mingled. Half the men were in black tie. The women wore elaborate gowns. A nine-piece orchestra played over the din. Mauve-coated attendants passed silently among the celebrants offering food and drink from silver trays.

Anna knew everyone. He was introduced to old school chums, old sorority sisters, old roommates. Each of the old pals had a husband or escort who also had a name. After ten minutes of polite concentration, O'Malley's eyes began glazing over.

The affair was a birthday party. During one introduction, O'Malley heard a reference to "Armstead's thirty-fourth." At another, someone couldn't believe "old Binky" had reached his mid-thirties. The giveaway was a huge cake in the middle of the floor where a freckled man held court. He was often slapped heartily on the back by passersby. Binky, himself, O'Malley concluded.

O'Malley didn't want to offend anyone, but the plain fact was he hadn't seen this many stiffs in one room since his J & D days. Yet there were compensations. He found the bar and elbowed his way toward it.

"Hello again," a voice said.

O'Malley turned and squinted through the smoke at a dark-haired woman smiling at him. She had a familiar young face and a small, round body. She carried herself in a challenging, lighthearted way. She looked the same as she had last time, like a young woman who took nothing too seriously, who always wanted to play. And had always been allowed to.

"I remember you, Harriet." He extended a hand. "Nice to see you again. I'm here with . . ."

"You're here with Anna, of course," she said. "I know that. As a matter of fact, everyone knows that." Her voice was teasing but not unkind.

Harriet moved over near O'Malley's Jack Daniels. "May I?" she asked. She said it mischievously, the way an indulged six-year-old asks for a sip of beer at his parents' party. O'Malley said nothing. Harriet took a sip, crinkling her nose at the whiskey. "A few of these and I'd forget all the good advice Anna's been given over the years."

Whatever that meant. O'Malley said, "I have the feeling you came over here for a reason. And not just to taste my drink."

Harriet put down his drink and her face darkened. "My, aren't we stern. I love stern men. Of course, if they get too stern, then I go away. And if I go away, it's a big loss for them."

O'Malley didn't want her to do that just yet. He took the tips of her fingers in his hand as the band began playing again. "Let's talk out there," he suggested.

Harriet was the sort of dancer a man could spend a long time on the floor with. As he held her, his touch necessarily fell on her bare shoulders. She seemed to enjoy that and relaxed easily in his arms.

"You're a lovely dancer," he told her.

She liked that. "You'll make me blush," she said. "By the way, you don't think I'm being too forward, do you?"

"Not yet. I'll tell you when."

She smiled and moved closer to him. "I'm teasing you because you came with Anna. For as long as I can remember, I've always wanted anything Anna had. In college, it was usually a stereo or a dress." Her voice dropped a bit, and she looked up at him. "But sometimes it was a man."

O'Malley didn't think she was alone. Notwithstanding the opulence around them, every glance in the room seemed covetous. Money, like a drug, had bought everyone a burning desire for more.

He looked more closely at Harriet. She was about Anna's age, about twenty-eight, but looked much younger. She wore a girlish pout that seemed born of long indulgence. Her black hair was full and curly, wildly kept. She had a tomboy's mien but definitely not a tomboy's body. The lips that formed her pout were full and rich. Her arms and shoulders were tan and bare, her dress light colored, her jewelry eclectic and multicolored. Harriet conveyed an impression of lightness, of youth, of willingness bordering on excitement.

They danced through one number and into another. O'Malley had long lost sight of Anna. The last he had noticed, she was off in a far corner of the room, still the center of a crowd. He decided to get back to business.

"How long have you known Anna?"

Harriet had been sleepily resting against his arm. The question was slightly abrupt and seemed to jolt her. "Where did that come from?" When he didn't answer, she shrugged slightly and nestled back into his arms. "Years and years. Past new years and into old years. All the way back. We've known each other for years and years."

"So you must know all about her father."

"Sure, I knew her father," she said. "A little self-satisfied but a nice man. He and Anna were very close."

"What was he like?"

She thought for a moment. "Well, I hate to say it but the first thing that always struck you about Mr. Kendall was his money. Maybe because it was the first thing he told you about. Everybody in this room has money, of course, but we're really paupers compared to Anna. Anna's father had the kind of money that comes from owning industries and factories and all that. I'm talking serious money."

The band ended the song and they walked back toward the bar. "Anyway," Harriet went on when they got there, "I knew Anna's father because I knew Anna. I guess over the years I've known her as well as anyone."

"What was Anna like as a kid?"

"As a kid? Well, the best way to describe her is a bit of a zombie. She had no real friends except for me. She was sort of antisocial, if you know what I mean."

"No, tell me what you mean."

"Let's just say she was different than me," Harriet said.

"I liked parties and as you might guess, I loved boys. With Anna, it was always work hard at school, get good grades, and go home to Daddy. Always Daddy."

"Did she ever break out of that?" O'Malley asked.

"I heard a few years ago that she broke out of it in a big way," Harriet said. "So much so that they had to put her in a home for a while."

"You're talking about just before her marriage to John Bradley?"

"Yes, that's right. She had been living with John after her father died. Anna must have thought that was a very rebellious gesture. After she went crazy and started screwing anything that would buy her a drink, they had this big legal thing out in California. As punishment for being a bad girl, they made her marry John."

O'Malley looked across the room and saw Anna leaning against a column with a glass of champagne in her hand. A fellow in a tux leaned against the same post looking as if he'd just stepped out of a Scotch ad. O'Malley caught her eye and made a small gesture. She shook her head with a smile and threw him a kiss, telling him she was fine. Harriet saw the gesture. "Asking permission?"

"Yes, I'm a traditionalist."

"I hear they've got pills for that now," Harriet told him.

They got some drinks and went into a corner. O'Malley began again without pleasantries. "Why do you think she went crazy? That time a few years ago, I mean?"

Harriet shrugged. "My guess is it's something she's wanted to do her whole life. When her father was . . . died, it sort of set her off."

"You almost said 'murdered.'"

"You're right. I almost said it. And he was murdered."

"How?"

"On the island. With an icepick."

"And Anna found him?"

"That's right. If she wasn't crazy before, she was then."

"Did they ever find who did it?"

Harriet shook her head. "No. The best they ever did was track down the car. It was stolen and left by a pier. There're hundreds of private boats on and off the island every day so there was no way to follow through."

"Poor kid." It was no wonder she blew apart. "Any relapses?" he asked. "After the time in California, I mean."

Harriet gestured across the room. "Look at her. She's as self-possessed as anyone you're likely to meet." Then she reached up and patted his cheek. "But I think your lady wants your attention again." O'Malley looked up to see Anna striding purposefully across the room. Her eyes were clouded. Harriet was laughing. She thrust a card into O'Malley's hand. "Here's my address out on Long Island. It's a lovely place right on the water. You want to invite yourself out, I'll be there for a week beginning tonight. Just me and the help." Then she gave a toss of her curls and was gone.

Anna came up looking slightly flushed. "Was that Harriet Resnick I saw you talking with?" Her voice was concerned.

"That's what the lady said."

"And the two of you talked about me, I suppose?"

"I did, or at least I wanted to," O'Malley said. "She seemed to want to discuss other things."

Anna seemed to relax at that. "You mean she wanted you to go to bed with her." She shook her head in disapproval. "That's very typical. I must tell you, Benjamin, if you decide to take Harriet up on her offer you certainly won't be the first man to share her bed." She said it in a high, catty way.

"I seldom am," O'Malley answered simply.

Anna dropped her head with a slightly chastened look. "I'm sorry," she said. "I know I shouldn't talk like that. Harriet and I were once very close but have since drifted apart. I have . . . have concerns of what she might say about me."

"She was quite complimentary," O'Malley lied. "But

let's not talk about unpleasantness. Are you having a good time at your party?"

Anna shrugged and waved an arm toward the room. "It's the same old people, the same people I've known for years and years. We grow older together, and that's a shared experience. There must be others." She smiled a bit and even managed to laugh at herself for once. "For example, we're all rich." Then her eyes darkened. "To be frank, though, when I come to these things, it seems I've done it all a hundred times before." She smiled again. "Which I have, of course."

"That happens to everybody," O'Malley told her. "You people just have more reunions than most."

She said, "Yes, we chase fond memories of days that at the time were as boring as today." She looked up. "Let me say goodbye to some people and let's get out of here. Is that O.K.?"

"Sure." He watched her go off. She moved with grace, a bearing common to the people in the room, yet her manner made clear she was extraordinary even in this company. She cut a swath without effort. When she paused for a moment, the others drew close to her as bits of lint around a charged rod. First, just a few; then, more and more.

O'Malley compared this with what Harriet had told him about Anna. Here was a woman who had grown up friendless, and who now attracted crowds. She had even managed to convince herself that in a dim past these people had been close to her, that they had shared important experiences. It was all a lie.

19

Baird accepted with considerable reluctance the ivory dice that flew at him off the stick of the pit boss. The crowd behind him began bouncing off each other to see where he placed his chips. "The Come Line?" the pit boss suggested solicitously. Baird shrugged. A couple of fifty-dollar chips landed on the table; he had no idea where they came from any more. Brenda huddled next to him excitedly. The crowd almost killed each other betting on his point. "Hard six," the pit boss intoned. Baird flung the hunks of bone at the far green barrier. The roar of the crowd cut off the pit man's call. Brenda threw herself into his arms. Baird yawned.

Las Vegas on someone else's money takes all the fun out of things, Baird observed. Vegas without risk is a desert and bad architecture, nothing more. Yet the solicitations of Newsome's functionaries ensured that risk was no part of his Nevada experience. Every time he walked to a gambling table a man in a black tuxedo would come up, welcome him to the room, escort him to the twenty-dollar tables, throw out one of the bums taking up a seat, and place a stack of chips "on the house" in front of him. The first time Baird lost all the house's money and actually felt bad about it. The man came over and made a small gesture with his head to the dealer. That was the last time Baird had lost at anything.

Brenda was as excited as Baird was bored. As night fell she dressed up in her finest and made Baird put on a tie. They went downstairs to the front of the hotel where a man in a red coat snapped his fingers three times. A black car

134

with an Italian driver pulled up for them. They sat in the back, sipped champagne, and were driven to a lovely restaurant. The maitres d' treated them as visiting royalty. No payment was permitted, and at the end of the meal the long black car was there to take them back.

Twenty-four hours after the first interview, Baird got the word the great man wanted to see him again. It was almost midnight when he arrived at the casino's top floor. Newsome sat as before, but this time flanked only by Stephen Karshan. This time there were no vignettes about Las Vegas or inquiries about his health. Newsome's eyes were as hard as his voice.

"Mr. Baird, we've examined in great detail the matters you raised at our last meeting. With your permission, we would like to discuss additional items with you today."

Baird felt himself tense. "All right."

Newsome turned to Karshan, who shook his head to say he had nothing to add. When Newsome turned back, the gesture told Baird this meeting would involve only the two of them. Karshan would watch and make his decision. "Describe your understanding of the relationship between Mr. Jacoby and David Perino," Newsome ordered.

Baird cleared his throat. "It's simple. Your company paid twenty times in cash to Jacoby's company what you could have paid to Roth's clients over time. Bradley and Perino were involved."

"Why would anyone acting on my behalf pay such inflated prices?"

"The first and most obvious answer is to steal from you," Baird answered simply.

Newsome didn't even flinch. It was obviously not a new notion to him. "Assuming you are right, then we must assume Mr. Perino is entitled to a share of Simon Jacoby's profit."

"Of course."

"How did he get paid?"

Baird raised his shoulders and dropped them. "There

135

are a thousand possibilities. The most obvious are phony business deals between Perino and Jacoby, deals designed to funnel money back to Perino." Baird had thought about this question and began talking excitedly. "A man like Perino wouldn't take cash in a large paper sack or even get involved in fancy Swiss bank accounts. He's too old for that. Perino has to have some legitimate way to get his money into the United States fast. My guess is he and Jacoby have what I call compensating business transactions."

"What exactly does that mean?" Newsome asked.

"Here's an example," Baird told him. "Jacoby is a broker, not only of film rights but also anything else that can be bought and sold on European exchanges. Let's say Perino sends a telex to Jacoby telling Jacoby to invest a few million D-marks against Perino's margin account. Jacoby complies by taking the millions they stole from you and invests that money instead. But it's invested in a very strange way. For every 'buy' transaction, there's a 'sell' transaction. In other words, every transaction is a wash."

"So far it doesn't sound like a real good deal," Newsome observed.

"So far it isn't. But here comes the good part. Fifty percent of the transactions will be successful and fifty percent unsuccessful. When Jacoby reports the results back to Perino, however, you will be amazed at how many of Perino's transactions were successful."

Newsome was quiet for a moment, then said, "You mean Jacoby just says all of the good ones were Perino's and all the bad ones were his?"

"That's right. Perino gets millions transmitted to the United States in superficially legitimate transactions. He reports it to the IRS and pays his taxes like a good citizen. If he's a pig, he waits long enough to get capital gains treatment."

After a moment Newsome asked quietly, "Is this what you think happened, Mr. Baird?"

Thus far they had only been talking about Perino. This was a different question. "No."

"What do you believe happened?"

Here was the Rubicon. The slow voice and carefully modulated tones masked the fact that these people were very dangerous men. There ought to be some gain to be made from rash gestures. Baird found himself licking his lips nervously.

"Yes, Mr. Baird," Newsome prodded.

"I can't believe Perino and Jacoby acted alone," Baird said quickly.

There was a long silence in the room. Baird could hear the ticking of a large clock he didn't even know was there. It seemed to click for two or three minutes before Newsome spoke again. In that interim, the atmosphere in the room was surreal. Newsome had kept his eyes fixed on Baird without a quiver or a blink. The half smile was as rigid as if penned by an artist. When Newsome spoke again, the question was so soft it was hard for Baird to hear it.

"Who do you think acted with Mr. Perino in addition to his European partner?"

Baird swallowed hard. "You, Mr. Newsome," he said evenly.

Newsome's neck darkened. Stephen Karshan cupped his head in his hand and leaned forward.

"You are an insolent pup," Newsome barked. "This is my company. Why would I steal from my own company?"

"Mr. Newsome, it's well known you have a silent partner in New York named James Silver. Mr. Silver is a front for the Cappicis. He supplies the money, you operate the companies. He is also a major international trader in everything from bullion to pork bellies."

"Mr. Baird, I don't know what you're talking about when you speak of 'fronts.' As for Mr. Silver, yes, he is my partner. So what?"

"So logically, the only thing that can possibly be going

137

on is you stealing from him. Which means you're stealing from the Cappicis. Unless they're in on it too, of course."

Newsome turned his head to Stephen Karshan. "Stephen," he began. Karshan raised his hand, then said to Baird, "You go ahead, Mr. Baird. You just tell us everything you think you know."

Baird rose from his chair and began walking around like a professor. "If the company makes a million dollars, on paper Mr. Newsome has earned five hundred thousand dollars. Question: How does he get it?"

The lawyer answered. "The company declares a dividend."

"If the company declares a million-dollar dividend, Silver, which means the Cappicis, gets half of that," Baird responded. "But before anybody gets anything, Uncle Sam gets his cut. At a fifty percent tax rate, that eats up five hundred thousand dollars, leaving only five hundred to distribute to the two shareholders."

"So Mr. Newsome gets two hundred fifty thousand dollars," Karshan said.

"No," Baird said. "A dividend is ordinary income to him. So give the government half of Mr. Newsome's payment. That leaves him with a hundred twenty-five." Baird spoke directly to Newsome. "Stated simply, if the company makes a million dollars in profit and you play it straight, you only get to keep one twenty-five, even though you and Silver control every paper clip in the company."

Newsome yawned. "What you're telling me is well known to me, Mr. Baird. That's why I spend a great deal of time in meetings with tax lawyers. How does that prove anything?"

"Let's take that same million dollars profit and do it a different way. Let's assume you buy some property for twenty times true value. The difference is one million dollars."

"All right."

"That million dollars never comes into the corporation's coffers and the company never pays a dime of tax. Matter of fact the company deducts it. Second, it's not a dividend so you don't share it with the Cappicis. Third, you don't pay tax on it either. So instead of keeping only a hundred and twenty-five out of your million in profit, you get to keep the whole million, plus a million in write-offs." Baird stopped for a moment, then added: "That's on one deal. My understanding is that you and Perino have lots of sweet deals going."

The room was silent then, Newsome looking straight ahead and Karshan looking at the floor in thought. Then Karshan spoke. "You'd be a foolish young man to come here and say these things if you believed them to be true. I can only assume you are trying either to learn something or warn us of something."

Baird was about to deny it but then stopped. Everyone he told the story to reached the same conclusion, even his clients off the Sunset Boulevard pavement. And when Baird put the numbers together, it didn't make sense any other way. Nevertheless, there was something in the man's demeanor and in the open symmetry of the scam that set Baird's antennae twitching.

Baird said, "I'm actually much more reckless than you imagine, Mr. Karshan. I came here to accuse Mr. Newsome, to gauge his reaction, to find out what I could about John Bradley's death. I don't know whether you people are involved in Bradley's death or not. You must admit, however, it is not uncommon in your circles for enemies to expire before their time."

Karshan laughed heartily. "My goodness, Mr. Baird, you've been reading too many comics. I am the representative of very complicated businesses. It is our policy to surround ourselves with executives of prudence, vision, and integrity. None of these men would remain in our employ for one instant if they suspected we solved our problems with violence."

"That sounds very pretty. What about Dominic Cappici?"

"That was 1939, Mr. Baird. The world was different."

Newsome interrupted. His voice was strained. He seemed like a man trying desperately to make a very important point. "I have one question, Mr. Baird. If my involvement is so plainly obvious to you, it must be plainly obvious to others as well, right?"

"Anyone with a pencil and paper."

"Quite so. And someone might even wrongfully suggest they were acting on my behalf. Right?" He said it as though he were pleading with Baird.

The question surprised Baird. Perino was Newsome's most intimate counselor. Anything Perino said was presumed to come from the boss. John Bradley, with the ambition of three men and only the faintest hint of a moral code, would leap at the chance to play at the highest levels. Perino might never even have had to pay a dime. All he had to do was suggest the orders came straight from Newsome. John would understand.

And maybe at some point even a moron like Bradley could figure out the truth. Or get cold feet. Or threaten to check the whole thing out with the people in Las Vegas. When that happened the incentive for Perino to remove him would be all but irresistible.

Baird shook his head and looked at the floor, then looked up again to meet Newsome's questioning gaze. Karshan was listening intently. "I understand what you're saying. It's not something I'd considered before."

"Who at the studio was responsible for bringing financial irregularities to my attention?" Newsome asked with renewed confidence.

"Bradley, obviously."

"And who, therefore, might wish to see Mr. Bradley pass from among the ranks of the living?"

"Anybody engaging in financial irregularities you were not aware of."

"So you've got it down to a few choices. Maybe I'm a crook, maybe Perino is a crook, maybe both of us are crooks, maybe neither of us is a crook. How are you going to figure out which is right?"

Baird felt the fog close in. His voice was weak. "I don't know."

Stephen Karshan sighed in exasperation and rose, signaling the end of the interview. "You have our cards, Mr. Baird. Call us when you do know."

20

The black limousine rolled easily through the early morning New York streets. Anna sat back with a satisfied sigh. O'Malley worked the gold lighter for her and tried to study her face. The shadows came and went as the car slipped through the lights of the city.

Who killed Cock Robin? Fancy parties and fancy ladies made it all so easy to forget work. Musings about other murders, about estates and guardianships, about tax scams at movie studios, about round, small bodies and sassy manners, all made it even easier to forget that the only thing he had ever been hired to do was find out who tied a cord around John Bradley's neck and hung him from an extraordinarily sturdy shower rod at the Park Lane Hotel. Why was it so easy to forget poor John Bradley?

Anna broke the silence between them.

"May I ask you a question?"

"Of course."

"You know how I feel about you," she said earnestly. "I know you do. I can also tell you're going to make this difficult for me." When he didn't answer, she said, "Benjamin, I don't make offers of myself lightly and I don't make them very often. What would you like? Would you like me to be explicit? Would that excite you? I'm happy to do that for you if it would."

O'Malley nodded. "Let's drive around for a little first," he said.

Anna moved closer to him. "Of course. We can go anywhere in the city you like. Where would you like to go?"

Like any kid growing up on the wrong side of the Hudson, O'Malley was an expert on untouchable New York nightspots. Now they were all his for the asking. Free of charge. Nothing to do but say the word and the man in front would take him anywhere he wanted. Then a frivolous thought hit him. "Jersey. Let's go to Jersey!"

Anna looked at him strangely. "You mean like *New Jersey*?"

"Sure. It's this big state just on the other side of the river. You know, Larry Doby, Danny O'Connell."

"I know what New Jersey is. My question is," she said reasonably, "why would we want to go there?"

"Because I know the most romantic unknown spot in the world right across the water," he promised.

"Are you going to make me walk out on some wharf?"

"No, I promise. This is foolproof. You'll love it."

Anna wasn't sure at all. She gestured to the driver hesitantly. "Tell him where to go."

The limo swept north. Soon it left the park behind and headed for the massive string of lights connecting New York and New Jersey. The driver took the upper deck for the view. Once on the other side, he paid the toll and looked back quizzically. O'Malley gave him careful directions. The driver passed through Fort Lee and signs appeared for Palisades Park.

"Oh goody. You're taking me on the roller coaster."

"You're losing trust again," O'Malley told her. "I can tell."

They drove until signs appeared for the town of Englewood Cliffs. He squinted against the frosted glass, trying to make out the streets. Times change; at seventeen he could have found the road blindfolded. When he saw something that looked promising, he told the driver to turn. It was a lucky guess. The road immediately got dark and windy. Anna huddled closer. The driver flipped on the high beams and began manuevering slowly. There was room for only one car on a road that soon dove precariously downward. For a moment O'Malley thought he had it wrong after all. Then, as if on cue, the road banked and turned and opened onto a wide, empty expanse of black asphalt. Overhead, thunderously brilliant, the George Washington Bridge shone like a fiery monument. Underneath, waves crashed against rocks and steel supports. Across the black water, the lights of New York blinked at them.

Anna was awestruck. Even the previously sanguine driver was impressed; his neck craned upward as he twisted to view the full expanse of the bridge. They were virtually directly underneath it. All three were rendered speechless by the noise and steel and concrete and luminance of it all.

"I've never seen anything like this," Anna shouted over the din. "It's frightening. It's so much bigger than anyone would expect."

"I know," O'Malley hollered back.

"What do people do down here?"

"It's primarily a parking lot for the bridge workers," O'Malley explained. He pointed toward the bridge. "There's a path along the water that runs under the bridge and out the other side. On weekends the kids go back there to neck. On Saturday night this place looks like Yankee Stadium during the Boston series."

Anna was quiet for a minute, then touched his arm. "Take me down there," she said. "Take me down there just like you used to take the girls when you were a kid." There was more than a small amount of intensity in her voice. "I didn't get taken down many secret roads by young men."

"O.K.," O'Malley said simply.

She gestured to the driver, and the man nodded, turned off the car and relaxed against the seat with his cap pulled down over his eyes. O'Malley got out and offered her an arm. They strolled down the walkway toward the bridge.

The night was clear and cool. The light from the New York skyscrapers came across the dark water without distortion. As they reached a point directly under the bridge, Anna stopped and looked across the water happily. Speech was impossible. When she was done looking, she gestured for him to put his arm around her.

"It's beautiful here," she hollered. The wind blew her hair in wild, crazy curves, and she laughed at that. O'Malley laughed with her.

"How many girls did you take here?" she asked. Her face had a teasing, happy look.

"Only the loose ones. Couple hundred maybe," O'Malley shouted back.

She slid more deeply into his arms. "I wish I were one of the loose ones," she said. "Where did you take them?"

O'Malley thought she was kidding until he saw her face. He pointed down the path. Anna craned her neck to see. The path meandered down toward the water's edge and then hooked back. As it came back, the retaining wall ended and was replaced by a barrier of shoreline boulders. The path slipped behind them and led to a wide open area covered with soft green grass. The boulders gave some protection from the noise of the traffic. On a hot summer weekend you had to take a number to get a spot.

He took her hand, and they walked under the bridge and out the other side. When she saw the expanse of green, she laughed with delight. "O'Malley, you filthy old man."

"It was actually a lot harder than you think," he told her. "That was before liberation."

O'Malley led her to a small plateau at the top of the grassy area with an unobstructed view of New York City. It was called the "High Ground" and for the most part was hidden from the path below. On a Saturday night people would kill to get on the High Ground. Now it was empty. They sat in the soft grass and looked back across the water.

Now, they could speak without shouting. Anna said: "Do you have any idea how many Saturday nights I sat at home hoping some boy would take me to a place like this?"

"You should have come around to Bayonne," O'Malley told her. "You would have had no problem."

She laughed. "That was my problem. I was never allowed to date the bad boys, only the ones from good families and fine schools."

"We didn't see too many of those on the High Ground," O'Malley admitted. "Not too many good girls either." It was the bad ones he remembered, the ones who loved to come to the "cliffs." The memories passed over him in waves.

He knew it was just a matter of time before she asked to be kissed. When it happened, her head turned to him and her eyes asked the question. Then she leaned back and pulled him to her, the expensive black cocktail dress hiking up her slim legs to her waist. He followed her down, feeling her warm skin, reaching with now resolute fingers for the elastic under her dress. His questions were fast evaporating. He was about to tell her that but never got the chance. Later on he thought he remembered hearing a soft footfall, a brief hush of a sound that wouldn't have told him anything anyway. A sixth sense caused him to flinch just before the softball-sized rock came down on the back of his head. His nose blasted a divot out of the High Ground and he began the sleep that would continue until noon the following day.

21

O'Malley woke slowly, unsure whether the pain in his head was caused by the lump of rock or the bright sun beating into his eyes. He blinked repeatedly, trying to focus. The bridge shimmered. Across the now bright blue water, the city was enshrouded in a bit of midday fog. He lowered his eyes and was blinded anew by the glare of the sun bouncing off the Hudson.

He tried to turn. The remnants of twelve hours of unconsciousness were as true a barrier as shackles and chains. Movement brought on waves of nausea. He rolled on his back, breathing deeply to cut off the sickness. As he turned, the left side of his face washed against the still wet blood escaping from the gash in the back of his head. He recoiled, twisting in repugnance. He crawled to his knees with his head buried in the low grass.

For a long time he knelt silently, breathing heavily. The sun was high and hot. The rocks on the face of the cliff looked white. The grass in front of him was dry, stripped of dew by the high sun and smelling of dank meadow. He fought unsuccessfully against the rushes of nausea. After many minutes, he was able to stand shakily. He looked across the blue water to the shimmering city. That was when he noticed the body bouncing against the rocks below him.

It was a moment of horror he would never forget. The body was twenty feet below, slapping as a bunch of rags against the shiny rocks. He shouted "Anna" once without thinking. Then he spun like a fool, looking for an adversary, the adrenaline momentarily quieting his pain. He wanted to

146

fight like an animal. But all he did was spin aimlessly, searching the High Ground for a killer who had long since gone.

O'Malley ran straight down from the bank into the cold water, fighting against the shock. He scrambled onto the rocks, the slime causing him to slip and fall, cursing. The rocks gripped the body below the shoulders; the arms flapped like broken wings in time with the motion of the waves. O'Malley pulled the head up by the hair and looked full into the face.

He had seen death before, but never a corpse that had been lying in the water for twelve hours. The face was a dull blue. The eyes were staring; the neck was distended. The mouth was open wide as though fully appreciating the horror of it all. Nevertheless, in spite of the unspeakable sight, he was relieved. The face looking back at him was a man's.

He felt with his fingers along the neck and head. The nose and cheekbones were shattered; the neck twisted. It was as if a single, tremendous blow had done all the damage that would ever be necessary. After that someone, for no reason at all, tossed the man, dead or not, into the green waves.

O'Malley yanked at the material of the coat, and it ripped in his hands. He was past caring about preserving any evidence for the cops. He pulled again, and the man's shoulders broke freely from the rock pincers. O'Malley fell backwards with a splash. The man, floating, began drifting seaward.

O'Malley slashed through the wet and grabbed an ankle, dragging the man back toward the shore. When he yanked the man onto the grass, the pressure on the bloated stomach caused dark, red liquid to rush out of the nose and mouth. O'Malley knelt beside the man and watched, letting the sensations seep through him. He wanted to be as outraged as the situation demanded. Only when the water slowed did he turn the man on his back and begin going through the pockets.

There was a wallet in the inside breast pocket. O'Malley

went through it and found forty-seven dollars in cash, a faded chauffeur's license, an expired MasterCard and a folio of pictures. The license declared the dead man to be one James L. Moran, Jr., born June 23, 1946, standing 5'10", and weighing 160 pounds. He once had blue eyes, said the license. Stapled on the back of the license was a business card for Metropolitan Area Chauffeurs with an office address that was the same as James L. Moran's home address. Stapled in back of that card was the registration for the limo, showing it to be the property of Metropolitan. A one-man operation. The kind that wouldn't spend a lot of time keeping records.

O'Malley forced himself to look at the folio of pictures. There was a faded shot of James Moran in an army uniform with an older man and woman smiling on each side of him. Another showed him in a tuxedo looking skinny and pimpled next to a formally clad girl. She had a pretty and open face. The next had the pretty girl in a wedding dress; after that the girl and their kid. O'Malley studied the photo for a long time. He had once known lots of guys who married the girl they took to the prom.

In O'Malley's mind there were certain crimes that could not be forgiven, only avenged. He put the man's wallet back in the soggy jacket. He quickly went through the pockets, but found nothing of interest: a water-logged pack of cigarettes, some coins, a cleaning ticket, a parking stub. O'Malley got up and dragged James Moran farther back on the grass to a spot where there was no possibility the river might reclaim him. He left the corpse in as dignified a position as he could. Then he cursed once more and began his search for Anna by the walk up the long hill back to the city.

22

The man leaning over the green felt table was young. The shaded lamp above his head cast a wide, glaring light that bounced off the slate bed, leaving his face in harsh shadows. Even so, it was clear the man had led a hard life. There was a quivering around the lips and a tiredness in the eyes. The man was also afraid.

Above the table, stretching the length of the room, was a metal string intersected by brown wooden beads. A brass divider separated the counters. The frightened man glanced hurriedly at his side of the brass divider, as if to reassure himself that yes, he did have a lead and yes, if but three more of the colored balls slipped down the felt pockets the money would be his. And the glory. And the opportunity to relax.

He picked up the chalk for the third time and ground it with a fury into the end of the cue. Then, as if seized by purpose, he crouched over the table, eyeing the purple ball sitting in the middle of the green sea. It wouldn't be easy; the cue ball was against the rail. He'd have to squeeze his fingers into a cramped bridge. It didn't feel right, not at all, and he licked the salt off his lip. "Four in the side," he murmured.

"Nice shot," a voice answered pleasantly.

The encouragement did nothing to help. He could feel himself seizing up. Shoot and get it over with, his mind told him. He stroked easily and surely; it was, after all, a shot he had made a hundred times before. A thousand. Just do it the same way. He let the stick fly and knew right away it was wrong. The carefully placed high right English was too much. It twisted the 4 too much to the left. The ball rolled surely toward the pocket, then turned, caught the point, and came back to the table. It sat like some repugnant thing a millimeter from the gaping hole of the pocket.

"Point Pleasant," a voice behind him said. "Used to spend summers there. Great town." A large man came out of the shadows and into the light. He had a sloping face, almost Indian, and wide shoulders. His frame was draped in wonderful clothes: a neat Italian knit shirt; matching pants; highly polished dark shoes. His hair was perfectly in place and the soft young face shaved smooth. James "Hoot" De-Marco had always been an extraordinarily handsome man.

"Hoot," the frightened man began. He still hadn't left the table.

"You got to go now, Sammy," Hoot told him gently.

The man finally stepped away, reaching up with his stick to slide eighteen of the wooden markers across the wire track. Three more and he would have been out. He looked over at his enemy's side of the brass divider. Hope springs eternal, and all that, but . . .

Hoot DeMarco had the sweetest stroke that ever passed over a table; maybe too sweet, too dramatic, the form being as important to Hoot as the result. He had nurtured it over the years so that it fit the man he was, matching his personality the way his trousers matched his shirts. It was a slow, even, sleepy stroke with no wasted motion. Balls seemed eager to leap into the pocket, and the white cue ball, once having done its job, returned to the middle of the table like a well-trained bird dog. The frightened man watched as the table emptied. Soon there was just one lonely striped 11-ball sitting patiently an inch and a half from where the new rack would go. The white ball sat in its usual place in the middle of the table.

"You got to make this one, Hoot," the man said nervously as he racked up the balls.

Hoot smiled as he chalked the end of the stick. When the man took the wooden rack off the table, Hoot answered him: "That I do, Sammy, that I do." Then he bent his six-foot-five frame over the table and with barely a glance sent the cue ball hurtling forward. The 11 raced into the left-hand corner pocket and the rack exploded as though hit with cannon fire. The cue came back to the middle of the table.

The frightened man was finished. He threw his stick into the middle of the balls. "That's it, Hoot, I can't stand to watch anymore. Next time you got to give me more."

Hoot shrugged. "You had me, Sammy. You had me dead." Then he walked over to the bartender to collect his money.

From the side O'Malley chuckled.

Hoot turned at the sound. He focused through the dimness, then his face broke into a wide grin. "Well Lord, look at this. Mama, get the tickets to Bermuda, our ship just came in." He walked over and draped a long arm around O'Malley's shoulder. "Times been tough since you left me, son."

O'Malley shook his hand. "I almost gagged when you told Sammy how close he came. That's what you used to tell me."

"Aw, but that was different," Hoot said. "I could never give a shooter like you any balls. It was straight up and winner walk away with it."

That was true. Except Hoot always walked away with it. Nevertheless, like Sisyphus, O'Malley would charge up the hill of each new game with a purpose he could never remember bringing to anything else in his life, racing ahead of Hoot, getting within sight of the top, almost pushing it over. Then he would watch those long graceful arms snap a few racks into the pocket until it was all over. O'Malley would stand where the frightened man had stood and watch his rock slide back down the hill. But he was always close. He said that, now. "I was always close, wasn't I, Hoot?"

"Every single time, Benjamin," Hoot agreed.

They sat at the bar drinking juice together because Hoot was working. Hoot turned to him with a questioning look.

"You look a little pale, Benjamin."

"I know." He turned slightly and showed Hoot the bandages on the back of his head. "I just got out of the emergency room. It's part of the business I've got to talk to you about."

"The business can wait, Benjamin. First, bring me up to date. It's been years, you know. What have you done?"

"Some very strange things, actually. For one thing I became a lawyer."

Hoot's face didn't change, but there was a slight embarrassed silence. O'Malley decided to reassure him. "Then I got indicted, thrown in jail, and almost disbarred."

Hoot's head nodded with genuine delight. "That's better, Benjamin, that's better." The words were, as always, slow and graceful, as if there really was an Indian in the genes someplace.

They sipped and reminisced for a time, interrupted only by the demands of Hoot's business. O'Malley didn't mind; he had, after all, caught him unexpectedly at the office. Although it had indeed been years, Hoot's business day hadn't changed. There were the same strange conferences with funny-looking men who came in with lots of slips of paper. Then there were truck drivers with quiet reports, reports that caused Hoot to leave O'Malley and walk to the end of the bar to discuss matters in peace. Hoot did a lot of different kinds of business in the next hour or so, and none of it involved a pool cue.

Around four in the afternoon things got quieter. Hoot turned to him. "You've been here a long time, Benjamin. Shall we talk about your business now?"

"Yes."

Hoot nodded. "You're in trouble? If it's local I can take care of it."

"It is local, but it's not me. A man was murdered last night and it involves something I'm working on."

"Where?"

O'Malley grinned. "On the High Ground, if you can believe that."

Hoot roared with laughter. "You're too old for that, Benjamin." He scratched his chin. "Anyway, that's not my land. Paterson, Newark, Passaic maybe. Not down there."

"I know. Maybe you can make a phone call for me."

"That I can do for you. Tell me what you need."

"Not a great deal. I want to know the status of the investigation, who the cops are looking to, whether they're dropping the whole thing. That sort of thing."

"And that's it?"

"Almost. I also want it passed around that a fellow by the name of David Perino was operating in this territory."

Hoot grew silent, playing with his glass for a moment. "Did he snuff this guy?"

"Yes."

Hoot nodded. "It is a name I know, Benjamin, although I've not had the pleasure and all that." His lips grew tight. "It is not the name of a man who should be found in this state unless his airplane happened to make a wrong turn. For myself"—he spread his hands—"I don't care." The hands came back together with a loud clap. "Others will care."

O'Malley nodded. "That's what I thought. One more thing. I'd like the word to get to the Cappicis that Perino was here, and he hit this man on the cliffs. It affects their business."

"That will be easy. On this one I am not doing you a favor, you have done one for me. There will be people who will be pleased I know this information."

"You need the name of the man on the coast? He's in Las Vegas last I heard."

Hoot clapped O'Malley on the back patronizingly. "Thank you, Benjamin, but that won't be necessary."

*   *   *

Six hours later and a continent away Baird eased his car into the parking lot of his office. The sun had now given up all pretense of shining on the city and Baird had to use the car's inside lights to make out his notes. As he read them over he mentally congratulated himself. All in all not a bad day's work.

He had spent the morning in the bowels of the clerk's office at the Los Angeles Superior Court, a dusty, drab morning among tattered files. Clerks openly resentful of the fact that they were clerks put in his way every bureaucratic roadblock years of experience had taught them; but ultimately, with patience, with threats sprinkled with tact, he got to see what he wanted. There it was, spread over an entire shelf: *In re Conservatorship of Kendall.*

He was surprised he could find it; from what O'Malley had told him he expected the transcripts to be sealed as tight as a drum. What neither of them figured on, however, was the notorious inefficiency of the Los Angeles Superior Court, the largest single court in the world, 140 judges strong, so constipated it takes five years to get from the filing of a complaint to the first day of trial. He made a mental note to drink a glass of champagne that evening as a toast to the good old clerk's office. On the first page of every one of these public transcripts, in large black letters, was stamped: SEALED—TO BE OPENED ONLY BY ORDER OF THE COURT.

He sat in a dark corner flipping pages rapidly, terrified that any moment someone would come out and notice the big red stamp. Baird passed by the preliminaries quickly and found the important testimony beginning on the third day. On that day the lawyer for the estate put on the first of a series of aimless and unemployed young men for the purpose of demonstrating Anna's mental illness. These men forthrightly described in detail for the judge their lack of worth. Then they described in equal detail what they had done with Anna.

The testimony was unsavory. A fellow named Bristol

154

testified he was a bartender at a place called the Brass Knuckle in Hollywood. He said Anna was a regular, a virtual nightly attraction. The night was rare when she didn't drink too much and cause a fight. She used to like to leave with the winner. But even that wouldn't have been too bad if it weren't for the drugs. At the beginning it was just Anna and a few of his less savory patrons, passing a few pills, sneaking into a corner of his bar to sniff a little coke from the face of her makeup mirror. Later on came the long heated arguments, the strange people arriving at all hours of the day asking to see Anna, the locked bathroom doors, the syringes found in the morning. At first she was great for business because she always had money to spend, but when things got too bad he kicked her out and told her to stay out. His was a fine family bar and he wanted to keep it that way.

Bristol was followed by a series of young men in their early twenties who claimed to have either slept with Anna, purchased drugs from Anna, or both. One Henderson, for example, said he made love to Anna at least once a week for a period of four months in the alley back of the Brass Knuckle. Henderson added bits of interesting detail, like the fact that they usually went back on Wednesdays because the trash was taken away on Tuesdays. Apparently full cans were too much even for Henderson's sensibilities. Further examination disclosed that Henderson's outdoor lovemaking was not the only thing he liked to do under the stars; indeed, sleeping was what he did best out there, the recession and his previous felony convictions making gainful employment somewhat difficult. Bristol testified Henderson had never had the wit to put two dollars for a drink together until Anna came along.

Throughout the first week the testimony was all pretty much more of the same. In the second week, however, things got more pointed. The estate called to the stand Anna's investment advisors, men whose three-piece professionalism came through loud and clear on the transcript pages. These witnesses spoke of the midnight phone calls from a woman on the other end of the line, a woman speaking garbled incoherent phrases, a woman demanding that brokers sell securities and remit the proceeds in cash for her account. This testimony was the icing on the cake. Anna's lawyer made a feeble effort at cross-examination, but the amiable and aging Mr. Glendon, selected for Anna by the estate, rarely did more than inspire the judge's patronizing remarks. Even a competent lawyer wouldn't have had much of a chance.

By the ninth day it was time for the key witness, Anna's executor and guardian, the man who for all practical purposes controlled her life. Baird read the words on the white pages. They didn't make sense; he read the words again. They still didn't make sense. He got up and ran out of the cramped room, ignoring the surprised looks of the clerks. In the hall a herd of lawyers and convicts milled around him as he dialed New York. O'Malley's phone rang and rang, but nothing happened. The convicts and lawyers stared at him as he ran cursing out of the building.

Now he was ready to try again. He leapt up the stairs to his office and dialed the Park Lane. From his window he could see the more ambitious of his clients punching in on the night shift. When the phone was finally picked up, the voice on the other end was tired.

"O'Malley, you've got to take better care of yourself."

"I'll keep that in mind. What's going on?" O'Malley's voice was abrupt.

"I've got to read you something. You don't have to do anything but sit and listen." Baird didn't wait for an answer. He just began reading from the transcript.

| "THE COURT: | If it's possible I'd like to break early today. We've all had a hard week. Do you anticipate any further witnesses, Mr. Edmonton? |
| MR. EDMONTON: | Your Honor, the estate will only have one further witness and that is the executor. He has some knowledge of these events |

156

	and is also the man we propose be made guardian of Miss Kendall's affairs.
THE COURT:	All right, go ahead.
MR. EDMONTON:	Your Honor, the Estate of Edward Kendall calls Mr. David Anthony Perino.
THE CLERK:	Do you swear to tell the truth, the whole truth, and nothing but the truth, so help you God?
MR. PERINO:	I do.
THE CLERK:	State your full name, occupation, and present business address for the record.
MR. PERINO:	David Anthony Perino. Attorney. 7523 Century Park East, Los Angeles, California.
MR. EDMONTON:	Mr. Perino, would you please advise the Court of your present duties and responsibilities with respect to this estate?
MR. PERINO:	I am presently the Executor of the Estate. I have been asked by the attorneys for the Estate to assume the role of Guardian over Miss Kendall's affairs in the event the Court rules her incompetent. If the Court wishes, I will, of course, be pleased to so serve."

Baird closed the transcript with a clap. "There are about twenty pages of unction after that where Perino tells what a great privilege it would be to serve the court and the estate, etc. I could barely keep down my lunch reading it so I assume you don't want to hear any of it."

"That's right," O'Malley said. He was quiet for a moment and then said, "What does it mean?"

"It means that in addition to everything else Perino is Anna's guardian and the executor of the estate. He gets to parcel out her every quarter, always has and always will. He also effectively controls every business in Kendall Industries."

"Is that it?" O'Malley asked.

"No. I found something else first that this casts a whole new light on, but it can wait."

"I'll get back to you," O'Malley said.

23

O'Malley hung up the phone and stared at a wall. It was amazing that he had stayed on this planet so long armed with such incredible stupidity. Perino as Anna's guardian, mentor, executor, and surrogate father. It made all the rest of it fade into insignificance.

But first things first. He picked up the phone again and dialed the New Jersey Highway Patrol. He had given passing thought to calling from a booth outside the hotel, but ultimately decided he really didn't care if they traced the call. He just wanted Moran's body found and disposed of in a civilized manner. The sergeant on the desk did his job, trying to keep the conversation going as long as possible. When O'Malley was sure the man had the essential information, he cut the connection.

For a moment, he thought about calling Mrs. Moran. He checked his watch. It was 9:30 at night. Patrick Moran had fidgeted all day in a fourth-grade classroom. Mrs. Moran would come on the line and O'Malley could tell her that her husband, the man who had taken her to the prom, married her in a blue tux, and risen to corporal in the United States Army, spent the night lying in a patch of grass called the High Ground next to the Hudson River with his head smashed in by a lowlife named Larry Reynolds, 13–10 at the Olympic. Then he could tell the woman how sorry he was.

Some men might have had the courage to make that phone call but O'Malley was not among them.

He walked over to the window to look out at the expanse of park twenty stories below. The traffic sat noisy and clogged on Central Park South. The view didn't give him a clue.

O'Malley could not remember ever feeling so helpless. He was completely shut out from this affair and neither bravery nor cleverness was good enough to get him back in. The list of unanswered questions was endless. Who killed John Bradley? Why did they kill James Moran? Why didn't they kill him? Where was Anna Bradley now? Was she with them voluntarily or not? Why didn't Anna tell him about Perino? Why did she hire him to begin with? What did the embezzlements at the studio have to do with any of this? Who were the good guys and who were the bad guys? Where was Monica these days?

The thought hit him square between the eyes. Monica. The little hooker who ran away with John. A tart undoubtedly in possession of enough information to hang all of them. He and Baird were as stupid as the day is long.

He wheeled nervously at the sound of knock at the door. For one weird moment, he had a notion it was Monica at the door, arriving at the precise time that his mind told him he needed her. But it was only room service bringing him some food, the first food he had touched all day.

"Thanks," O'Malley said. He handed the man a few dollars.

The bellman took the money, but didn't leave. He studied his shoes for awhile while O'Malley stared at him. "Problems?"

The man looked up. "I know you been getting information from a lot of people around the hotel, but they really don't know what they're talking about. I'm the room service guy, and I . . ."

O'Malley was already leading him to the door. "I'll be in

159

touch." The man was still protesting as O'Malley slammed the door in his face.

He went to his food, drank cold coffee, stared at a wall. Why didn't it make any sense? In the middle of a bite, he jumped up, ran to the desk, and brought back a pad and pencil. He held a pencil poised over the pad as though something important were going to happen. It didn't. He drew Xs and Os for awhile, then dropped the pencil in frustration. He felt clammy and uncomfortable, his day-old clothes clinging to him. Finally he jumped up and tore off his clothes on the way to the shower. He was in the bathroom when Harriet Resnick's card tumbled out of his pants pocket to his feet. He was in the shower under the cold, stinging rays of water when he realized just how important it was for him to see her.

The yellow cab cruised slowly along the road running adjacent to the beach houses. There were no addresses visible. The cabbie was a Manhattan cabbie and had never known this part of the world existed. Now that he did, he wasn't impressed.

"Lousy fucking place to drive around in. Can't even tell the numbers. I told my wife once, 'If I ever tell you I want to go live on Long Island, shoot me with a big gun.' That was good advice."

"Look at the card. I think you can tell we're getting close."

"I'm lookin' at the fuckin' card. The fuckin' card don't tell me shit. If the fuckin' card said '114 East Eighty-sixth Street,' I'd know where the fuck I was. But we're on Long Island, you know what I mean? And we ain't in any part of Long Island I ever heard of before."

"Just do the best you can."

The man grumbled, squinting at the big houses, looking for some information. O'Malley kept telling him it was only a matter of minutes. They turned a corner. A weathered white frame house was set closer to the road than the others. A nice elderly lady was watering yellow flowers.

"Hey, Toots," the cabbie howled.

The lady stood bolt upright and began looking around with a certain fear. She pointed to her chest. "Me?" she mouthed.

"No, I'm talkin' to your rake. Shake it over here for a second so I can ask you a question."

O'Malley began to hide his head until he saw the lady's face beam with pleasure. She almost trotted as she came over to the car. The cabbie handed her the card. "You know where this is, Toots?" The lady nodded excitedly and pointed to a white colonial across the way set well back from the street. The cabbie thanked her and winked. "Next time I come out we'll look at your petunias, you and me," he promised her. The little old lady ran away howling with delight.

"You just gotta know how to talk to broads," the cabbie told O'Malley solemnly.

O'Malley paid the man and the cab left. In front of him a large expanse of well-tended grass led to a white house. In the back was enough room for a good-sized par-three. The blue of the ocean lapped gently against a dock. He went up and knocked for Harriet Resnick.

When there was no response, he walked around to the back. The colonial was two stories high and sat flush in the middle of a sea of green lawns. No trees or fences separated the house from neighbors so far away no barriers were needed.

In the back of the house, a brick path led down to the dock. A small sailboat was tied to the east side of the pier. A table and chairs were set in the middle of the lawn about fifty feet from the dock, the umbrella rolled down so the sun could wash over the dark hair of the woman sitting cross-legged facing the water.

O'Malley walked up to Harriet. She had a towel wrapped around her neck. A white cotton T-shirt clung wetly to her body. She wore ordinary cotton running shorts and a pair of white tennis shoes. Her legs were crossed in a fetching manner. As O'Malley approached, a woman in an apron handed Harriet a pale green drink. Harriet's face was flushed.

She looked up as O'Malley got near, and her eyes registered surprise and delight. "I don't believe it. You came after all."

"I was dying to see how the other half lived. I had a feeling your house would be a pretty good example."

"I think that's a compliment," she said. "Anyway, I'm glad you came. Why don't you sit down and I'll have Ethel get you some grapefruit juice." She signaled to the maid, and the woman went away. Harriet smiled as O'Malley sat down. She pulled the wet shirt away from her body. "Don't mind all this sweat. I've just come back from a run on the beach. I try to do about six miles a day. Do you run?"

"Lately only when somebody's chasing me. But isn't running a little lower class? Shouldn't you be playing polo or something?"

Harriet laughed. "You've not read your *Gatsby*. Nowadays rich young girls are fabulous jocks. I was once a terrific tennis player as a stripling, even ranked nationally." She smiled. "Now I only play if I have a good partner."

"I'll save you a question. I don't play that either."

Harriet shrugged. "Pity."

The maid arrived with grapefruit juice. For a moment they sipped silently, watching the sun dance on the blue water. O'Malley half expected the grapefruit juice to be spiked with vodka, but it was just fresh-squeezed and pure. Harriet was idle and rich, but not dissolute. Her body was not only deliciously round, but firm, her eyes clear. She seemed to be very intelligently enjoying her money without guile or guilt. O'Malley had no quarrel with her.

"Let's walk down by the water," he suggested.

They walked quietly for awhile. Then O'Malley said, "I came out here for a reason."

"You mean a reason other than wanting to see me?"

"Yes."

"I'm not surprised," she said, "although a little disappointed. What can I do for you?"

"I'd like some more information about Anna."

"More? What more is there? I've already told you what I know."

"That's not even partly true," he said abruptly. "Last night, it didn't matter, but today I have to find out everything you know." His voice was harsher than it needed to have been.

She looked up into his eyes surprised, then turned and walked away from him down the grassy bank toward the beach. He walked behind her for a moment, then reached out and gripped her arm. She attempted to yank away, and he tightened his hold. Her look was indignant. "Let me go immediately."

O'Malley spun her around so she was facing him. He held both her shoulders. "I told you I need your help. This isn't a game anymore."

"I don't like your tone of voice," she told him. "I'd like you to go now."

O'Malley let Harriet's shoulders drop. He was sure under the white cotton material of her running shirt there were now angry red marks left by his fingers. She rubbed her right shoulder. "A man was killed night before last," O'Malley told her simply.

Her rubbing stopped and she looked up into his face. "What do you mean, killed?"

"I mean killed. Dead. Dead like a corpse. Have you ever seen anybody who's dead?"

Harriet ignored him. "Who was he?"

"James Moran. A chauffeur. Anna's chauffeur. There wasn't a goddamned reason in the world for him to die, but he did. If you want to make a phone call, I know a nine-year-old in Jackson Heights who can verify by now the man is dead."

163

"Oh, God, I don't believe this." Harriet looked legitimately distraught. She shook her head and looked out over the water. She was still staring that way when she spoke again. "What does Anna have to do with that? What do I have to do with that?"

"Anna was with me. Now she's gone—I don't know where but I'm certain she's with Perino. I don't even know if she's in danger or not—I guess it kind of depends on whether Anna's agreed to what he wants. As for you, I'm here because I think you can help me."

Harriet took a long sigh. "Come on," she said. They walked out to where the water lapped luxuriously against the soft sand. "Take off your shoes," she suggested. O'Malley did and the two of them dangled their feet in the small waves.

"What do you want to know?" she asked.

24

O'Malley's red-eye sailed over the blackness of the Mojave Desert toward the brilliance of Los Angeles. O'Malley sat in the first-class section all but exhausted. The plane had left New York at midnight, and although the clocks on Los Angeles walls argued it was only 2:00 A.M., O'Malley's body told him he had been up all night. For the hundredth time, he tried unsuccessfully to twist into a position comfortable enough for sleeping. Just when he thought he had one, a stewardess with all the warmth of a prison matron ordered him to bring his seat back to an upright position. He sat like a stickman until the plane skimmed over the cars on the San Diego Freeway and went bouncing down the thousand feet of concrete runway at LAX.

O'Malley ignored the throngs heading for the baggage area and went straight for the bar. Baird was sitting there surrounded by badly stylized prints of dead actors. He had four Styrofoam cups in front of him. A fifth was filled with black coffee.

"That stuff's gonna make you sick."

Baird was staring more or less hypnotized at the planes going and coming on the runway below. He closed a thick legal pad filled with thirty pages of cramped script. "I've been sitting here for two hours trying to put some of this stuff together. It makes less sense than it ever did."

"You're losing faith," O'Malley said cheerfully. "I can tell."

"Lost faith, O'Malley. This ship is going nowhere but down. I'm watching the waves splash over the gunwales."

The waitress came over, and O'Malley ordered a coffee to keep Baird company. There'd be no problem sleeping tonight. "I hate to ask the same old question again," O'Malley said, "but what's happening?"

"What's happening is we've got to go to the cops," Baird said firmly. "I'm sitting here looking at dead bodies all over the country, a missing client, and probably a massive laundering scam. I'm a very conservative person, O'Malley."

"You forgot the estate. You know—Perino as Anna's guardian."

"That's too kinky even for me," Baird said. "You go figure that one out."

"Don't push it aside so easily. It's the most important thing we've got."

Baird sniffed. "What's important is a dead dinner companion of yours lying unattended in an alley in New York City, a dead chauffeur lying unattended under a bridge in New Jersey, and our client's former husband lying in a plot of ground someplace. Where did they bury him anyway?"

165

"Forest Lawn. When you say it like that it makes it all sound very sinister."

"O'Malley, I realize this is going to come as a shock to you, but if you're present when somebody gets killed—even if they just get hit by a car—you're supposed to call the cops. It's a custom."

"What are we going to tell them?" O'Malley asked. "The first thing they'd want to know is why didn't we tell them before?"

"That is an argument that does not lend great support to your position here."

"And what about Perino? What are we going to tell them about him? And Anna, have you thought about her? Baird, she's our client and we don't even know where she is."

"You took the words right out of my mouth."

"Besides," O'Malley argued, "you know what will happen if we get the cops involved. It's just going to be a swearing contest between Perino and us, and we've got nothing on our side. What am I going to tell them, that I know Larry killed the chauffeur because I could smell him? And as far as Brent is concerned, Larry was at the other end of a pitch-black alley. And besides, what if we could even prove it was Larry? The only way we can tie Larry into Perino is because you got beat up by Larry in the bottom of Perino's building. What does that prove? Maybe you scratched his Mercedes or something."

Baird shook his head. "I will select the cop. I will do the talking. When I am through, they will understand."

"That's very nice. I remember that line from *Ghandi*. Didn't help him in the end, either."

Baird smiled. "A religious metaphor is appropriate, O'Malley, because I've been to the mountain."

"I see, Las Vegas. I think I'm going to be sick. How did God look?"

"A bit out of shape," Baird admitted. "He tries to convey the image that he's just a regular fellow, a businessman.

166

But there's something in the way he and his friends look at you that makes it clear they're all much more than that."

"Does he like having his money stolen from him by his pal, Perino?" O'Malley asked.

"O'Malley, that question has more assumptions in it than you will ever know."

"Or care about." He yawned. "Believe it or not, Baird, the only things that interest me these days are the murders and Anna's whereabouts. The other stuff is nonsense."

"That's where you're wrong. The angles these people are playing are fascinating. You could spend a lifetime looking into them."

"Be my guest. Something tells me notwithstanding your stated concerns about Anna, what you really want to go to the cops about are all these sweet deals you now know so much about."

Baird was about to protest that charge but was interrupted. O'Malley followed his friend's eyes to the door. A woman was walking through with a bright step and a wide smile. There was still a bit of puffiness around the cheekbones and a faint discoloration under the eyes. Nevertheless three men at the bar stopped their conversation while she walked by.

O'Malley stood to greet her. She lifted her cheek in a dainty way for him to kiss. O'Malley said: "You're gorgeous, kid. That man's hands didn't do a thing to hurt you."

Baird was standing too, a serious, solicitous look on his face. They embraced and kissed. When they sat down they held hands. O'Malley had had no idea this sort of thing was still going on.

"You guys want to neck for a while, I'll just go home."

Brenda smiled easily. "That's O.K. I can wait, long as it's not too long." She turned to Baird. "I hope you're not mad. I got bored and thought you might be lonely down here. You guys go ahead and talk business."

O'Malley looked down at his watch, then shook his

head. "No more business for tonight, please. It's almost six A.M. New York time. I'm through."

Baird agreed. "We won't lose any time. We haven't said anything yet that's the least bit meaningful."

Brenda ordered a drink. "You mean you still don't know who killed John Bradley?" she asked.

Both Baird and O'Malley laughed. "Not only do we not know who killed John Bradley," O'Malley said, "we don't have any answers. Beginning with why a guy like Bradley would run off with his secretary when he had one of the richest, most beautiful women in town waiting at home for him." O'Malley could have gone on with that description a lot longer. "Not to mention the better question of where the hell is the secretary."

Brenda took a sip. "You're kidding, right?" She looked back and forth between them, but neither of them was laughing. "About Monica, I mean. You're kidding, right?"

O'Malley looked at her quizzically. "No, we don't have the foggiest idea where she is."

Brenda shook her head, then leaned forward on her elbows. "Don't you two heroes realize Monica Davis is probably the easiest chick in the world to find?"

25

Brenda walked up and down Baird's office in front of the window that faced out onto Sunset. Her hands were folded behind her back; her chin jutted forward like a marine sergeant's. In front of her, standing more or less at attention, were six lovely, well-mannered, conservatively dressed, and quite fetching young ladies.

Brenda peeked out the window and saw the sun had moved a few notches toward the west. Time was getting short. She took her hands from behind her back and began primping the girls, removing a bit of lint from Cheryl's charcoal gray business suit, fixing Sandra's hair so it didn't spill onto her new cocktail dress, holding out her hand so Doris could give up the cigarette nub. She stepped back and took a last long look at her charges. "We're ready now," she told Baird confidently.

O'Malley had been trying without much success to remain serious, but he lost it each time he looked up to see Baird's ladies of the evening in their finery. Outside on Sunset Boulevard, cops were no doubt scratching heads at the lack of action. They would be scratching even more if they had witnessed the scenes that had been taking place in Baird's office for the last twenty-four hours.

"O.K., O'Malley, it's all yours," Baird told him.

O'Malley sat on the corner of Baird's desk. The ladies regarded him with a mixture of boredom and mild interest. They were intrigued by the assignment. Professional decorum required, however, the appearance of total disinterest.

"Ladies, you're beautiful," he told them. "Brenda, fabulous job." Brenda gave a curtsy. The evening before, the six ladies had arrived in halter tops and skintight pants. Now each would pass for a Harvard MBA. Until they opened their mouths, of course.

O'Malley picked up a brown manila envelope, pulling out six copies of a photograph of two women. He handed one to each of the women.

"Look at this picture closely," he said. "The girl on the left is Brenda. Take particular notice of the lady on the right. Her name is Monica Davis."

O'Malley let the six study the photograph. "The plan is to find this lady. She's a working girl like you, or at least used to be. She also used to be Brenda's roommate. We're trying to find her. Brenda, why don't you tell them what you know."

Brenda said: "Monica and I used to work together. I liked to work out of my house, but Monica used to get bored. She loved to get all dressed up and hang around the bars in the big hotels in Beverly Hills and Bel Air. It was her entertainment as much as a job. Also she figured what better way to meet the prince."

A couple of the women smiled weakly at the familiar dream. Brenda went on. "We want to cover all the places she used to hang out." She handed each of them a card. "On that card is the name of a bar at a hotel. Go there tonight and do your thing. Whatever you make you keep. You'll find this is a lot better than Sunset."

The women were noncommittal, preferring to wait for the bottom line. "We'd like you to do this for six nights," she went on. "Each night you'll switch bars. Monica told me the bartenders will let you work once a week, and that's all. They don't want the same chicks hanging out every night. So after you make your round of the six bars, you can go back to the first one without a problem."

Brenda hopped off the desk and walked closer to the women. "There's a couple of things you've got to know," she said, holding up her fingers. "First, you've got to look good to get in. Second, you can't act like a slob. Go up to the bar, sit down, and smile sweetly at the bartender. Order something light like white wine. Ask him to light your cigarette for you. When you pay for your first drink, leave him a huge tip—maybe twenty. Then give him another big smile like he's your partner for the night. After that, he should send some folks over to see you."

"Now, for the good part," she said grinning. "The price is a hundred fifty a hit." The girls looked at each other with surprise. "The bartender gets forty, the doorman twenty. That leaves you ninety." Brenda looked over at Baird slightly apologetically. "That's what Monica told me," she said.

O'Malley walked over near Brenda and faced the ladies. "If you spot her, please don't say anything to her. Just call the number on the back of the card right away." He thought for a second, then said, "It's like hide and seek, except if you tag this girl, you make a thousand extra."

The elegant ladies were all smiling and chatting as they walked out the door.

O'Malley had the phone cradled against his ear, listening to it ring as he had many times before. This time he was determined not to hang up. He sat on the hotel floor cross-legged and cramped. The cigarette in his fingers was burned to the nub. He lit another one with the burning end of the old and crushed the stub out. The ashtray next to him was filled to overflowing.

He felt himself drifting to sleep. To counteract that, he stood and began pacing back and forth. He was so mesmerized by the repetitive ringing he didn't hear it stop at first, didn't hear the weak "Hello" on the other end of the line. The old man had to say it two or three times before O'Malley reacted.

"I said hello, who is this?"

"Mr. Thurston?" O'Malley asked. "Is this James McDowell Thurston?"

"Who wants to know?"

"Mr. Thurston, my name is Benjamin O'Malley. I need to talk to you on a matter of great importance."

"You a bill collector?" the man asked.

"No, I'm not." O'Malley hesitated. "I'm a friend of Anna Bradley's."

There was no sound except the static of a long-distance wire. Finally the man spoke. "I got nothing to talk to you about. You understand? Nothing."

"Mr. Thurston, please. I've gone to a great deal of time and effort to locate you, and I must speak to you. It's a . . . ."

The old man interrupted him with a laugh. "A matter of life and death? That what you're going to tell me?" Then he laughed again.

"In a way, yes." O'Malley's voice was insistent. "I want to find out what you know about Edward Kendall's death. How did Anna's father die, Mr. Thurston?"

O'Malley could hear the man sigh. "She killed her pa," he said. "Right there in his sleep. Drove that pick into his head just as cold as ice."

O'Malley breathed slowly, closing his eyes. He tried to keep his voice calm.

"You were the investigating officer?"

"Son, I was the whole force. This happened at the country house. I was responsible for the whole island alone. Every once in a while I got Jeff from the gas station to help out if he was broke, but as soon as he got two quarters ahead, he was back to the bars."

"Was there an autopsy?" O'Malley asked.

"You're a real ghoul. You want to know how far it went in? I'm telling you the handle of that pick was sticking out the back of his head and that was all you could see. Not even blood, 'cept a trickle."

"How old was Anna at the time?"

"She was about seventeen, maybe a year or two more. Just old enough to be jealous of her pa running around with a bunch of young ladies."

"Is that why you think she did it? Because her father had girlfriends?"

"That's my opinion," Thurston said firmly. "I can't prove it, but that's the way I read it. I watched Anna grow up out on that island every summer, and you never saw a girl more in love with her father in your life. Her father was a good man, but every summer Anna had a new mama, if you know what I mean. Actually, more like a new sister."

"So she was used to it, right?"

"I ain't no shrink," Thurston told him. "Girls grow up. She was seven and eight years old, she didn't care. It was just somebody new to play with every summer. She got older, she wanted her pa all to herself. She couldn't get him, so she decided to make sure nobody gets him."

"Do you have any evidence she did it?" O'Malley asked.

"Sure," the man said. "The night it happened, I was on duty like always. It was about four A.M., and I was cruising by the good parts of town. All of a sudden, I see this white ghost in the middle of the road. I throw on the big light and I see it's Anna in a white nightgown. She's just walking down the middle of the road staring straight ahead. I catch up to her and grab her by the arms and look in her face. Her face is as pale as her nightgown and streaked with red. I look down at her hands, and her hands are covered with red also. Her eyes were crazy and just staring straight ahead. I took her back to the house, and we found her pa in the bedroom. There wasn't nobody else in the house. We took the pick down for prints, and hers were the only ones on it."

"How much blood was around the icepick when you went back and looked at it?"

"Like I say, just a little trickle coming out near the point. Those things just slide right in. Of course, if you jostle 'em or try to pull 'em out, it can get messy. There was some red streaks on his back, but that was all."

"He didn't have a shirt on?"

"That's right," Thurston said. "Didn't have no pants on either."

"What happened to Anna after the killing?" O'Malley asked. "After you found her on the road, I mean?"

"I wanted to throw her in the jug. But on a big case like this, they dragged in the people from the county. They did a complete investigation and didn't charge her with anything. Just threw her in the bin for a while."

"What do you mean, threw her into the bin?"

"I mean she was put away because she was crazy," Thurston said. "They do that with rich kids who kill people. Except in her case, they didn't put her away long enough."

That was the first he had ever heard of Anna being put away twice. If Perino had known of the earlier commitment it would give him incredible leverage. And Perino knew everything. "What if I told you Anna didn't kill anybody?" O'Malley asked calmly.

"What's that you say?" Thurston shouted. "Whaddya mean didn't kill anybody? What about the blood?"

"What about the blood? You told me yourself that the icepick slid right in. No blood at all."

"So how'd she get it all over her hands?"

"Grabbing at the pick in horror after it was already in there. Jiggling it around, like you say. That's also how it got smeared on her father's back. He was already dead by the time Anna found him."

"How do you know," the man shouted. "I conducted an investigation."

"You conducted shit," O'Malley told him, not really sure who he was angry at or why. "He was naked because he was sleeping with a woman is my guess. I agree with you that somebody killed Edward Kendall in a moment of sexual rage. But it wasn't Anna."

"Who then? Who did it?"

O'Malley's weariness was getting to him and he had no desire to continue the conversation. Harriet's information had panned out and he now knew all Thurston could tell him. Was Thurston right? Who knew.

The old man was shouting something else at him when O'Malley hung up the phone.

26

It was another two days before Baird finally broke through and convinced O'Malley to go to the cops. Baird's method of persuasion was simple: By never talking about anything else he finally just drove O'Malley nuts. But Baird had help. For every hour of those two days O'Malley waited for some word, any word, of Anna's whereabouts, of her safety. When he didn't get it he knew it was time to throw in the towel.

The cop Baird selected was the United States Attorney, or rather one of her underlings. They arrived for their appointment and were led by a close-cropped FBI type to a windowless waiting room on the seventeenth floor of the federal courthouse. Jimmy Carter smiled warmly at them from the wall above. A square patch of less faded paint to Jimmy's left heralded the coming change of administration and the fact that as recently as yesterday the vice-president had stood beside him.

The assistant assigned to them was a gruff and cheerful sort in his early thirties, the kind who would do well in private practice in another couple of years. He sat in a metal chair behind a metal desk with a gray pad over it. On one corner of his bookcase was a picture of his wife. On the east side of the room, what had once been a plant was going through its death throes. The room was littered with sheaves of seemingly unrelated pieces of paper.

He introduced himself as James Chapman, a good solid prosecutor's name. He motioned Baird and O'Malley to two chairs in front of him and then motioned again to tell them where to dump the paper.

Chapman checked his watch and punched a button to his secretary. "Don't let me forget I have that sentencing at eleven," he told her. Chapman was obviously a guy running one step ahead of disaster at all times.

He turned back to O'Malley and Baird. "Sarah sent me your letter," he said curtly. Sarah was Sarah Levine, the first woman appointee to a United States Attorney's slot in the country. She would not remain after the forthcoming Republican takeover. "She didn't tell me anything about the case because she doesn't know anything. The only thing I've been able to do in the last twenty-four hours is have the FBI run a quick check on you fellows." He smiled at them.

O'Malley didn't even get angry anymore when this sort of thing happened. "Did they turn up my Congressional Medal of Honor?" he asked.

Chapman stopped smiling. "No, they missed that one. They did pick up certain honors bestowed on you by the grand jury, however. Both state and federal."

Baird had no patience for joking of this sort, especially about a case he believed he had won. His voice was flat. "I assume your sources also informed you of the disposition of those cases."

"Yes, I understand the charges were dismissed," Chapman said. "That doesn't mean he didn't do it."

The scarlet rose quickly to Baird's neck. "Mr. Chapman," he began, "the United States Attorney's Office—this very office—prosecuted the action against Mr. O'Malley. They did it quite poorly, and I am certain if the matter had gone to trial, we would have prevailed, both because Mr. O'Malley was not guilty of the crimes alleged and also because of the general incompetence of the personnel prosecuting the matter. As it turned out, the humiliation of your colleagues was not necessary. The true perpetrators of the crime were tried and punished. Mr. O'Malley was completely exonerated and the charges dropped. We keep waiting for the apology from this office, but perhaps the mails have been slow for the past three years."

Chapman tried to look stern but his face betrayed him. He broke into a grin. "Off the record, I know the assistant who had that case. He's a lifer who's off in Washington now working for Justice Lands. He didn't have the slightest idea what was going on. Some big firm downtown was feeding him information."

"That's correct," Baird said. "Jenkins and Dorman. Mr. O'Malley and I are both from that firm."

"I remember it now. Someone over there was trying to lay it all off on your boy here. It worked for awhile, and then they got 'em."

"That, in essence, is correct."

Chapman leaned back. "So tell me what I can do for you."

Baird opened his briefcase and began examining a yellow pad. Then he looked up. "I'd like to discuss with you a murder. Three, in fact."

Chapman yawned. "You got the wrong building. You see that picture of the guy in the lobby? He's the president of the United States for the moment. They've got another building a few blocks away where the district attorney hangs out. He's got a picture of the board of supervisors in his lobby. They're real interested in murders over there."

"Ordinary murders, maybe. This may be RICO," Baird said.

Chapman's eyes came alive. RICO was the acronym for the Racketeer Influenced and Corrupt Organizations Act, a phrase that brought a warm glow to the heart of every federal prosecutor. It was originally supposed to be nothing more than an omnibus racketeering statute, but the way it was written the vast net of RICO caught everything: state crimes, federal crimes, the Mafia, wife-beating, everything. RICO made it a federal felony to think about doing something unpleasant by or to anyone who had ever made an interstate telephone call.

Chapman knew RICO. "Everything's RICO. So what are you trying to say to me?"

"What I'm trying to explain to you is Mr. O'Malley and I have run across a laundry operation," Baird said. "A laundry operation connected to three murders. A laundry operation that involves the film business and some very important people in New York, Los Angeles, and Las Vegas. A laundry operation that may involve millions of dollars of tax fraud engineered through respected international commodity brokers." Baird hesitated for the big one. "A laundry operation that involves the Cappici organization." Chapman's eyes were now ablaze. "Now if you still think we should trot over to the D.A.'s office, just say the word."

"No, no, relax, relax. We probably got off on the wrong foot here." Chapman grabbed a pad. "You just go ahead and tell me what you've got to say."

Baird talked in slow, even tones. He spoke for forty-five minutes straight and Chapman didn't interrupt once. At the end of the forty-five minutes Baird reached his conclusion, stated it to Chapman, and stopped. Chapman scribbled for a few more minutes and then also stopped. He casually flipped through the fifteen to twenty pages of notes he had taken, then leaned back and stretched. That done, he walked to the window and examined the street below. He spoke to himself. "Nine fucking years doing this shit, and they still got me looking at the freeway."

He walked back over and sat down. "They just don't give a shit, you know that? They just take and take and take. They don't care about law; they don't care about anything but money. And here I sit working like a pig for nine years looking out on a freeway. You know what a GS-15 makes?"

"Fifty thousand dollars?"

"Thirty-eight thousand, five hundred and forty-two dollars," Chapman said. "That's after nine years of doing this shit. Last month I had to go to New York on a case and the government gave me a per diem of fifty dollars. That's for everything: hotel, meals, taxicabs, the whole works. Fifty dollars! I got the cheapest room in the city, and it cost me ninety-five dollars. That's before I put a bite of food in my mouth. And you know what they tell us around here when we complain? 'You pay any extra over your per diem, you can deduct it.'" He laughed. "That's our tax shelter."

Baird and O'Malley were silent. Then Chapman said, "What do you want me to do?"

O'Malley said: "We haven't seen any of them since New York. Not Perino, not Anna, not Monica. I understand the Justice Department has an agency with some experience in investigations. Maybe you could call upon their services."

Chapman smiled. "We'll be in touch," he said.

For the next two days Baird and Chapman were wary, circling each other like a pair of Sumo wrestlers. On the third day each seemed to realize simultaneously just how good the other was. Then they shook hands and went after Perino like two starved dogs.

By the end of the sixth day, Chapman had a grand jury cranked up, subpoenas out the door, and the FBI swarming. By the eleventh day, strange men in ill-fitting suits began showing up at Chapman's office with their lawyers at their sides. These were the informants, men eager to be the first in the door to exchange information for immunity. As they talked, layer after layer fell from the cover of one of the most ambitious laundry schemes in Nevada history.

Baird became transformed by the process, working day and night with Chapman on the subpoenas, on the documents, on the witnesses. The few times O'Malley actually got to see him in the flesh his friend's face was puffy from lack of sleep but nonetheless animated, the eyes ablaze with the excitement of the quest. Even Brenda was complaining at the lack of attention.

The grand jury probe was top secret until the first subpoena hit the desk of the first recipient. Then it blew like a bomb all over town.

27

Two weeks and a lot of wasted time after their visit to Chapman, O'Malley listened for what seemed the thousandth time to the answering machine in Baird's office. This time he got what he wanted.

O'Malley was too cheap to pay the fortune the crimson bedecked valet demanded at the Beverly Wilshire Hotel, so he parked a few blocks away. The walk back was through verdant residential landscape. At the Beverly Wilshire he entered a glittering alleyway between the new and old parts of the hotel. Men in long, red coats opened the doors of exotic automobiles with theatrical flourishes. At night a thousand lights illuminated the display. The show cost about fifteen dollars per car.

O'Malley squeezed past all the nonsense into the old part of the hotel. Inside were a jewelry store and a shop peddling antique Chinese pottery, each emphasizing its importance with an armed guard stationed outside, each slightly embarrassed by the barbershop sitting between them. Further in was the marble lobby and a tasteful sign pointing toward the Hideaway Bar.

O'Malley sat down at the bar and looked around. Nothing familiar. He ordered a bit of evil Jack from the man waiting patiently before him. The bartender poured one and said, "That'll be seven-fifty."

O'Malley stopped the drink halfway to his mouth. "They ought to give you a mask and a gun," he told the man. "You'd feel more at home."

"I know this is going to be a surprise to you, pal, but I only get fifty percent of the take here. Why, if it was up to me I'd give you the drink for free, just because you look like such an interesting person."

O'Malley paid the money. "Do I get anything with this? Like a steak dinner?"

"You get my condolences," the man said. But he wore a small smile when he left.

O'Malley sipped but couldn't taste any difference. He lit a cigarette and was preparing to pass the time with a little banter when he felt a tap on his shoulder. He smelled, rather than saw, the woman next to him. The perfume made no effort at subtlety.

"Would you like a little company, sir?"

O'Malley squinted. "Marsha?"

"Yes, sir." She sat up on the barstool and held up her cigarette. "You know if I'd discovered this place three years ago I'd be retired now."

O'Malley laughed. "And here I thought rich people were all very moral."

"Yeah," Marsha said. "They all pay cash."

O'Malley nodded in understanding. "But now you're going to tell me you've been able to help me out?"

"Only if you buy me a drink," she countered.

O'Malley held up his finger for the bartender, but she stopped him. "Let me or he'll bring another club soda."

The bartender came by and gave her a real drink. "Christ, that's great," she said. "After this job, I ever see another club soda I'm gonna throw up. I found your girl."

"Where?"

Marsha tilted her head at some tables in the rear of the room. O'Malley looked back and saw a curtained area. Waiters scurried in and out with food. "She's having dinner?" he asked.

"Not now, before. I thought I saw her back there with some people when I was here a week ago. But you told me she'd be working, so I thought I must have it wrong."

"So what happened?"

"I noticed the dress she was wearing, a wild, sexy, red thing, looked totally out of place back there. Before I could get close and really check her out though, I got a customer. I got back down she was gone."

O'Malley felt disappointment rise. "So you didn't get to see her?"

"Not that night. But when I came tonight, who should I see sitting at the bar but the lady herself, wearing the same red dress. It's like a uniform or something."

"Are you sure it was her?"

"Yes, I almost forgot to tell you the most important thing," Marsha said. "I talked to her."

"What do you mean you talked to her?"

"I mean we had a great little chat. We talked about business and the weather. I told her I was looking for a place to stay and asked her if she needed a roommate."

"What did she say to that?"

The woman smiled. "Do I get extra for being smart?"

"I thought you were doing this as a favor to Baird." When the woman's smile remained, O'Malley sighed. "Yes, you get extra for being smart."

"She said right now she didn't have a place because she was staying at a friend's house at the beach. She said she expected to be looking for her own place right away. Said we could get together and look around."

O'Malley felt like kissing her. "Great job. Did she tell you anything else?"

"Not much, just the phone number of the place at the beach where she's staying." A few minutes later the bartender had to come over and tell them to keep it down because they were laughing too hard.

The man left and O'Malley said, "Where is she now?"

The woman pointed to the sky. "The guy looked like an Arab. Monica said she could smell the money from across the room." She took a last sip of her drink. "By the way, speaking about money and upstairs, you're sort of blocking traffic if you know what I mean."

"I know what you mean. Do me one quick favor when you see Monica again."

"Sure."

"Find out when she expects to be back here. Make up some excuse like it's always good to have a girlfriend around." The woman made a face. "Well, you can think of something. Anyway I just want to know when she'll be back."

"O.K."

O'Malley actually ran into the lobby looking for a phone booth. When he found one he dialed Perino's office immediately.

"Hello," he said to the female voice who answered. "This is Mr. Steven Spielberg's secretary. He's calling for Mr. Perino if he's available?"

The answer wasn't surprising. "No, I'm afraid Mr. Perino is not in today. He's on vacation. He'll be out of the office for at least thirty days."

"Oh dear, this is most important," O'Malley whined. "May I reach him at home?"

"I believe so, yes." The woman didn't say anything more.

"Now let's see if I've got this right," O'Malley said. He reached in his pocket for the scrap of paper Marsha had given him in the bar. "I have 422-8102. Do we have it right?"

"Yes, that's correct. I'm sure Mr. Perino will be quite delighted to hear from you."

"Quite," O'Malley said.

28

He left the phone booth laughing out loud. An old lady looked at him strangely and he blew her a kiss. What a nice day. What a nice lady. He checked his watch. What better way to kill some time than a stroll up Rodeo Drive; see what the locals were up to. It was a beautiful clear day in L.A., smog-free and eighty degrees. The sky was nothing but blue. Nice-looking ladies in strange outfits bobbed haughtily between the shops. They were thick with jewelry. The shops were marblefaced, with extravagant prices next to extravagant clothes behind high, squeaky clean windows. Rolls and Mercedes were parked ticketless in the red zones outside each shop.

This was Anna's country. This is where she shopped and shallied and spent the fortune of an allowance Perino allowed her. It was a fine, useless life that even made John Bradley look productive. They must have found her easy to control.

He was aimlessly wondering how much of the whole thing was real and how much hustle when his thoughts were jolted by a plain gold plaque over a women's clothing store. It was a simple brass plaque engraved with a simple name. Inside, a variety of colorfully dressed women ran their fingers over expensive fabric. He stopped and looked in, then back at the sign. There was something strangely familiar about it all, and nothing on this stretch of road should have been familiar. As he watched, a woman walked out with three or four boxes followed by a chauffeur with a number more. Then it hit him. Anna Bradley's garage. And a honey-blond woman dropping fine embossed boxes at the sight of a man with a pockmarked face.

Inside, two salespersons stood idly behind the counter. The women were groping at the fabric. He strolled in.

"Yes, sir," the woman said automatically. She had a strangely accented voice. It sounded almost Russian.

O'Malley affected his best North Jersey truckdriver twang. "Afternoon. I came for Mrs. Bradley. You got some boxes to be picked up?"

The woman actually warmed when she realized O'Malley was a fellow working stiff. The rudeness was only because the customers liked it that way. "I don't remember her leaving anything," she said amiably, "but come in the back and I'll look at the books. You can have a cup of coffee."

"Thanks," O'Malley said. He followed her toward an ordinary office. As they walked, one of the patrons whined about a gown. The lady quickly soothed her with a soft Russian-accented tone. In the safety of her office she muttered, "Fucking cow," in a snarl that came straight from Manhattan.

They laughed together. O'Malley drank a cup of coffee while she went through her books. "Let's see. I have her down five times this year." She flipped some more pages. "And except for an alteration she's picked up all of her boxes." She shrugged. "Looks like you made a trip for nothing."

O'Malley's brow knitted in thought. "It's just not like her to make mistakes like that." He stroked his chin and said, "May I see that?"

The woman shrugged and pushed the book over. O'Malley turned it and ran his finger down the page until he saw the name of Anna Bradley. There was a series of dates next to her name and a signature next to each one. One more column over and there was a seven-digit order number. The final column was skinny, had an asterisk and the number "43" next to it.

"What's the asterisk mean?"

The woman came over and stood close to him. "That means there's an alteration."

"What's the 43 mean?"

"That's the page that tells me what to do with the jacket." She licked her fingers and began flipping the pages rapidly. Then she ran her finger down another column of entries. "Let's see, Bradley, Bradley. Here it is. Yes. We're supposed to send it out by special messenger before Saturday. That must mean it was our fault." She looked up at O'Malley. "But it's still not ready," she said. "Probably be tomorrow sometime. Anything wrong?"

"Where will you be sending the jacket?" He hoped his voice was casual, but he doubted it.

"Let's see. Should say so right here." She squinted at the page again. "Yes, here it is. 11711 Pacific Coast Highway, Malibu. The number is . . ."

"422-8102," O'Malley interrupted.

"Yes," she said.

O'Malley leaned over, grabbed the woman by both

shoulders, pulled her close, and kissed her long and flush on the lips. The woman was only slightly taken aback; she looked up with expectancy. O'Malley shook a finger at her. "I will be back for you. Bet the ranch on it." They laughed together. O'Malley left the little boutique with a spring in his step he had not felt for a month. It must be getting awfully crowded out there at the beach.

29

O'Malley left Beverly Hills and drove east down the length of Sunset to the seedy hotel he called home. He had originally picked the Hollywood Dunes because it was near Baird's office; now his only excuse was he was too lazy to move. Anna Bradley was not only getting great service, she was saving a bundle on expenses.

The Hollywood Dunes was the sort of hotel that prided itself on its friendly service. There were two perfectly acceptable ways to pay: a week ahead by cash, or a day ahead by cash. There was a sign in back of the front desk that said, "We Don't Like Checks, We Don't Like Credit Cards, and We Don't Like People Who Try to Use Them." Underneath the words was a little cartoon figure being kicked into the street.

The squat man behind the desk had been unsure of O'Malley from the first day and the long New York hiatus had only added to his qualms. Each time O'Malley came in the man stared at him with squinty eyes, his fingers itching to dial the cops. When O'Malley paid his money, the man would lick his fingers, count each bill carefully, turn it over on both sides, and occasionally hold a representative one to the light. Only very reluctantly would he turn over the key for another week at the spa.

When O'Malley came in this time the man wore his standard squinty look. O'Malley tried to smile and walk on, but the man crooked a dirty finger. O'Malley walked over.

"Somebody's up there."

"Up where?"

"In your room. Where the fuck you think I'm talking about?"

"What do you mean, there's somebody in my room?"

The man smirked. "You don't speak the English language too good do you? I said there's somebody in your room. Which of them words don't you understand?"

O'Malley realized that the sudden urge to reach over the desk and strangle the little fuck was probably just a throwback to less rational days. He tried mentally counting to five.

"Let's try this again. Who is in my room?"

"Some broad."

"Why is the woman in my room?"

"What do I look like, a fucking psychiatrist? Maybe she wants your autograph."

That was enough. O'Malley leaned over and grabbed the man's tie in a big fist, then yanked straight down. The man's face bounced off the desk twice. He wailed and red appeared under his nose. O'Malley held the man's face flush to the wood. "Now, Mr. Desk Clerk, if you don't stop fooling around and tell me immediately what this person is doing in my room, I am going to wring your scrawny neck like a chicken's."

The man spoke quickly. "She said she knew you. I didn't think there'd be any harm."

"What did she look like?"

The man gave the description quickly and without further banter.

O'Malley relaxed his hold. "Thank you."

He went up the three flights of steps quickly, then

turned down the hall on the third floor. He slowed when he reached his door.

The door was locked. He used his key softly, trying to feel the tumblers before moving them. The door opened noiselessly.

The room was dark. The white sheet on the bed was hilly. He walked over, lifted his hand and delivered a loud, resounding smack to the top of the hill.

Harriet Resnick screeched and spun out of the bed. She jumped up and down rubbing the back of her tight jeans with both hands. "That hurt," she wailed.

"It was supposed to hurt," O'Malley told her. "I realize this is a liberated age, but I'm old-fashioned enough not to want to find people sleeping in my bed unless they've been invited."

Harriet continued rubbing. "I just wanted to come and see you," she protested. "Maybe help out, even. What's so wrong with that? The man downstairs said I could come up."

"I know," O'Malley said. "And the man downstairs is now sorry he said that. But that's beside the point. You still weren't invited."

Harriet finished rubbing and walked over to a chair, sitting down in a huff. "You're the strangest person I've met in a long time. Just when I think you're interested in me, you change your mind."

"I never change my mind," O'Malley said.

Harriet looked at him quizzically for a moment, then her gaze softened. She crossed her legs and smiled. "You know, you're not nearly so tough as you make out. Now that I'm here, what are you going to do?"

"I don't know, maybe toss you out into the hall."

"I doubt it."

O'Malley had a retort on the tip of his tongue that never came out. Harriet was wearing a nice woolly sweater on top of her jeans. The combination was one that emphasized how warm and cozy Harriet could make a cold winter's night.

Even in L.A. Harriet's look made clear the lady was very sure of her ultimate success, even if her quest might take a little time. O'Malley felt his stern look dissolve into a grin. "How about a drink?" he suggested.

They sipped Jack Daniels from plastic tumblers after the chastened desk clerk brought them up a bottle. They talked about lots of things while they sipped. At one point Harriet said, "It's getting late."

O'Malley looked out at the gathering darkness. "I know. You hungry?"

"No. I don't want to eat. What I'd like to do is go to bed with you immediately." She grinned saucily. "If you invite me, that is."

Not now, not yet. He shook his head from right to left.

Harriet couldn't believe it. "O'Malley, are you nuts?"

A very rational question. "I must be," he said. As if to emphasize that obvious proposition Harriet turned and walked away from him to her chair. He didn't turn away.

"Why?" she asked.

"I don't know."

"It's Anna, isn't it?"

"Yes."

"You're in love with her?"

He coughed. "I want to find out what happened to her. I also want to find out why certain things were done. After that . . ." He spread his hands and left the sentence unfinished.

"You mean there's hope for me." She said it in a catty, sardonic way.

"Only if you stop talking like that."

"Christ, O'Malley," she complained.

He tossed a pillow at her feet. "I think you'll find that chair very comfortable."

They woke when the sun fought its way through the dust on the windows and the open drapes. It was a glaring, harsh light. The Naugahyde furniture shone dully in it. It was a light that would be unflattering to anything and any-body, anybody except Harriet. O'Malley got up and wan-dered over to the cute bundle of blanket and jeans curled into the chair.

"Good morning."

She turned a sleepy face to him, then curled back up into a ball. "Go to hell, O'Malley," she said cheerfully.

"Don't be a baby. If you're good maybe you can sleep in the bed sometime."

"If you'd let me sleep in the bed you'd find out just how good I am."

But she was game. An hour later they were showered and clear-eyed over some watery scrambled eggs at a very shaky neighborhood coffee shop. Local workers were at all the other tables.

"You know between having my body refused, sleeping in a chair, and being poisoned at breakfast, I'm having a really shitty time."

O'Malley laughed. "Think of it as paying your dues."

"You better be worth it."

They were both surprised at how easy it was for them to be together. Inevitably, however, the talk turned back to Anna. Harriet said: "We have to talk about her some more, you know."

"Why?"

"Because she's a part of me and she's become a tremen-dous part of you. She's also sort of standing in my way. I'm entitled to know what the story is."

"The story is I was retained to do an investigation into John Bradley's disappearance," he told her. "I've now been diverted from that investigation somewhat."

"Why?"

"A lot of reasons. For one, everytime I try to concen-trate on John and Anna I run into some side road like Anna's father's murder. By the time I get back to business I'm lost."

"All right, then I'll keep my question simple. Are you working for her or against her now?"

That was easy. "For her. Always for her."

"Is she in danger?"

"In my judgment, yes."

"Is she alive?" Harriet's voice had a slight break in it.

O'Malley thought about the question. "I don't know," he said evenly. "Sort of, I would guess."

Harriet started crying immediately. When she stopped she seemed embarrassed. "It shouldn't matter. I mean, it doesn't matter. She hasn't let me be close in years. Nevertheless, the thought of her like she was before is just . . . is just . . ."

"I know." O'Malley put his arm around her and held her close. She looked up.

"Is there anything I can do?" She sniffed a few times. "I mean, I'll do anything."

He had given a lot of thought to that question. It was the whole purpose of the breakfast. "Yes, there is something," he said.

She looked up quizzically.

"Do you think you can get me about twenty thousand dollars in small bills?"

The good home cooking had him back again the next morning. He had the coffee halfway to his mouth when the headline leaped off the page and grabbed him.

U.S. JURY PROBING CHARGES OF TAX SCAM

By Wallace Charles, Times Staff Writer

A federal grand jury is looking into charges that a major underworld tax avoidance scheme may have been engineered in Los Angeles and Nevada using the resources of a number of businesses, including local movie studios, government sources said Friday.

The Times has also learned that the Justice Department's Organized Crime Strike Force has become involved because of charges that the tax avoidance scheme was aided by reputed underworld figures who have been the target of several government investigations, including members of the so-called Cappici organization.

The grand jury has begun issuing subpoenas for the financial records of the companies involved, including one major Los Angeles-based movie studio. There was no estimate of how long the grand jury was expected to continue.

The Times has learned that the investigation is being conducted by Assistant United States Attorney James N. Chapman. Mr. Chapman refused comment on the purposes of the probe.

So now it was official. To the left of the article was a picture of Baird and Chapman walking smilingly down the steps of the federal courthouse. The caption identified Baird as "an unidentified federal agent," a reasonably approximate description.

O'Malley was glad Chapman and Baird were having such a good time and getting in the newspapers and all, but it was as clear as day to him that the question of John Bradley's death was getting all the attention of a discarded hot dog wrapper at a baseball game. It would have taken Baird a good ten minutes to recall who Anna Bradley was.

O'Malley pushed some cold eggs around a plate, feeling grumpy at the thought. Then he looked up and saw a fresh face grinning at him beneath tousled curly hair. It was a sassy face with juice in it, a face that was like an open window in a stuffy room. This was a face that wouldn't leave him for pictures in the paper or her name in the news. "I've got it," she said excitedly, sounding simply like a girl about to have some more fun. "One day and I got it." He leaned over and grabbed her by the unkempt mass of hair and kissed her. "Let's go," he said, "we've got a lot to do."

30

It was four nights before they struck pay dirt, an expensive hiatus given the rate for the Beverly Wilshire's suites. But at least Harriet had a bed.

When O'Malley first saw the woman in the bar, he wasn't sure it was she. The four days of inactivity, of hanging around inconspicuously, of staring at every woman who came in, of ironically being offered one of Baird's ladies each night by the helpful bartender, had all combined to make him jittery, ready to jump at flashes. He decided to make sure before making a fool of himself.

She sat down at the end of the bar. O'Malley watched the bartender slide a drink before her without even taking her order. She put a few bills in front of her and he discreetly whisked them away. There was no change. Even from a distance O'Malley could tell the bills were large.

He held up a finger and the man was there instantly. "Jimmy, lemme have a Jack Daniels and do me a favor. Tell that lovely young lady at the end of the bar I've got her next round." The bartender nodded, went down to the other end of the bar, leaned across and whispered something, then pointed back at O'Malley. The woman turned to him and smiled, raising her glass in what appeared to be gratitude. Then she held up her cigarette and silently mouthed the word, "Light?"

O'Malley picked up his drink and went to sit next to the lovely Monica Davis.

He snapped a lighter in her face, then lit one of his own.

"Terrible habit," he told her. "We'll probably be dead at forty."

Monica smiled easily. "Who wants to live past forty?"

O'Malley intentionally laughed too loud. Monica picked up on it and smoothly moved in, glibly chatting about the city and the hotel, then moving expertly into O'Malley's life. O'Malley was impressed; Monica was very, very good at this sort of thing.

"So what brings you to Beverly Hills?" she asked.

"I'm in the export business," he said. "My father's company buys American products and resells them in Europe. We're based in London."

"I see," Monica said. Her eyes grew large with interest. "So it's all your father's business?"

"It was. He passed away last year unexpectedly. I'm afraid it's all my burden now."

Monica tried to hide her glee. She muttered condolences.

"That's why I'm the one making the trips to the States now," O'Malley told her.

"So you're European?"

"I suppose so. I was born in Amsterdam, educated at Princeton, and presently live in London. I've picked up American mannerisms from my father."

Monica was nodding delightedly. "It's remarkable. You sound like you were born in New York City."

"So tell me about you," O'Malley said quickly.

Monica shrugged. "There's really not much to tell. I'm an actress and model."

O'Malley bit the inside of his lip. "Really? That's very exciting. What sort of acting have you done?"

"Well, at the moment I'm sort of, uh, between projects I guess you'd say. In the past though, I've done a number of important American films. And of course TV and magazine covers and all that."

"Is that right! Well, you certainly do look familiar."

Monica shrugged with a nonchalance that said she'd heard it all before. O'Malley wondered how to move the conversation from Monica's phony career to her real one. Monica saved him the trouble of wondering too long.

"But there's one thing I've got to tell you," she said sadly.

"What's that?"

Her lip trembled slightly. "It's hard to admit this, but times have been terrible recently in the entertainment business."

"I've heard that. They're laying off people right and left. Even the most promising talent."

Monica nodded in agreement. "That's what I mean. Even actresses who are relatively successful find that they suddenly have to . . . have to . . . supplement their income."

What could that possibly mean? "It must be very difficult for you," O'Malley agreed. He took a deep breath, as though contemplating an important decision. "I'd like to help. I know I shouldn't say this after knowing you so briefly, but I'm tremendously attracted to you. Maybe it's simply the glamour of your profession. Does that sound silly?"

Monica shook her head from right to left hurriedly. "Doesn't sound silly at all. Matter of fact . . ." She actually managed to blush. "If the truth be known, I'm actually very attracted to you also." She flashed an absolutely gorgeous smile.

O'Malley hung his head, nervous and embarrassed. He shuffled his feet and said: "Well, what now? I suppose we should try to get to know each other a little better. Shall we go out to dinner, maybe?"

Monica came close to shuddering. "No, let's just go up to your room," she said.

They walked through the ornate doors hand in hand. "Nice suite you've got here," she said. She walked around

195

inspecting knickknacks and bric-a-brac. "Next time get one of the penthouses, though. They're the best."

"I'll make a mental note."

Monica walked behind the stand-up bar. She knew the territory well. "Can I make you a drink?"

"Jack Daniels, rocks, with a twist."

She manipulated some glasses and ice expertly, then handed him one. She took a long sip from her own. "That's nice. I been waiting for that all day."

O'Malley said nothing. He watched her move around the room, comfortable and serene. This was her business, her turf.

"Why did you kill John Bradley?"

Monica's head snapped over her drink. Her eyes changed from languorous to fiery. There was a bit of recognition at the corners. "What did you say?"

"You heard what I said. I asked about John Bradley's death. To be specific, I asked what you had to do with it."

"I'm getting out of here." She grabbed her wrap and started for the door. O'Malley let her go, leaned back against the sink in the kitchen, lit a cigarette, took a sip off the Jack Daniels. Monica was halfway to the door when a woman appeared; an athletic and most capable woman. She put her hand against Monica's throat and pushed hard. Monica fell sprawling on the couch.

"You'll leave when we tell you to leave, girl." Harriet's voice was cruel. O'Malley had no idea where she picked up the language.

Monica's eyes were filled with hate. "Who the fuck are you? What is this scam?"

O'Malley went in and stood across from her. Harriet grabbed her by the hair, yanking back suddenly. "Who we are don't matter. You just listen and do what he tells you." Harriet was really getting into it.

Monica shook her hair free of Harriet's hold and stepped back. "Hey, bitch, stay away." She turned quickly back to O'Malley. "I said what the fuck's going on."

O'Malley said, "We want to make a deal, a simple deal."

"What deal?" Monica asked the question out of habit. Her eyes were still outraged.

O'Malley said to Harriet, "Bring in the suitcase."

Harriet went into the other room and returned with a polished burgundy case. It had gold hardware and soft leather. Monica stared at the gold buckles. She licked her lips unconsciously.

With studied casualness, Harriet flipped the clasps and dropped the case. It split open. Green bills cascaded over the white pile rug.

Monica was transfixed. When she spoke, she spoke into the floor. "May I touch it?"

Harriet didn't answer. Monica dropped to her knees and ran her hands through the bills. There were thousands of bills in all kinds of denominations. O'Malley had told Harriet to mix it up, get old bills, don't band them, and don't be afraid to get lots of ones. Monica was a girl who loved cash more than anything in this world. He wanted her to be awash in a green sea.

Monica looked up at the two of them. She asked in a little girl voice, "Is this for me?"

"It is if you do what we tell you," O'Malley told her.

Monica said in a hushed voice, "I'll do anything."

"I want some information."

"What kind of information?" Monica's voice developed a hint of caution.

"I want to know everything you know about John and Anna Bradley." O'Malley said it straight out, without softening the blow.

Monica breathed deeply, but she understood. Whatever primitive notions of loyalty she had were being scoured clean in the green tide. The only question now was the size of the risk. O'Malley answered the question for her. "Nobody ever has to know you've been here. You just take the briefcase and walk on out of here like a real estate broker."

"I don't know," she said to herself.

O'Malley gave a brief flick of his head toward Harriet. Harriet reached for the case and began to close it. Monica's eyes grew wild and she shouted, "No!" She slapped Harriet's hand away and began gathering the money together, then snapped the case shut. She said, "Don't touch this." Then she turned to O'Malley. "What do you want to know?"

O'Malley set up a chair in front of Monica and turned it around, sitting so he could lean against the cane back. He said, "How long were you blackmailing Anna Bradley?"

Monica looked startled. "You're fucking nuts. You've got it absolutely one hundred percent backwards."

O'Malley picked up a pad and flipped it near the beginning. "From 1974 through 1979, you were paid as much as twenty thousand dollars per year in monthly increments that reached as high as seventeen hundred dollars." He raised his head. "So why were you blackmailing her?"

This time Monica's laugh had some mirth in it. "Blackmailing her! Honey, I was working for her."

O'Malley stared dumbly. He tried to rearrange things so they fit again, but he couldn't do it. "What do you mean you were working for her?"

"I mean I was on her payroll," Monica Davis said simply. "I was working for her." She spread her hands. "What else can I say?"

"Is this before or after you became John Bradley's lover?"

"John Bradley's lover?" Monica laughed. "Sure, I was John Bradley's lover, the same way I'm the lover of all those guys downstairs. I was being paid to do a job."

"By who?"

"I just told you, darling. I was working for her. Always for her."

"Are you telling me Anna Bradley was paying you to sleep with her husband?"

Monica laughed at him. "That's exactly what I'm saying. Except when John and me got together I didn't get much sleep."

198

"Why would she do a thing like that?"

Monica shrugged. "To find out what they were up to."

"Who?"

"Who do you think? Perino and John Bradley. My job was to find out what they were doing and tell Anna about it."

"Are you talking about the estate? Anna's inheritance? How would you know anything about that?"

Monica shook her head. "I don't know anything about her inheritance. I was supposed to find out how they were screwing the company. You know, stealing." Monica paused and smiled. "You see, Anna had blackmail in mind, all right, but it was her that was gonna do it."

"So for five years you slept with John Bradley and tried to find something Anna could use to blackmail them with. Ever find anything?"

"Sure, lots of things, but nothing big. Perino steals out of habit and everybody knows it. Then one day this deal came along that was different."

"A deal in France, maybe?"

Monica was surprised. "Not bad. That's right, a deal in France. It was clear as day to me and my girlfriend Brenda they was rippin' off the company for a bundle. I told Anna right away. She was happy as hell." Monica shrugged again. "I didn't know shit about what was going on. But Anna sure as hell did."

She crossed her legs and lit a cigarette. The slit in her skirt showed creamy white thighs, legs that had driven John Bradley to give up everything. But that was the next chapter. "Why did you kill John Bradley?"

This time Monica didn't even get angry. "You're just trying to make me mad. But now that I'm relaxed over here with my money, it doesn't even make me shiver. Ask me nice and maybe you'll get an answer."

"O.K. How did John Bradley die?"

"He hung himself in a room at the Park Lane Hotel. From the shower."

"I keep getting smart answers, your chances of getting that cash are gonna go way down," O'Malley told her.

She bristled at that. "I'm telling you the truth as far as I know it. He hung himself. I mean that's really all I know. I was gone when he did it."

"Let's back up. Why did you leave town with John?"

"I was told to."

"By whom?"

"Anna, of course," she said. "That's who I took all my orders from."

"Why would Anna Bradley tell you to leave town with her husband?"

Monica shrugged. "I don't know. But she did."

"Before or after you told her about the French deal?"

"After." Monica smiled. "Right after."

"What if he didn't want to go?"

Monica laughed this time. "You must be kidding."

"No. Anna Bradley is a very rich and beautiful woman."

"But John hated her and hated her money." Monica's face took on a confident air. "He loved me. He'd been asking me to go away with him for years. He said he had a nest egg stashed away."

"Did you know there was an investigation after you and John left?"

"Now I do," she said. "And I know Perino buried it. That's when Anna went out and hired two guys—lawyers or detectives or something—to try to stir things up for her." A little glimmer of understanding flickered in Monica's eyes. "And one of them was supposed to be this big guy with a bad attitude."

"What a coincidence," O'Malley said. "Where did you go with John when you took him away?"

"All over. Only thing Anna told me was keep away for six weeks. So I told John I wanted to go to all these bizarre places. First, we went to this little fishing village in Mexico called Nueva Puerta. Nothing there but lobsters and poor people. Then after a couple of weeks, we started traveling all over Mexico. I kept him inland from the hot spots like Acapulco and Puerta Vallarta. Told him I had an interest in Mexican antiquities." She laughed at that one. "Anyway, after a while he got worried. Maybe he could see I was playing games. That's when we went to New York."

"Were you in contact with Anna all that time?"

"Most of the time," she said. "Every day or two I'd make a call to the States. I told her right away when I knew we were coming back to New York. She's the one who told me to ask to go to the Park Lane."

"And then she came to New York to meet you?"

Monica nodded her head up and down. "That's right. She came out and stayed at the Carlyle. That's when the blowup happened."

O'Malley remembered the information he had received from the hotel employees about the breakup between Monica and John. "What exactly happened?"

"When I got back to New York, I called Anna and we met for lunch at the Tavern on the Green. She must have been followed there because after we left a guy followed me back to the hotel. He grabbed me as soon as I got out of the cab."

"Was it Larry? Do you know Larry?"

"Now I do. Larry is Perino's muscle. Yeah, it was Larry."

"So what happened?" O'Malley asked.

She shrugged. "I'm no hero. When he asked me where John was, I told him."

"And he also gave you a little money, I assume."

"Sure. Five grand."

"Then what?"

"Then I called Anna and told her exactly what had happened. Later on, Larry called John and set up a meeting with him in the hotel bar. I told Anna about that, too."

Dead solid perfect. Now the big question. "Tell me what happened at that meeting in the bar. Every detail you can remember."

"I don't know anything about that."

O'Malley's voice cracked at her. "Don't screw around with me, Monica, or you won't get a quarter. I know you were there. What happened?"

"I wasn't there." She said the three words slowly and with great assurance. There was no doubt she was telling the truth. O'Malley just stared at her for a moment. His house of cards came tumbling around him.

"O.K., I understand," he said finally. "What did John tell you?"

"He said Larry threatened him."

"How?"

"He said Larry wanted him to come back to Los Angeles and meet with Perino. If he didn't come back, Larry said John would be blamed for everything."

"How did he take that?"

"He went upstairs and wrapped a belt around the shower curtain."

"Right away?"

"No, not right away," she said. "At first he came up to me and started screaming at me, asking a lot of strange questions. He accused me of setting him up. When I got a free moment, I called Anna." She shrugged. "Anna told me to dump him in a public place."

O'Malley again remembered the information he had received from the hotel employees. "So you picked the lobby of the hotel?"

"That's right, right out front by the cab stand. I got into a fight with him, told him I was leaving him for good, then went upstairs and got my stuff. I came downstairs and got out of there in a hurry and went over to Anna's suite at the Carlyle."

"Then what?"

"As far as I'm concerned? I stayed the night at Anna's and the next morning she got me a first-class ticket back to L.A. I was supposed to lie low for awhile until Anna called me. But as soon as I got off the airplane, Larry was waiting for me. How he knew I don't know. He popped me in the back of a limo and took me out to Perino's place by the beach." She grinned. "It's been kind of like prison."

"When did you find out about John's death?"

"Later, way later," she said. "Larry told me one day while I was sitting out by the pool. He just came right out and said it. I think it gave him a kick to tell me." Her face reflected a certain seriousness for a moment. "I'm not saying I was in love with him or anything like that, but the news hit me pretty hard. You can't stay with someone all that time and not be sad when he goes."

"That's sweet. Did it bother you enough to go to the cops?"

"No," Monica said simply. "Not that much."

"When was the next time you saw Anna?"

She shook her head. "I didn't see Anna until they dragged her in about three or four weeks ago."

"What do you mean dragged her in?"

"She was drugged," Monica said. "They dragged her in like a bag of chicken. Flew her back in a private jet is what Larry said."

"So she's their prisoner?"

"Yes. Or at least she was. They're trying to make her see things his way."

"What way is that?"

She shook her head in genuine ignorance. "I don't know what they're talking about. It has to do with her inheritance and who's going to control it and all that stuff. They've had a lock on her for years, if you know what I mean."

"I know what you mean. Let me ask you something. Does she ever mention her father?"

"Her father?" She thought for a moment. "That must be

203

the picture she keeps by her bed. A nice-looking dude in a suit? That him?"

"That's him," Harriet said from the door. O'Malley looked over at her. "She's always had that picture, even at college," Harriet said. Harriet turned to Monica. "How did that picture get out to the beach house?"

Before Monica could answer, O'Malley waved the question away. "Never mind," he told her.

O'Malley was silent then, drinking in what he had heard. He asked Monica a few more questions about the layout and location of the beach house and then lapsed into quiet again. Finally Monica interrupted. "Can I go now?" she asked sweetly.

O'Malley spoke absently. "No, you're not going anywhere. You're going to get to know Harriet a little better."

Monica didn't respond, but her lips grew tighter. Her hand moved toward her purse. O'Malley saw the gesture out of the corner of his eye and jumped like a cat. He grabbed her wrist roughly. She tried to resist for a moment, then gave up the fight.

O'Malley dumped the contents of the purse onto the middle of the floor. A police .38 clunked out with a bunch of coins and cosmetics. Not exactly a ladies' gun but then again Monica wasn't exactly a lady. O'Malley picked it up and inspected it. It gave off no smell. It was loaded with four rounds, one of which was already fitted into the firing chamber. Crowded among the debris from the purse were an additional eleven bullets.

O'Malley moved the bullet away from the firing chamber and clipped the safety on, then slipped the .38 into his belt. He stuffed the bullets into his jacket pocket. Monica had by this time stood up with the briefcase in her hand. She had a nice, pretty glare, the kind that if converted to a smile could easily melt a man's heart. He knew that only one thing warmed this lady's heart.

"Don't worry, baby, the suitcase is yours. We're paying for our information fair and square."

"So can I leave?"

"Sure. In a couple of days." He turned to Harriet and nodded. She seemed to be waiting for the moment and came over with relish. She pushed Monica hard at the shoulders, and the woman fell back roughly into a chair. "Sit, bitch." O'Malley hid his head a little at that one.

Monica began a soft series of incredibly abusive curses against O'Malley and Harriet. The curses got louder as Harriet revealed long strands of cord. "I spent hours looking for these," she told Monica. "They're supposed to be the best there is. Here, hold this end," she ordered.

Harriet trundled every inch of Monica into the straight-backed chair. An expert could have done with a tenth of the rope; Harriet just made up for inexperience with more knots. When she was done, most of Monica was hidden away under the coarse hemp.

Monica's curses were now hysterical. "You fucking cow. You fucking bitch cow. I'm gonna kill you. I'm gonna have you torn apart, you miserable cunt." The last was screamed. Harriet listened to it, waited for Monica to open her mouth wide for another epithet, then jammed a handkerchief into the gaping maw. She wrapped a final strand of rope around Monica's head. The room became quiet.

Harriet stepped back and admired her handiwork. "Not bad," she concluded. She slipped her arm through his and walked him to the door. When she got there she looked up at him with eyes that were different from those of the confident little rich girl looks he had come to know. These eyes was vulnerable and more than a bit frightened. O'Malley kissed her, and the kiss was as sweet and genuine as any he could remember. He broke it and moved toward the door. "I've got to go."

She nodded. "I'm going to be really pissed off if you don't come back."

31

In many ways, in all the important ways, he was operating alone now. Chapman and Baird had fish to fry that had nothing to do with him. To Chapman, Perino and the Cappicis were quests that promised glitter and bracing energy, a case that could catapult him forever out of his drab, GS-15, freeway-view existence. This could be the big one, a headline-grabbing, news-interviews-with-sexy-blond-reporter kind of case. It was the sort of case that caused an ambitious prosecutor to go out and buy new suits for trial days. Yet maybe that was cheapening Chapman's motivations. He'd probably go after Perino just for fun.

For Baird, that was all it was, the fun. Baird was simply eccentric enough to work against Perino for no other reason than the moral satisfaction of lighting the fuse all the way to the top. O'Malley could tell from the light in Baird's eyes when he talked about the grand jury that his friend now had a cause.

O'Malley had little interest in the grand jury, and less in whether Perino and Newsome were stealing from the company, from each other, from the government, from Newsome's partner, from the Cappicis, whatever. He had originally been asked to find John Bradley, then to find out why Bradley died, and he now knew the answers to both questions. Now he was free to work for himself and maybe, if it was possible, save the Anna he knew from the Anna at Perino's beach house.

The night was black when he reached the Pacific Coast Highway. A harsh squall was just beginning, bending the coastline palms with rushes of Pacific wind. The rains would not be far behind. He traveled north with the dark, roiling ocean to his left. A flimsy bar formed the border between Santa Monica and Malibu, set precariously a few yards from the now endangered beach. He pulled into the parking lot and hurried inside.

He had barely avoided the wet. He took a seat near the window and watched shafts of water clatter like pebbles against the glass. Workers were furiously laboring on the beach below to drag in furniture. A pretty dark-haired waitress came over to look out the glass with him.

"It's going to be a very bad night," she observed.

"Yes, it is," he agreed.

She gave him a glass of evil Jack and left him alone. The bar had tables set up for ocean viewing, now all empty. Waiters were pulling on jackets for an early departure, some sliding up to the bar and transforming from the help to the customers. No one expected much business tonight.

He snapped a pocket flashlight at a gas station map. The Coast Highway runs true north and south through most of the state, even Gualala for that matter, but not through Malibu. The famous beach, as aberrant as ever, makes a dramatic ninety-degree turn to the west, yanking the highway with it, creating a large mass of land jutting into the Pacific. In that dark mass lies the colony, secure in its very inaccessibility. Many people lived their entire lives in L.A. and had no clue how one might enter this most glamorous of Malibu locations.

The only access roads were shown cutting directly from the highway into Malibu and Trancas, rare, barely visible, thin lines of red on the map. One of the access roads led to a guard station, which, assuming one got past it, led to more little roads. At the end of these roads people like Perino had their carefully protected beachfront homes.

He wasn't about to drive to the guard station and ask to be buzzed in. That left only one means of access—from the west, from the beach and the now foaming ocean.

He left the bar and drove north again. The rain had let up somewhat but the access road he had decided upon was still almost impossible to see. He drove past it once and had to double back. After he found it he turned right and traveled three miles in blackness to a bluff overlooking the beach.

Before getting out he changed clothes, pulling on dark sweatclothes. The jacket had a hood in the back and a pocket in the front. He put the .38 in the pocket, taking care it was adequately protected. Then he got out and walked to the tip of the cliff.

It was at least forty feet down to the beach. The top of the rise was covered with rusting wires. An ancient conduit once used for runoff ran broken from the bluff to the beach accompanied by what at one time had been a metal handrail. This was the "access point" to the Malibu beach mandated by the ever vigilant Coastal Commission, designed to insure the public always had a way to get to the public beaches. It had all the accessibility of the Normandy beach during the Allied landings.

O'Malley turned his back to the ocean and began inching his way down, holding firmly to the metal handrail. The side of the bluff was not vertical; it was, mercifully, gently banked. Nevertheless, the rain, now increasing again, made the footing treacherous. He slipped repeatedly, cursing, gripping the cold, wet metal bar tightly. At the last the whole thing gave way beneath him. He toppled the final twelve feet, landing in an undignified lump among the broken concrete at the bottom.

No wonder nobody bothered the stars. He got up and checked for broken bones, then wiped off the wet sand and rock. That done he turned to the north. The rain splashed in his face. He began running heavily along the hard sand to the colony.

It was still five miles away and he spent the first of them blessing the time spent jogging on Gualala beaches. The rain came harder, washing away the sweat and the grime, but also obliterating most landmarks. He gave up trying to figure out where he was and ran by his watch. Thirty-six minutes after landing on the sand he slowed, squinting against the wet, puffing balls of steam into the night. In time his eyes focused, framing an enormous palm and the six landmarks that followed it: an oriental teahouse, a lifeguard station, a wildly tiled swimming pool, a beachside tennis court, a rusting flagpole. The flagpole had a beacon on top placed there by the city to keep aircraft and vessels out of the living rooms of the famous. From Monica's description it told O'Malley that one house beyond was David Perino's.

He ran past and tried to steal a look inside. Perino's place was well back from the beach, set high beyond a granite retaining wall. A patio area visible from the beach was lit by outside lights. The rain beat on the empty tables. The lower portion of the massive but nondescript house was dark; a single light burned in what appeared to be an upstairs bedroom.

He continued further past the house. If spotted he would appear to be nothing more than a crazy jogger without sense enough to come out of the rain, a common enough sight. A half mile further down he found a dry spot under a concrete staircase and slowed.

Although the run had been measured, the dark hooded sweatshirt and cotton sweat pants now clung wetly to him. The beat-up tennis shoes were caked with wet sand. He sat and took deep breaths until his normal breathing returned. As he sat he pulled Monica's .38 from his jacket pocket and filled it with cold bullets.

The night air and driving rain cooled him quickly. He found himself shivering. He left a free chamber in the weapon, turned on the safety, and walked quickly to the south again, staying huddled and close to the large retaining walls set on the eastern boundary of the beach.

Unlike most of the beach houses, Perino's staircase to the beach was protected by a six-foot metal door set securely between concrete braces. The estate two doors north was not so inhospitable. Their staircase was gateless. He scurried up the steps to a lawn area and, from there, to the top of a retaining wall. One retaining wall led to another. In a short time he was kneeling silently, staring like a black cat from the top of the wall fronting Perino's house.

When O'Malley saw nothing move, he dropped noise-lessly into the patio area. He held the gun in a clammy hand. Rushes of fear now dominated his senses. The exterior of the house remained black and still. It was the stillness more than anything else that gave him an eerie sense of the presence of death.

He kept his left hand gripped tightly around the wrist of the right, the gun pointed skyward. He was ready to kneel and fire at anything that moved, shadows included. When he was sure he was alone, he ran low and fast along the grass abutting the patio until he reached the house.

There was a small service porch to the left of the main door. He knelt near it and listened closely. There was no sound except the pounding of the waves, now muffled by the retaining wall. The fear wouldn't go away; indeed, as he sat there, he imagined the smell of death. It was an evil smell of decay that sapped him, eating his strength and courage. His fear became loathing. He hated the aura of disease that seemed to spread from the inside of the house.

He gripped the .38 tighter, wheeling it around and about in little arcs, hoping for an excuse to open fire. When he didn't get one, he decided to provoke an excuse. Standing, he took a deep breath and rammed a thick shoulder into the locked door of the service porch.

It broke easily and noisily. Splinters flew from the wooden frame of the door as the metal deadbolt broke through rotten molding. Inside was a concrete floor and more darkness. He elbowed his way through the door leading into the kitchen, then sat back with the gun pointed forward. He knew in his stomach Larry was in the house. He also knew if they met, Larry would kill easily, certainly without remorse and probably with satisfaction. O'Malley's best defense was that now he would kill as quickly as his enemy.

He stepped forward, leading with the gun, the only sound the muffled background beat of the sea washing against the seawall. A long, straight center hall divided the house in two. On either side were openings into dark rooms. At the end a stairway led to the second floor.

As he turned spinning into each empty room, O'Malley stayed low, his eyes and ears straining for shapes or sounds. He could only see a few feet into each opening. That's why it came as no real surprise when he felt the cold metal next to his ear.

"Well, look at this," Larry said. His voice was soft. "Just open that hand real slow."

"You got it." O'Malley dropped Monica's .38 quickly. It clattered against the wood floor. Larry picked up the gun and jammed it in his belt. He gestured toward the staircase. "Up there," he ordered.

On the way up the steps O'Malley thought about turning and kicking but rejected the idea quickly enough. At the top he listened for the sounds of others in the house, but heard nothing. The upstairs rooms were as dim as those below. O'Malley again felt the metal dig into his back. "Straight ahead," Larry said.

Larry led him to a large empty room, devoid of all furnishings. A rough, stone fireplace dominated one wall. Three adjacent floor-to-ceiling windows let in faint light from the courtyard below, light that revealed black burglar bars bolted to the outside of the building. That was the problem with burglar bars. As surely as they kept outsiders out, they kept insiders in. The room was a superb jail.

O'Malley turned to Larry, who was standing leisurely by the only door. As he watched, Larry took off his jacket and flipped it onto a chair in the hall. Then he tossed the gun and shoulder harness on top of it as well. O'Malley stared quizzically. Larry grinned and shut the door with a bang, then turned a dead bolt. He put the key in his pocket.

"Oh, shit," O'Malley said softly.

Larry walked forward like a man who had been waiting for something for a long time. O'Malley backed up, circling warily. He had a chance now; all he had to do was take the key out of Larry's pocket. That's all.

He ran out of space near the fireplace. He reached back and felt the rough stone. There was no place to go. Without options there was only one option. He took a deep breath, ducked his head, and charged straight at Larry's belt.

Larry didn't even flinch. He braced and came up hard with a left uppercut. The punch landed flush and straightened O'Malley like a palace guard. O'Malley couldn't believe the sudden pain; all he wanted to do was go down and die in peace. Larry wouldn't have it. As O'Malley's head sagged, Larry caught him under the chin and drove the right hand hard to the body. The air rushed out and didn't come back. O'Malley began choking and flailing. Larry backed him against the wall and started working hard.

By the third shot O'Malley was unconscious, but Larry still didn't let him fall. He snapped two more hard lefts to the side of O'Malley's head and then followed with a right cross. O'Malley didn't feel any of them; his head just whipped dangerously back and forth in response to each blow. Mercifully, Larry soon got greedy. He took a step back to brace for a hook and let go of O'Malley's neck. O'Malley slid down the side of the wall and sat in a lump on the floor. He stared without sight for a moment before toppling to the left. His head bounced twice off the hard wooden floor and then stopped.

He woke at dawn. The sun was only weakly forcing its way through the still ominous clouds. He staggered to his knees and felt a jagged pain in his jaw. His eyes felt puffed and thick. Larry sat quietly across from him in a straight-back metal chair.

O'Malley got up and stared out through bruised eyes with a mixture of fear and hatred. Larry walked over slowly, rubbing his right hand with his left. "You hurt my hand, fucker, you know that? Look how red it is."

He realized with sudden horror that Larry was going to beat him to death. He didn't know why it wasn't obvious before. It would take some time yet and cause Larry some exertion but there was no question of the purpose of all this. Each time he awoke he would find Larry in that chair, and each time he would be weaker and more broken. Over time the professional, unimpeded shots to the head would take their toll. Larry would hit one last time and he wouldn't ever wake up.

And there wasn't a thing he could do about it. The room was a fortress, one way in, no way out. There was nothing in the room that could be used as a weapon; indeed except for the metal chair there was nothing in the room at all. His only choice was to fight each time, against a man who on O'Malley's best day would have little trouble with him. To fight back was a choice that would do little more than amuse Larry.

Larry closed in slowly, humorlessly, avoiding all chances. They had rolled and scrapped on the floor of Anna's garage and Larry didn't want to repeat that. Larry kept his distance, faking and patiently waiting for his opening. When O'Malley swung clumsily, the fast left hand flashed twice, then hooked. O'Malley blocked about half of it but the half that hit was enough. He felt himself start to go out again and fought against it. A left to the kidneys spun him around; mercifully he was now far past pain. He swung out of habit and missed completely. Larry administered a quick jolting right as the coup de grace. The last thing O'Malley saw was a pair of black shoes rush up at him.

When he woke again the room held only the remnants of a sun now setting over the water behind him. He could barely make out the details in the room. One detail was Larry sitting in his metal chair.

He realized now that this was the last time. His head

was badly damaged and he felt a sharp, dangerous pain deep inside. He coughed and blood rose in his throat. He grimaced at the effort of straightening. Larry laughed softly.

Larry walked to the windows and spread the drapes. "Take a long look, son. It's gonna be dark in here pretty soon. For you it's gonna stay that way."

That's what he figured. O'Malley rose and tried to walk. It was all but impossible. He tripped and fell, then painfully rose again. This time he stayed up. He began staggering toward the metal chair.

Larry watched with interest, then started to chuckle. He folded his arms to enjoy the spectacle. When O'Malley finally reached the chair he had to pause to catch his breath. Then he grabbed his only possible weapon with both hands and strained; a simple ordinary card-table chair, but the strain was almost unbearable. The veins on his neck stood out and Larry roared. He beckoned to O'Malley with his chin held out. "Come on over. Hit me with it. Come on. Try real hard." Then Larry broke up again.

O'Malley finally got the chair in the air and walked forward again. Larry began dancing around the room on the balls of his feet, holding clownish bouts with the chair. O'Malley ignored him; he just kept staggering forward with his chair like a man on the way to Calvary. When he reached Larry he had to stop again, his breath coming in labored bursts. He could barely hear the taunts anymore. When he was rested he smiled at Larry. Then he turned quickly and coolly threw the metal chair through the ten-foot-high expanse of window.

The crash was deafening. Jangled shards of shiny glass rackishly transformed the final rays of the almost departed sun; half of them landed in the driveway and the other half rebounded off the burglar bars and returned to the room. Larry stopped laughing and stared dumbly at the carnage. "What the fuck . . ." he began. O'Malley dove into the mess and came up with a four-inch hunk of glass as sharp as a carbide cutter.

Larry backed away, the grin now completely gone. He reached with his right hand for a shoulder holster that wasn't there anymore. His eyes took on the first light of fear O'Malley had seen.

"Drop the key on the ground," O'Malley said evenly. The words were slurred.

Larry looked intently at O'Malley to find out how real the whole thing was. The hand that gripped the heavy glass shard was now running red with blood. It was a sight that convinced Larry that O'Malley was very serious indeed.

"Go ahead and pick one up for yourself," O'Malley challenged. "Then we'll be even."

Larry shook his head from right to left. But he didn't drop the key.

O'Malley backed up three steps to prepare for the charge. He yanked at the fabric of his shirt with his free left hand, then quickly wrapped the cloth around the open wound of the right hand. He held the glass tightly now. "Drop the key," he ordered Larry again.

Larry shrugged, then came hard.

O'Malley had only the briefest of moments to react. As Larry made a grab he slashed blindly. Larry screamed and stumbled. The glass stayed intact in O'Malley's hand and described a vicious red line down the side of Larry's face. Larry was on his knees; O'Malley slashed again and caught him on the neck. Larry spun away, howling louder now. He reached back and recoiled in disgust at the red on his hand. The sight of it seemed to paralyze him and he stared at it open mouthed. As he did O'Malley attacked again, thrusting downward twice. One missed but one sank deep into the thick muscle of the man's shoulder. O'Malley twisted the shard and felt it break, half now in his hand and half imbedded in Larry. Larry screamed, "Jesus, look what you done." He began pulling at it feverishly. A piece broke free and a veritable fountain of blood followed. "Oh, God, oh God. . ." Larry wailed. O'Malley stumbled back to his ammunition dump for a new blade. Then he came at Larry again.

At bottom, Larry was a profound coward. "Wait, wait
. . . hold on," he begged. He dug into his pants pocket and
dropped the key on the ground. "O.K. That O.K.?" he
asked. His eyes were wide.

"Move away from it," O'Malley said.

Larry backed off quickly, even cooperating a little bit by
kicking it across the wooden floor in O'Malley's direction.

O'Malley bent over and picked it up. "Where's the
gun," he said. Larry pointed dumbly toward the hall.

O'Malley unlocked the door and looked outside into a
dark hall. Another small metal chair held Larry's coat and
shoulder harness.

"Where's Perino?"

Larry seemed to consider refusing for a moment, then
remembered not only the glittering glass in O'Malley's fist
but the gun in the harness as well. He nodded toward the
other wing of the house.

"Fine," O'Malley said. He grabbed the gun and walked
back inside the room. "First we talk."

32

When he was done he locked the door behind
him, strapped the harness on, and checked the .38 for bullets. The squat weapon was full. He jammed it into the harness and went walking down the stairs toward the other side
of the house.

The house was shaped in the form of a U, with the open
end to the west. The north and south wings were separated
by an open rock garden. A hallway on the first floor connected the two wings.

He walked quietly through the connecting corridor to the north wing, where he found a duplicate staircase to the upstairs. He went up with the .38 in front of him. This time, no matter what happened, he was not going to let go of that gun.

The upper level was a series of bedrooms dominated by a master suite. The bedrooms were large, dark, and unoccupied. What he assumed to be the master suite had huge double doors left partially open. Light came from the inside. O'Malley went over and looked in.

Anna Bradley sat at an ornate dressing table with her back to him. She was staring at her image in a glass, slowly brushing tangles out of her long blond hair with a silver-backed brush. The hair, now loose, fell gracefully onto her bare shoulders and the thin straps of a satin dressing gown.

Fifteen feet to the left of Anna, David Perino stood next to a monstrous bed. A small lamp on the table was the only illumination. Perino, too, had his back to O'Malley. A phone was to his ear and his eyes trailed like beacons over the street below. He wore a bottle green robe and little old man's slippers. His free hand was waving excitedly at the person on the other end of the line.

O'Malley could only listen to half the conversation, but it was pretty clear what was going on. Perino was begging for his life. He didn't do it obviously, or with any hysterics. But there wasn't any doubt he was doing it.

"Eliot, look, I know your position," Perino said. "But you must realize I had nothing to do with setting this up.

"O.K., so that was stupid. But I had no idea this would wind up in front of a grand jury.

"What was that question? Did I do what? Of course I haven't been down to see the U.S. Attorney. What do you take me for? I've got as much to lose in this thing as you do.

"Eliot, I know how much is involved. But you don't have to worry about me. I been here before. I'm the laundryman, remember? I'll take the high five and that will be that." Perino gave a nervous laugh.

"What was that? . . . Sure, I do. Eliot, Simon Jacoby and me go back a lot of years. . . . What? . . . I don't know if it's commodities or what it is. I just send over money and Simon invests for me. You really ought to get into it yourself. . . . Sure, he's very successful.

"This evening?" Perino hesitated and ran his hands through his hair, quickly peering out the window again. "Well, as it happens, Eliot, me and my lady were all packed up and ready to go on a little vacation. I figured to be gone for about eight days.

"Can I stay? Well, Eliot, I got a problem there. You see I already bought the tickets and . . .

"Well, sure, if it's that important, I suppose I can. Tonight? Well, we'll probably go out to dinner and won't be around much, you know. . . . Who wants to meet? Stephen Karhan!" Perino literally stiffened with fear. "When did . . . I know it don't matter, but . . .

"I guess we could. Sure, don't you worry about it. You get done with your meeting you just call. We can wait an hour.

"Sure, Eliot, you too. Just relax and it'll all blow over. Say hello to Rita for me." Perino gave a little cackle at some sort of parting joke from Newsome. Then he slammed the phone down hard. He spoke to the wall without turning. "Baby, get dressed quick. We gotta get the fuck out of here."

When O'Malley first walked into the room they didn't notice him. When they finally did they both just stared dumbly. O'Malley knew he must look bad, yet didn't expect they'd be quite this blown away.

"Don't mind me, you guys go ahead with what you're doing. And from the sound of it you better be quick too." He turned to Anna. "Nice gown."

Perino recovered first. His hand moved toward the dresser drawer.

"Don't even think about it, Perino." O'Malley waved

the gun in a small circle. "I use this there'll be nothing left for the Cappicis." Perino's hand stopped.

O'Malley turned to Anna. "I hope you're O.K. I ran along the beach and got wet and all out of breath, not to mention almost getting killed a few moments ago, just to make sure you were O.K. You are O.K., aren't you?"

Anna didn't say anything. She just stared at him in a preoccupied way, as though her mind had escaped to a safer place. Her lip didn't quiver and there were no tears in her eyes. The sight saddened O'Malley. He didn't think the Anna he'd come for was here anymore.

O'Malley turned back to Perino. "I know you're not O.K., but that's your problem. Wages of sin and all that, I suppose."

"What do you want?" Perino had a lot on his mind. He couldn't have cared less how O'Malley got in the house, how he got beat up, how he was feeling these days. Perino just wanted to move things along.

"I want to find out what happened," O'Malley said, "for my own peace of mind. After that you go your way and she"—he gestured toward Anna—"she goes with me."

"Fair enough," Perino said. "You don't mind if I pack in the meantime, do you?"

"Go ahead," O'Malley told him. "I just need a couple of details. Who was Hamilton Brent working for?"

Both of them looked up in surprise. "Who?" Perino asked.

"Hamilton Brent. A little guy who liked to carry a big gun. Knew a lot about restaurants and a lot about Anna's affairs. He's not with us anymore. Who was he working for?"

Perino snorted. "Never heard of him." He grabbed a suitcase and started jamming socks into it.

O'Malley turned to Anna. "So who was he working for, Anna?"

Anna was pale. "I don't know."

"Bullshit," O'Malley said softly. "With all respect, of course."

"Why would you believe him and not believe me?"

"Because his man killed Mr. Brent for one thing. Now maybe Larry kills his own people for the fun of it, but you have to admit it doesn't make a whole lot of sense. Anyway, Larry just told me he didn't buy Brent until the morning of the day Brent tried to set me up. Before that our little gourmand was working for someone else."

"And you think that's me?"

"Sure. Besides, you had to have someone besides Monica working with you in New York. How else would you have managed to murder your husband?"

Anna's head snapped. Her mouth tightened. "That's ridiculous."

"Is it?" O'Malley turned to Perino. "What do you have to say about that, champ?"

Perino just shrugged and went on packing. O'Malley went over and kicked the suitcase shut. Then he held the gun under Perino's nose. "I said what do you have to say about that?"

"All right, just relax."

"Did she kill Bradley?"

"Maybe. I know I didn't do it. I always thought the little fuck just hung himself because that hooker didn't love him anymore."

"That would be Monica. Did you know Monica was working for her?"

"I do now," he said. "We grabbed Monica as soon as she got off the plane and brought her back here. She told us what we wanted to know after we gave her a few bucks."

"But you didn't know it then?"

"That's right. When John Bradley left town it was like the end of the world for me. Kill John Bradley? If that little prick had come back I would have married him. My whole world fell apart when Bradley left."

220

"Which is what she wanted, right?"

"Sure." Perino looked at her with something approaching admiration. "She set me up and did a good job of it. Tried it once before and we had to put her in the bin for a while. This time she was smarter. She got that slut to fuck her husband and tell her everything going on. At the right time she disappeared with that sorry little prick." He shook his head in exasperation. "Christ, I thought the whole world was investigating that French deal."

"You get accused of corruption and you're off the estate. That about it?"

"That's it. They get a tight ass downtown and I'm out in the cold. She's back in charge."

"And without control of the estate, you can't launder the Cappicis' profits through Kendall Industries anymore, right? The laundryman is out of business."

This time Perino didn't answer. He just stood quietly. "I don't know what you're talking about."

"Sure you do," O'Malley said agreeably. "You didn't do all this to get into Anna's pants or even to get her money. That's just icing. You need companies, lots of companies, to run your little scam with your friends in Las Vegas. That French deal had nothing to do with anything, right? Other than jeopardizing your control of Kendall, that is."

"I'm not saying anything more."

"Then you're not leaving," O'Malley said simply. Perino involuntarily glanced outside the window. The sun was now completely gone and the outside lights burned bright through the black. It had been fifteen minutes since he had hung up the phone with Newsome. "All right, you're right. We needed the companies."

"Now all we need is a tape recorder."

"Sorry, I can't remember where I put mine." Perino shrugged.

"That's O.K." O'Malley walked over to the table and picked up the phone, then dialed Baird's number. He listened for the beep on the office tape recorder, then handed the phone to Perino. "Start talking. If you throw in a lot of detail the whole thing can be over in ten minutes. If you fuck around we'll just keep trying till you get it right."

Perino held the phone in his hand and thought about it. The very sight of the darkness through the window seemed to send a chill through him. He began talking rapidly into the phone. For a man who usually spoke with the grace of a hoodlum, Perino made a sudden transformation. The words were clear and lawyerlike. It took only eight minutes to say it all, but in that eight minutes Perino put in enough detail to hang all of them. When he was done he handed the phone back to O'Malley. "That about do it for you, champ?"

"That'll be fine, Mr. Perino," O'Malley said.

"And it's fine with me, too," a feminine voice said.

O'Malley didn't even bother to turn around, just began cursing himself for ignoring Anna this long. "Just drop it right there on the floor," she ordered.

O'Malley did as he was told. Then he turned around to look at the beautiful yellow-haired woman holding the ugly square automatic. There was nothing in her face that looked familiar to him. She waved the gun. "Sit down over there." Then she turned to Perino. "If I were you I'd find out what happened to your friend."

When Perino scurried from the room, Anna turned to O'Malley and smiled. "Don't look so surprised. It's a woman's job to help her husband any way she can."

33

O'Malley sat on the edge of the desk with his hands folded, the broken parts of his face beginning to ache once again. Anna stood across from him with the gun held steady. With her free hand she ripped clothes down from closet rods.

"I'm in too much pain to be either angry or surprised," O'Malley said. "But when did you two tie the knot? I assume you're not a bigamist along with everything else."

Anna tossed the clothes over on the bed. "Yesterday," she said briefly. "In Las Vegas."

"Why?" When she didn't answer he said it again. "Come on, what does it matter, now?"

"Maybe I'm in love."

"Yeah, that's possible. He's a real prince. Cause any girl to get moist at the edges."

"Then maybe I owe him."

"For what. Stealing your money?"

She turned and looked at him. "No, keeping you alive," she said simply.

O'Malley opened his mouth to respond but no sound came out. The bridge. Anna gone, the chauffeur dead, and O'Malley with no more damage than a bump on the head. That didn't happen because Larry loved him like a brother.

"Don't let them do this to you, Anna." His voice was intense. "We'll get out of here together."

Anna's eyes were weary. She began packing again. "It's too late now. I can't fight them anymore." Her voice was weak.

Her tone exasperated him. "O.K., stay with him. Answer me one thing, though. Why did you kill your husband? Your other one, I mean."

She just glared at him. "I'm not sorry he died. He wanted to come back and reconcile with Perino. It would have destroyed everything."

"And you knew that because you met him, right? In the bar of the Park Lane?"

Anna gave a little nod as a compliment. "That's actually very good. You used to think it was Monica who met with him in that bar."

"That was when I was even stupider than I am now. Anyway, I take it that's when you learned Larry had talked him into coming back."

"That's right," she said. "I tried to make him see things my way, I really did. I begged him to help me but he was afraid." She shrugged. "I had no choice."

"How did you convince him to hang himself? Did you just suggest it would be a good idea?"

She stiffened at the question. "I didn't do it. Mr. Brent did it."

"And just how did Mr. Brent do it?"

"With a drug of some sort . . . . One that's . . . that's hard to detect. I . . . I held a gun on him. Mr. Brent . . . Mr. Brent dipped the liquid on a rag. I left then."

"Very nice. What was John Bradley doing while all this was going on?"

This time Anna did more than simply stiffen. Even now her lip quivered at the memory and the gun in her hand shook. Her voice cracked. "He cried," Anna said. "He seemed to know exactly what was going to happen to him. He cried and cried. The whole thing took so long." Then she began breathing deeply.

O'Malley never got a chance to say anything else. She cut him off with a shrill voice. "No more. I don't want to hear anymore. Just shut up and sit there."

O'Malley saw a face close to hysterics and a hand shaking uncontrollably. He decided to shut up.

It took only a few moments for Perino and Larry to return. Larry was holding his right shoulder in pain. The left one was the one with the glass in it. Perino said to Anna, "I found this moron trying to butt his way out like a fucking goat." He looked up at Larry. "You are a fucking imbecile. Start packing and do something right for a change."

The two of them started jamming things in suitcases while Perino stared at O'Malley. O'Malley sat quietly on the edge of the desk watching the show. He paid particular attention to Anna, wondering if marriage to Perino had changed her. There really wasn't any reason why it should have. Anna and Perino had undoubtedly been lovers for many years, maybe before Anna ever heard of John Bradley. Now they were married. Was Anna's whole scheme designed to get away from Perino, or simply to get close to him? As close as she had been to her father? The answer wasn't that easy. It depended on which Anna you were talking about.

But O'Malley knew she didn't have the whole thing put together yet. She couldn't. Even Anna couldn't know.

"Anna, I have a question," he said amiably.

She looked up from her packing with an impatient look.

"How does it feel to fuck your father's murderer?" he asked.

The question hung in the room. All three of them stopped packing. Larry looked at Perino for instructions. Anna stared at O'Malley for a full thirty seconds. Then she threw her clothes to the floor and turned to Perino. "You son of a bitch."

Perino had been standing stock-still also. Even he seemed shaken. "You're crazy," he said quickly. "This man's talking trash to save himself. You listen—you're as crazy as everybody says."

Anna turned back to O'Malley. "Why did you say that?"

"Besides the fact that Larry, with a little prompting, told me about the night of your father's murder, it makes perfect sense. Perino was your father's advisor for years. He did the will and made sure he was named executor. When the Cappicis needed legit companies to run laundry operations through, he picked your father's. Matter of fact he was ripping off Kendall Industries for years before he had Edward Kendall murdered."

"That's a lie," Perino said.

"Is it?" O'Malley turned to Anna. "Baird went down to the courthouse to check out your insanity trial. He had to look it up in the card catalog under 'K' for 'Kendall'. It was easy enough to find. It was the listing right after the case of *Kendall Industries* v. *David Perino*."

Perino began backing up. O'Malley shouted, "Don't let him do it, Anna." Anna still had the gun in her hand and instinctively raised it. Perino's was lying on the bed next to the suitcase. He seemed to think about going for it and then stopped.

"What does it all mean?" Anna asked.

"It means your father found out Perino was stealing and they had a blowup. Your father even sued him, maybe was planning on going to the cops. The murder occurred nine days later."

"What did he sue him for?"

"Stealing, embezzlement, fraud, all sorts of things. The executor of the estate decided in the interest of economy not to pursue the litigation."

Perino snorted. "I get sued about once a week. I don't kill people for suing me."

"No, you kill them for trying to remove you as executor."

The room was silent now. Anna didn't need to be a lawyer to understand that. Then Perino spoke again. "That's just a lot of air, Anna. You know who killed him. It was that broad he was sleeping with. They found him naked as a jaybird with come all over his cock. Whoever he fucked that night did him in."

Anna laughed quietly, a seemingly incongruous laugh in the circumstances. Only O'Malley got the joke. "That can't possibly be true, can it, Anna?"

She still had a smile on her face. "No, Ben, it can't." She turned to Perino. "I didn't kill him. I just came out of the bathroom and found him."

Perino's jaw dropped and his eyes widened. Larry stared for a second. He began to say something, then simply shut up.

Anna still had the same enigmatic smile on her face. Then she laughed again in a small, manic way and walked across the room to a chair. She fell into it.

Perino recovered first. He slapped Larry hard across the chest. "Forget her. Let's just get the fuck out of here now. We're taking him with us."

34

The three of them walked down the dark steps like businessmen checking out of a hotel. Perino and Larry each carried a suitcase in the left hand and a gun in the right. O'Malley walked unburdened in front of them.

As they walked they dispassionately discussed O'Malley's fate. "Bring the limo around," Perino ordered. "We'll put him in the trunk and drive out to the canyon. We'll dust him there."

"Why don't I just hit him in the trunk?" Larry asked in a reasonable tone.

"If you ever do that I will personally see to it that you clean up every drop of blood from my trunk with your fucking tongue."

"Oh, yeah," Larry agreed.

As they exited, the night around them was even blacker than the inside of the house. The houses of the neighbors, each as secretive in its own way as Perino's, were all protected. The light from those houses remained hidden within the individual enclaves. Perino pushed O'Malley forward and then turned to Larry. "Well, what are you waiting for?"

Larry was shuffling his feet. "Can I ask you just one question, Mr. Perino?"

"What?"

"It's about when I dusted her old man. I was out on the balcony watching him boff this broad. Then when the broad left the room I went in and stuck him. Back in there she said . . . I mean I thought she said . . ."

"Shut up," Perino barked.

Larry went around quickly for the car. O'Malley sat on the edge of a massive potted plant. The sea air was cold around him. The sweat from his body chilled him deep inside. He was as frightened as he ever remembered.

He studied Perino. Perino was holding the gun with a natural nonchalance. His carriage said he had held guns often and knew how to use them. He wouldn't have the slightest hesitancy about shooting, blood or no blood, if O'Malley attacked. Could O'Malley take a bullet? Hope it didn't hit a vital spot? Keep going? Once he got to Perino he could get the gun. He doubted he could get there.

On the other hand, he had one ace left to play. "May I suggest a reason you shouldn't hit me?"

"Yeah, what? Your mother'll be upset or something?"

"Well, that too. But I thought you might like to know where that tape recording is."

It was obvious Perino had forgotten the tape. His head bobbed back and forth. "I'm getting old," he said to himself, "no doubt about it." But there was nothing he could do now

228

except cut his losses. "I think you just bought yourself some time, son," he said agreeably.

O'Malley breathed easier. In the middle of Hollywood he would take his chances.

They were prevented from further conversation by the screech of tires. Even Larry now realized the urgency of the situation. Seconds later a big gray Mercedes with frosted windows squealed to a stop in front of them.

Perino put his arm on O'Malley's shoulder and gripped hard. O'Malley was about to get up when he felt the grip suddenly relax. He looked up to see Larry standing next to the car with a strange look on his face. He followed the gazes of the two of them down the long driveway toward the access road. A pale set of beams bounced repeatedly against the trees lining the road. As they watched, the light from the beams intensified. A pair of bright headlights swerved into Perino's driveway.

Perino let go completely. Larry just stared at the bright beams like a frightened deer. Four doors from the dark automobile opened quickly and men in suits got out of each one. A voice barked: "Stay right where you are."

O'Malley was about eight feet from Perino's limo and even farther than that from anything that might be called protection. His eyes went back and forth in terror. He heard Larry say, "I know that man. I prayed my whole life he'd never come for me."

O'Malley didn't need to hear any more. He dove head first into the concrete of the driveway, trying to swim into a dried-up oil slick he found there. From in back of him he heard Larry curse and then a metallic click. He covered his head and flinched when the firing started. Larry's pistol spurted rapidly. From the opposite side of the driveway he heard deep thumps followed by explosions and screams, then a quick succession of thumps. The driveway filled with smoke. He heard howling from both sides of the driveway. Then there was a new sound, a new squeal of tires. He felt rather than saw more bright beams fill the area. "Freeze," a voice shouted. The voice had a nice official ring. There were more curses and more deep thumps. When it was finally quiet he looked up. Strong young men in dark suits were striding purposefully forward pumping the underside of shotguns to eject the spent shells.

Baird reached him first. He helped him up slowly. "I'm sorry," he said. "We had a tip Perino was going to get it tonight and we've been following that car for hours. We couldn't know you'd be here." O'Malley didn't answer. He was shaking so hard he could barely stand. Baird had to lead him over to the car to lean against it. The door to the limo was obliterated. In back of it Larry lay face down, filled with twelve-gauge shot.

Chapman walked in front of the dark suits and gave some orders. The men immediately began rummaging through the inside of Perino's car and the trunk. Perino stood smiling in front of Chapman with his hands outstretched. Old soldiers never die; they just make other folks die. Nevertheless, at least the grand jury was going to have a very important witness soon.

It took a long time for O'Malley to clear up. When he did he pushed himself off the car and reviewed the carnage. Two men lay face down in front of the car that had first driven into the driveway. One had his hands cuffed behind his back and was squirming. The other wasn't cuffed and wasn't moving.

So it looked like a complete success. Nevertheless a thought was nagging at him but he couldn't remember what it might be. He cursed his inability to concentrate. He again turned toward the four FBI men. Two were still rummaging in the car and the other two were walking toward the front door of the house. He watched them try the latch. He thought it was funny that they would try to open a locked door; he even giggled when one stepped back. The man seemed to move in slow motion: bracing his legs, raising the gun to the sky, pumping once.

Then it hit him. "No," he screamed.

The scream was lost in the roar of the shotgun. The bolt of the door was blown away. O'Malley ran toward the door. "Anna," he shouted, "it's all right."

He burst through the door just as the loud, unmistakable report of a proper lady's .32 exploded from the upstairs bedroom.

35

It was late morning when O'Malley found himself back in Baird's office. He felt beaten and defeated. For the last twelve hours he had been jostled around in FBI cars, ambulances, and hospital emergency rooms. Now he sat with white bandages on his face and white tape around his chest. The lines around his eyes were cracked like an old man's. In addition to everything else he felt clammy and cold inside a cotton pullover that had been on him for almost forty-eight hours.

He sat in the corner of the room, away from the action in the middle. As depressed as he was, the rest of the room was full into high celebration. It all looked like the winners' locker room after the Super Bowl. Swarms of young lawyers and FBI agents wandered around clapping each other on the back and shaking hands. In the center of the room a large copper coffee urn had been set up with stale pastries next to it. But the urn was only a sidelight. The real hit of the party was the duplicate tape of Perino's eight-minute confession. Like a gravelly chant, it played over and over as background through two giant speakers brought in specially for the occasion. The celebrants roared when particularly favorite lines were replayed.

O'Malley had no idea what he was doing back here, except someone from the hospital seemed to think this was where he belonged. He hadn't argued with whoever it was, just as he hadn't argued with any of them since hearing the crack and the thump signaling a sorry end to Anna Kendall Bradley Perino's sorry life. At first he had raced up the stairs, but stopped at the top. When one of the men put an arm on his shoulder, he accepted it without question. He never did go in to verify the obvious.

By the time he had made his way back downstairs, Larry had been swept away like so much rubbish. Perino was sitting in the back of the FBI car with his legs crossed like a man who owned the world.

O'Malley had wandered out to the low brick wall, sat upon it, watched the activity around him through glazed eyes for a while, and then calmly fell forward on his face in the oily driveway. They told him later that Baird had gone a bit berserk at the sight, and began screaming at Chapman, who in turn began screaming at an FBI agent. The ambulance was there shortly thereafter. It had arrived in the driveway simultaneously with the first of the dark blue vans from the coroner's office.

By the time O'Malley woke up, his face had been fixed, his ribs taped, and the FBI man was there to take him back. He refused the drugs offered at the hospital so he'd be clear to use his own. He cadged a little evil Jack from Baird and snuck off into a corner to suffer in peace.

Now the day neared noon and the celebration was really picking up. Someone suggested going out for champagne and giving everybody the day off. Everyone cheered. Then Chapman got up on Baird's desk and began pounding the copper urn with a bent spoon.

"Listen up everybody, listen up." Everybody cheered Chapman, their leader, and then became quiet.

"We got some more news here. And it's all good." Everybody whooped again. Chapman banged the urn some more.

"Perino and his lawyer just got out of a meeting with Sarah. They been going at it for four hours. The bottom line is Perino's going to testify. Tonight he sleeps in a fancy hotel under the witness protection program. Tomorrow he goes to the grand jury."

The roar was deafening. Chapman went on. "I don't know enough details to tell you the whole scam, but we do know the outlines now. The whole thing was centered on Kendall Industries. The Cappicis were laundering millions in profits through all of Kendall's companies. Not only that, when they weren't doing phony transactions through Kendall, they were looting Kendall itself. Over the past three years, Perino has put his own men into responsible positions at all levels of the company. By systematically selling the company's assets to their pals in the United States and abroad, they've reduced Kendall Industries' net worth by two hundred million alone over the past thirty-six months. In another six months, Kendall Industries would have been bankrupt."

"Who were Perino's partners?" a voice shouted.

"There were two," Chapman answered, "Newsome and Silver. We got agents swarming all over Silver's operation in New York right now. At six this morning they intercepted a truck full of documents on the way to a chartered Swiss plane at JFK. This is going to make the Marc Rich case look like a misdemeanor."

One of the FBI men had apparently found the champagne after all. His boisterous voice rose over all the others. "Get me to a telephone. I gotta tell my wife to sell the stock."

Everybody laughed. When it died down Chapman said, "You're wrong about that, Howard. The reason this deal was so sweet to the Cappicis was there was no stock, no nosy shareholders looking over their shoulders. Edward Kendall Jr. owned Kendall Industries one hundred percent, lock, stock, and barrel. When he died, it all went to his daughter."

Howard piped up again. "So now who owns it?"

Chapman raised his voice. "This is where it gets rich, guys. The reason Perino is so willing to testify is because there is now very little we can pin him with." The room got quiet at that remark. Even O'Malley paid attention. "You see," Chapman continued, "when Anna Kendall Bradley Perino put a gun in her mouth, she did more than make David Perino a widower. She made David Perino an heir."

Chapman didn't say anything after that, letting the obvious sink in, maybe, like a good trial lawyer, milking the drama. O'Malley couldn't believe it. He had a strange unbelievably sick feeling in his stomach. His mouth hung open, suspended only by the bandages. Chapman said, "You got it fellows. Kendall Industries is now owned one hundred percent by the laundryman."

Baird came over and sat next to O'Malley. O'Malley asked him. "Is it true?"

"Maybe."

"But how? I mean he . . . he . . ."

"He didn't kill her. If he had killed her, he couldn't inherit. She killed herself."

"But he had been stealing from Kendall Industries for years. That was the whole reason he . . ."

"I know that. But Anna must have known that too. And no matter what you may believe about the relationship between Anna and Perino, the plain fact is they go back a long time. Perino has letters from Anna that would make your hair stand on end."

It wasn't surprising. O'Malley said, "Let me get this straight. Anna loves Perino. Perino loves Anna's money. Perino puts Anna in the loony bin. Anna gets out by marrying John. Then Anna blackmails Perino." O'Malley shook his head. "For what? What was she blackmailing him for? If she knew he was looting Kendall Industries, what did she want?"

"Depends which Anna you're talking about."

O'Malley knew what that meant. He'd just never heard anybody say it out loud. "She was schizo? That what you're saying?"

"Not in any dramatic way. But there was one part of Anna, the part you and I saw, that wanted to be free of Perino. Then there was another, maybe unconscious part, that wanted to . . ." he began groping.

"Wanted what?" O'Malley asked.

Baird shrugged. "To marry daddy, I suppose. That's probably all she ever wanted."

O'Malley didn't argue with that either. But he had always known there was one problem with that theory. "Say you're right. How do you fit Perino in? If all she wanted to do was marry Perino, why not let her? Then he would have had it all."

"He didn't need that," Baird said. "What did he need to marry some crazy bitch for? He had John Bradley do that for him. And once he was executor and guardian, he really had everything. Simply put, being a guardian with sex privileges is a lot better than being a husband."

O'Malley remembered the Anna he once knew. "Depends on what you're after," he said.

By noon the room had pretty much thinned out. O'Malley had occasionally thought about getting up and leaving, but ultimately decided he was just as comfortable sitting in his corner. He slept fitfully a few times and otherwise paid little attention to the nonsense around him.

When he woke from his last nap he realized there were only three of them left. He walked over to where Chapman and Baird were sitting and said, "I'm getting out of here."

Baird nodded. "We can have a car take you back. Do you still want to go back to the Beverly Wilshire?"

O'Malley nodded yes, then said, "Holy shit, I just remembered. Monica is still out there."

Baird shook his head. "No she isn't. You told us all about that last night in the ambulance. We sent someone to pick her up."

"But there was . . ."

Baird laughed. "Yes, we know. Your girlfriend almost got arrested for assault. She said she was under strict instructions not to let anyone have Monica. That's quite a lady."

Yes she was, and it was time to get back to her.

O'Malley got up to leave, then stopped at the door. He had one question left. "Just for the record, and in twenty-five words or less, what the hell did that business with the studio and France and Simon Jacoby and all the rest have to do with any of this? None of that involved Kendall Industries at all."

Baird and Chapman both nodded agreement. Then Chapman said, "You're right. The studio deal was just Perino getting pocket money. It had absolutely nothing to do with Kendall. But it did give Anna Bradley the hook to come after Perino. That's what pissed Newsome and the rest of that bunch off so much. They didn't mind a little stealing. What enraged them was Perino's utter stupidity and the threat he caused to the Kendall operation."

Baird interceded, saying, "When I confronted Newsome in Las Vegas I thought the studio was the key to the whole thing. Instead it was nothing."

Chapman laughed uproariously at the irony of it all. Baird was polite enough not to join him. O'Malley got up and stretched. On the street below a man in a dark suit stood next to an FBI car. He went out the door and down the stairs. Chapman was still laughing when he left.

O'Malley went quickly in the back door of the Beverly Wilshire and up the elevator to avoid questions from nosy doormen. On the way up he felt for his key, then realized the key was in a pair of pants, which were in the back of a rented Ford Fairmont, which was sitting lonely on top of a bluff next to a broken concrete drainage pipe. It seemed the car had been there for a hundred years.

The quiet and elegance of the carpets and brilliantly polished wood stood in stark contrast to his mud-encased clothes and broken body. He was bone tired, dragging each step. At the door he fumbled for a moment and then knocked.

When he saw her face again, he smiled, in spite of everything. It was as fresh and open as it had ever been. Yet there was no question she had been crying.

He said, "I'm sorry. I guess you heard."

She nodded. "They told me. Are you all right?"

"Sure." Given the alternatives, and especially given the bodies that had trailed in Perino's wake, that was an accurate statement. Compared to how Perino made out, well, that was something else.

He went over and sat on the couch, the exhaustion flowing through him as a sickness. The dull, constant pain of his jaw and ribs formed the backdrop to a sense of despair that bordered on nausea. Yet when he looked up to see her, he almost smiled again. She was biting her lower lip and had her hands on her hips. She looked like a woman about to take charge.

"You know I hate to be insulting, but you really look bad."

"I know."

"Will you let me take care of you?"

He nodded. "Yes. I'd like that very much."

She grinned. O'Malley watched through half-opened eyes as she worked. He heard the warm bath bubbling in the bathroom, then heard her on the phone to room service ordering up a meal that would feed an army. For the first time he realized how ravenous he was; it had probably been thirty-six hours since he had touched food. After setting a wonderful table in the middle of the suite, she came back to him. She said, "Here comes the good part. Strip, O'Malley."

No problem. Whatever or whoever had once stood between them was now reduced to rubble and ash, silenced by the crack of a .32 and the tumble of a honey-blond woman against an ornate dressing table. She knelt to help him. They pulled together at the soggy running shoes. They got scissors and cut the heavy cotton pullover off his body because he couldn't raise his arms. She ran her tongue slowly over her upper lip as she fingered the drawstring of his sweatpants.

"Need a hand with this?" she asked.

"Sure," he said.

In the bath he had to act as a contortionist, twisting to avoid soaking the bandages and wrappings. Nevertheless, it was a gloriously restful experience. He stayed in the warm water for an hour, until it became cold and the rapping at the door told him that food had come. She had to help him from the tub and help him dry off. She spent a long time helping him dry off.

When she was through, she held his face gently and kissed him deeply. He responded easily. The ghost between them was now really a ghost. She felt his response to her and smiled. "Maybe this was worth the wait after all," she told him.

He came out wrapped at the waist in a white hotel towel to the food set out in the dining room; it was a wonderful feast, filled with good, healthy things like fruit and breads and champagne. She ate sparingly, watching him with interest while he attacked the food. At the end, he leaned back with a cigarette and coffee. He was still exhausted, but her ministrations had changed a deep, debilitating weariness into something approaching relaxation. She came over, stood behind him, and wordlessly kneaded his shoulders with strong hands.

He stubbed out the cigarette and stood up. Her smile was wide as any he could hope for. "Let's go, baby."

She brought the rest of the champagne into the now darkened bedroom with her. Together they toasted the commuters heading home in the gathering dusk. The Beverly Hills lights were going on and the people were departing. He reached for her hand.

She came easily and unhurried. Her kiss was warm with a tremor of excitement in it. Mischievously, she reached behind him and yanked at the towel. It fell at his feet. She stood back and inspected him once again. "That's what I like to see, O'Malley, a little appreciation."

She led him to the bed like an invalid, which was close enough. He lay back naked on the bed, sipping his champagne, and pulling on a cigarette while she undressed for him. When she was naked, she knelt next to him and put her lips near his ear. "Any requests, O'Malley?"

He laughed at that. "Yes. Take me someplace that makes me forget my name."

"No problem," she said. She moved against him and over him. Her mouth and hands were practiced. Harriet was a girl with either a lot of experience or a lot of imagination. O'Malley found himself zoning out into a wonderful world that involved no thought or sensation other than Harriet's warm body. At one point, he looked up and saw her smiling down at him.

"Now that I have you nice and relaxed, it's time to play spaceships. You're the Russian and I'm the American."

"Okay, what do we do?"

"We dock," she said. "In the interests of better relations."

O'Malley was still laughing as she led him into her. She sat astride him, rocking gently against him. He ran his hands over her slim hips, pulling her down into him. Soon they moved together, responding to a rhythm too long delayed. As the tension built, O'Malley found an anger growing in him, an anger left over from the night before. He held her

239

roughly and pushed against her with a force that bordered on violence. At the ultimate moment, he found himself gripping her hips so tightly his fingers ached.

Afterwards, she lay next to him. They were both breathing deeply. "Ow," she said softly.

He grinned. His anger was gone, and a lot of his pain too. He turned her over to inspect the damage. "Not too bad. I figure we'll work up to the big stuff."

She nodded her head in agreement. "That's O.K. with me."

It was almost 4:00 A.M. when O'Malley gave up staring at the plain white ceiling and got up. He left his sleeping companion next to him, naked, curled delightfully into a small ball. Neither holocaust nor tragedy seemed to disturb the innocence of her sleep.

He went into the living room and wandered around for a while, replaying in his mind the night Monica had stood there telling them about her employment by Anna Bradley. A strange story, that. Anna Bradley forced to take a husband, then arranges for the husband to take a lover, a lover in her employ. The one thing Perino never figured on was that Anna was smarter than they ever gave her credit for. Make that cleverer, not smarter. In the end she died trying to give everything to a man completely devoted to taking everything from her. Not very smart, that.

The thought of Perino brought home clearly why sleep had not come this night. No matter that Anna was as responsible for her fate as anyone could be. David Perino still spent the night dozing smugly in a fancy hotel, counting his money to fall asleep. To say it was all unfair was childish, a statement about the world that in this city would bring embarrassed lowering of the eyes. So if the question couldn't be fairness, it could at least be justice. Make that revenge.

A woman's voice answered the phone. It was a voice with more than a small amount of hostility in it.

"Hello, Mrs. Moran. My name is . . . is . . . it's not important. I know it's awfully early to be calling you, but I have some information for you about your husband."

The woman's tone softened. "Are you with the police?"

As good a lie as any. "Yes, Lieutenant Zukor." He hesitated. "We know how your husband died."

O'Malley could almost see the woman drinking this in. It was a weird tale to hear at 7:30 in the morning, but life had been weird lately. "I'm listening."

O'Malley talked until he said it all. In his mind the woman's greatest anguish must be uncertainty, the sense of losing a man for no purpose. O'Malley couldn't replace the man, couldn't even supply the purpose, but he could tell her how it happened. Most important, he could tell her about the large shotgun shells that plowed into her husband's killer as he stood behind the door of a stretch Mercedes.

"Good," she said when she heard that part. "I hope the son of a bitch suffered."

"Not much more than a second or two, I would expect," O'Malley said. He hesitated. "How's the boy?"

Mrs. Moran said, "Patrick? He's my hero. When we told him he went in his room and cried for most of one day. Then he came out and told me not to worry. Can you imagine?"

"I'm sorry. I can't tell you how sorry I am."

Mrs. Moran said, "That's O.K. We're all right."

O'Malley didn't need any more incentives. He dialed Baird. Baird's voice was cracked and sleepy. "Who the hell is it?"

"Baird, it's me, O'Malley. I'm sorry to wake you up but I have to ask for something."

Baird seemed to become instantly awake. "I don't mind. I was afraid you might be one of those imbecile FBI types still celebrating."

O'Malley said, "What hotel is he staying at?"

There was a long silence. O'Malley could hear his friend

breathe hard into the phone as he thought about the question. Finally Baird asked the inevitable, "Why?"

"You don't have to know."

"O'Malley, don't do anything stupid. It doesn't matter what the man said or what he's going to do. You're not a hero. I'm as angry about all this as you are, but the answer is not to rush off and do something stupid. The place is swarming with agents. You'd never get near the place."

"What do you mean, 'what the man said.' What did he say? What's he going to do?"

"I thought you knew." Baird hesitated. "He says you're a dead man. He also says he's reniging. He . . . he may not testify after all."

"Good. Baird, I'm asking a favor. I'm not asking for advice. You owe me this."

"Why? Because you saved my life at Guadalcanal? I don't owe you anything, O'Malley. Maybe if you tell me why, I'll give it to you for free."

"I can't do that." Then he thought for a second. "Where's Chapman?"

Baird chuckled. "Where you'd expect, watching over his charge. Trying to talk him back into it. He's got a big day tomorrow and wants to make sure he's got it all under control." Baird stopped laughing and his voice became serious. "That about do it for you, O'Malley?"

O'Malley said, "You know it does. Thanks."

He picked up the Beverly Hills phone book and began dialing at random. He went through the eight most important hotels in Beverly Hills and asked for James Chapman at each one, and at each one was told there was no such person there. Then he started on the big hotels in L.A., less of them, but each resulting in the same negative reply on the other end of the line. At the end of the process he watched with a defeated look while the sky grew pale. Time was definitely growing short. Then he started laughing. Of course. He picked up the phone and didn't dial anything. After a moment a voice on the other end said, "Desk, may I help you?"

"James Chapman, please."

There was a moment of rustling. "Certainly, sir. Just one moment." A few seconds later O'Malley heard a ringing and then a male voice spoke. "Chapman," the voice said quickly. It was a voice that had a good solid prosecutor's ring to it. O'Malley hung up the phone.

It took a long time for the people at the casinos to take him seriously. In time though, he was passed through increasingly higher levels of command; he knew he was getting close when he stopped talking to people working the night shift and was handed over to people who had to be awakened to speak to him. It was almost 6:00 A.M. before the man's voice came on the line. It was a gruff voice without the civility Baird had described. It was also a voice that spoke without pleasantry.

"This is Eliot Newsome. To whom am I speaking?"

"Benjamin O'Malley. I am Jerome Baird's partner. I want to make a deal with you."

"A deal. I see. Are you taping this call by chance?"

"No, but it wouldn't make any difference what I said, would it?"

"No," Eliot Newsome said. "What do you want?"

"Two things, actually," O'Malley told him. "First I want to give you some information. Second, I want a quarter of a million dollars."

"That's a lot of money, a quarter of a million dollars."

"It's peanuts. It's nothing, pocket money, compared to what is at stake for you."

Eliot Newsome said, "What's at stake for me, Mr. O'Malley?"

The whole idea was that Karshan couldn't possibly know yet. "David Perino's grand jury testimony this morning," O'Malley said, and held his breath.

There was a silence on the other end of the phone.

Newsome didn't get to be where he was making imprudent statements into tape recorders. "I don't know what you're talking about," he said finally. "I will, however, listen to what you have to say since you've gone to so much trouble to call me at this hour."

O'Malley let his breath out. He was home free. "Fair enough. I want the money sent to the following address." He read off the address. "It's the address of the widow of a man by the name of James Moran. Mr. Moran was . . ."

"Yes, I know. Your Mr. 'Hoot' has already contacted us."

O'Malley said, "Fine. Nice small bills. Be discreet. She shouldn't have to answer a lot of questions."

Eliot Newsome said, "I'm still listening, Mr. O'Malley."

O'Malley hesitated, finding himself savoring the moment. Bye-bye David Perino.

"The Beverly Wilshire Hotel," O'Malley said finally.

"Yes?"

"That's all. Small bills. Get it to her right away. I'm relying on your good faith."

Eliot Newsome said, "I'm sure I don't understand what you're talking about. I'm going to hang up now. Goodbye, Mr. O'Malley."

"Goodbye, Mr. Newsome."

He looked out the window at the commuters beginning to cram into the bank buildings. He felt for the remorse that didn't come. Then he felt a tug and looked up at a face with sleep in it. She clutched a robe warmly around her. "Don't worry about it, O'Malley. Don't even worry about it for a second."

"You heard?" She nodded.

"Any qualms?" She shook her head vigorously.

She stood in front of him and took his face in her hands. "Let's get out of here. Let's get to someplace we can forget all of it, all the corruption, all the deals. You want deals, I'll give you one so sweet you'll never look back. Just me and you, a nice beach, and a warm fire at night. Let's go someplace and spend my money for a while. You know any place like that?"

He was laughing. "Let's go," he said.

They were on the floor of the Golden Gate Bridge heading north when he turned on the radio. Perino's death was at the top of the news. Harriet was asleep in the seat next to him. O'Malley felt the anger, rage and frustration of the last forty-eight hours fade from his mind, becoming nothing more than a mist joining the other mists roiling around the red span and spilling over the hills into Sausalito. The boats in the marina far below were white and bobbed on dark blue water. He drove through all the mists toward the sunlight dancing on San Francisco Bay.